Shame

AN ENEMIES-TO-LOVERS COLLEGE ROMANCE

SKYLER MASON

Editing by Heidi Shoham

Cover Design by Cover Couture

www.bookcovercouture.com

Chapter One

anessa

"My name is Vanessa Gallo, and I'm a virgin raised in purity culture."

As I stare at the light of my phone camera, a tingle spreads over my skin. Why am I nervous? I've said those words hundreds of times. My eight hundred and forty-six thousand TikTok followers are probably getting tired of hearing them by now.

Plus, I don't even have to post this video. I can keep it in my drafts folder indefinitely, telling myself I'll post it when I'm ready. I could edit it perfectly and then just get rid of it, smashing my finger on the delete button for some kind of catharsis.

No. I won't be doing either of those things.

Something changed in me last night.

"I have a big announcement I'm going to make at the end of this video," I say, "but I'm going to start by giving you a little recap on my journey in my faith and ultimate rejection of purity culture. I haven't done one of these in a while, and I got a lot of new followers this week."

When my head grows fuzzy, I press the red button to turn off the camera. I plunge forward and grab my water glass from the coffee table.

Saanvi winces as she looks up from her textbook. "Hungover?"

I nod as I gulp down the water, gasping afterwards. "Wine gives me the worst hangovers."

I'm not even much of a drinker. I didn't even have my first full glass of wine until a year ago. It's not a coincidence that it was around the same time I decided to reject purity culture. Good Christian girls are taught that the buzz of alcohol causes our morals to relax, and getting drunk puts you in danger of forgetting what you've committed to.

Namely, not having sex before marriage or anything approaching it.

"Maybe you should do this another time," Saanvi says. "You look like you're breaking out into a sweat."

"I need to do it while my head is foggy to make sure I actually post it."

She winces. "Are you sure you should? What if you regret it?"

I plop back down on the couch in front of my tripod. "If I regret it, that's probably a sign it was the right thing to do. I've been dragging my feet on this."

Saanvi glances down at her textbook, probably to hide an eye roll. "Being traumatized by an asshole who doesn't know how to get a woman off is not the same as dragging your feet."

I shiver at the memory.

Graham. Six foot one with a smile that made my stomach flutter. The only guy who's ever touched me, almost a year ago now. I hated every moment of it. It repulsed me. The fire his smile ignited in me turned to ash in my stomach.

Jesus, is my body broken?

"I don't believe that," I tell Saanvi. "It's not fair to expect guys

2

to know what to do with our bodies. I certainly didn't help him by bursting into tears."

I huff out a laugh, but it sounds like a sob. I'm not really crying again over this, am I? I've laughed about this numerous times with Saanvi. When I glance up at her, she's giving me a sympathetic look. I clench my teeth to fight the mist rising to my eyes. "I'm too fucking exhausted, and it's making me emotional. I need to make my damn video."

"I'll just keep studying and leave you alone. Or I can go into my room if you want privacy."

"No." I fluff my hair at the temples, using my camera as a mirror, trying to make myself look less hungover and haggard. "I'd feel better if you were in here."

"Okay." Her voice is soft.

"I have to force myself to do it. I'm channeling my inner Livvy. I'm giving myself a deadline to lose my virginity. She did, and now she is so happy..." My throat grows tight. Oh God, I hate my jealousy even though I know Saanvi understands.

Livvy's happiness is driving my misery right now, because I'm apparently a terrible person. How can I be jealous of the kindest, most loving person in my life? My big sister, Livvy, has in many ways been my emotional anchor, and I ought to be overjoyed with the progress she's made since she broke out of purity culture three years ago. Last night, she came over with her brand-new fiancé, Cole, and two bottles of wine. I hope Saanvi's the only person who noticed that I consumed almost an entire bottle all by myself, but I doubt I'm that lucky.

Livvy knows me well. She's always been an attentive and almost motherly big sister. She could probably sense that her wonderful news sent me into a frenzy. I couldn't help but reflect on myself.

On my failure.

Livvy's twenty-four years old and living a full, healthy sexual life with her now fiancé and co-habitant for the last three years. She was raised the same way I was. Had all of my hang-ups.

But she got over them all in a flash. All it took was having sex with Cole, the best friend she had loved since she was a teenager, and her sexual shame vanished overnight. Literally.

My experience hasn't been even close to that.

"Livvy wasn't TikTok famous," Saanvi says, thankfully pulling me out of my head. "When you announce that you're ready to lose it, it's going to be seen as a campus challenge."

I laugh. It will be seen as a challenge. The UC Santa Barbara fraternity scene has turned my purity-culture TikTok into a big joke about who will finally take my virginity. I've heard some of the frats even have bet pools going. It's gross and misogynistic, but I don't care. Let them have their creepy fun. It has nothing to do with me.

Besides, maybe I'll have mind-blowing sex with one of them, and it will get back to Graham...

No. I can't think these petty thoughts. It's not Graham's fault my body is broken. It wasn't his fault he was turned off by me having a panic attack in the middle of a sexual encounter. Who wouldn't be?

I need to focus on the greater good—the reason I started my TikTok platform. It wasn't easy to do. Some of the videos I've made have been so embarrassing that I cringed when I edited them. Yet it's also been cathartic and given me a purpose. I'm providing a service. I have hundreds of thousands of followers, many of whom were also raised in purity culture, and I'm helping them see that they aren't alone. I share the ugly truth about how being raised this way can make living a full life almost impossible.

It isn't impossible, and I'm going to prove that to them.

But first, I have to prove it to myself.

Determination sizzles through my veins, giving me the energy I didn't have when I stumbled out of bed this morning. I straighten my spine, reach out, and press the red button on my screen.

"Just a year ago, I still fully bought into the purity-culture bullshit. I wore my purity ring and prayed daily for God to help take away my sexual thoughts. It was only after watching my sister and her now fiancé 'live in sin' for three years that I finally started to realize something was off in my beliefs."

At the mention of my sister, Saanvi lifts her head from her textbook. She probably wasn't expecting me to talk about Livvy in this video. She sensed my turmoil last night—probably because I was so quiet after the engagement announcement—and she even told me after my sister left that it's normal to feel a little off-kilter when a sibling gets engaged. Her brother's recent marriage left her listless and melancholy for weeks after the ceremony. But I was tight-lipped with her. I didn't want to admit what I was feeling, even to myself.

It's so damn selfish. All that should matter to me is Livvy's happiness. The fact that she was able to get over her sexual shame so quickly is a wonderful thing, and it doesn't have anything to do with me.

So why am I feeling this way?

"I couldn't be happier with how far she's come," I say, hating how robotic the words sound. "She's still a Christian, but she hasn't let that stop her from living a full sexual life with Cole, even after my parents told her she was putting her salvation in jeopardy. I know this might sound crazy to some of you, but at one time, I agreed with them. Not only did I think she might go to hell, I also thought she was damaging her relationship with Cole. I thought if he got sex from her regularly, he would eventually get bored and find someone else. That is what I was taught." I raise both hands in the air. "It's no wonder I find it so hard to explore my sexuality without shame. I feel like once a guy touches me, he's going to lose interest."

And what a self-fulfilling prophecy that became with Graham. He touched my clit, rubbed a little too hard and awkwardly, and that sent me into a panic attack.

He hasn't even spoken to me since.

"I also had..." I expel a shaky breath. "I had an experience that made my shame so much worse. I'm going to do a part two and

5

tell you the details of that story. It's really hard for me to talk about, but I know it's common, so I want other people to hear my story and know that they aren't alone. Anyway, that's enough background. Now, I'm ready to tell you my plan."

I feel Saanvi's gaze locked on me, but I can't look her way. I have to propel forward. I may not be ready, but it's time.

If I don't set a deadline, I'll drag my feet. I'll become a thirty-year-old virgin still jealous of my sister on her ten-year anniversary.

"I'm still a virgin," I say, "but not because I want to be. I've tried to experiment with my sexuality, and I failed. Being touched made me sick to my stomach. I felt like a sinner, even when I told myself over and over again that I'm just a normal, horny human being."

My expression grows hard. "I need to separate my feelings from the physical act. My feelings are fucked up because of the way I was raised. I can't change that overnight. My body wants sex. I experience desire, but shame intrudes. I need to make my body feel so good that I don't think."

My gaze narrows in on the record light of my phone. "I'm now in search of a sexual partner. I plan to lose my virginity within the next thirty days." I gulp back a laugh. "I know that sounds like a strange thing to say on TikTok—like I'm advertising myself—but I really would prefer someone who watches my purity-culture videos. They'll know my journey better than even some of my friends. I've been so open about it on here.

"I also would be remiss if I didn't mention that I'm aware of my sort of...celebrity status here on the UC Santa Barbara campus. Since I use all the big UCSB hashtags, I know I'll probably get a flood of DMs from male college students. I won't be checking my DMs for the next month. And if anyone approaches me on campus and the first thing out of their mouth is about my virginity—"

Saanvi's laughter makes a smile rise to my lips. "You're probably going to get a rejection from me," I say to the camera. "I need someone who can make me comfortable because I'm hoping whoever I choose will want to go live with me on here after we… do the deed."

When Saanvi gulps back a laugh, delight bubbles in my chest for the first time all morning, and I'm grateful for it. I reach out and press the red button on my camera. As soon as the ticking clock stops, I burst out laughing, and Saanvi joins me.

"Please tell me you really are ending the video there."

"I am," I say. "I'm ending it with a bang."

"Literally. Now you just have to prepare yourself for all the harassment you're going to get from frat guys."

I shrug. "I can handle it."

Chapter Two

C arter

"I'm on my way to dinner with Grandma and Grandpa," I say to my mom. "So how about I just go ahead and transfer you five grand? I'll be able to make something up when I see them. I'll say the frat needs a new washer and dryer."

She sighs heavily, sending a rush of feedback into the phone speaker. "Baby, five grand is too much. That's your money."

I roll my eyes as I flip on the turn signal, not wanting to get into another argument with her about my trust fund.

"It's Grandpa and Grandma's money, and they're probably going to cut me off as soon as they find out I'm taking the job with OvuTrac."

"I doubt that," she says. "But they might cut you off if they find out you transferred me five grand. Or at least have a serious talk with you about how you spend their money."

"Let me worry about that." When I pull up to the stoplight, I roll down the window and let the cool ocean air brush over my face. I glance to my right to see if Lacey minds the cold, but her oblivious gaze is fixed on her phone. "You're getting a new goddamn washer and dryer. I use them too when I visit. Your dryer is a piece of shit. It has one job, and it fails miserably."

"I'll just get a new dryer, then. There's no need to get both."

"The washer is a piece of shit, too."

She groans. "I just hate that we're even having this conversation. I'm supposed to be taking care of you."

My chest grows tight. I hate when she says things like that, because I can hear the shame in her voice. She really thinks she failed me as a mom. All because her worthless parents failed *her*. I shouldn't even have a trust fund from my grandparents. All of the money in that huge bank account should be hers.

"Well, I'm transferring you five grand whether you want it or not." I smirk. "And I don't want to hear you whine about it."

She's quiet for a long moment, probably because she's getting emotional.

"I love you, baby."

Her brittle voice confirms my suspicion, and I swallow to ease the tightness in my throat. "Love you too, Mom." I quickly hang up.

"You're so cute," Lacey says, smiling at the screen of her phone. "I've never met a fuckboy who loves his mama as much as you do." She scowls at her phone. "Goddammit. There's no reception in the whole fucking city of Santa Barbara, I swear. Did you happen to watch Vanessa Gallo's latest video?"

Heat sizzles through my veins as I flip on the turn signal. So she posted a new one. She must have done it this afternoon, because I checked her page this morning.

I don't know why her stupid TikTok series about purity culture gives me so much delight. I've been hate-watching her for months now. I've even scrolled back and watched some of her older videos from before she made her entire brand revolve around her so-called virginity.

Probably because she's unbelievably gorgeous with her big,

Disney princess eyes and her plump heart-shaped mouth. I love looking at her face. It's a tragedy that she's so irritatingly prim. I've put my hand on my cock so many times and imagined fucking that stick right out of her tight little ass.

If only she'd own her hypocrisy and admit that she runs her stupid purity-culture TikTok for sponsorships and small-time celebrity, I might admire her. But from what I've heard from Graham, she's a stuck-up bitch who pretends like she really believes her bullshit.

Even when I know for a fact that she's not a virgin, thanks to Graham.

"I haven't seen it yet." I turn into the parking garage. "But I'm fucking obsessed with her. Her videos are so cringe."

Lacey giggles. "They really are, but she seems like a really sweet girl, so I feel kind of bad saying that."

I snort. "Why would you feel bad? She has basically the entire UCSB fraternity scene salivating over her. Our pool is almost up to five K now. And I've heard Phi Gamma Tau's is over ten. Whoever takes her virginity can get suite tickets to the Lakers."

"I think she'd be so creeped out if she knew about the bets."

"Oh my God, Lacey, really? Has she fooled you too? She loves them because they add to her celebrity. She knew what she was doing when she claimed to be a twenty-year-old virgin."

As I pull into a parking spot, Lacey whips around to face me. "Wait a second! What do you mean 'claimed'? If you have inside knowledge, I need details!"

I set my hand on her thigh and give it a squeeze. "My shameless girl."

"I need to hear it. We have like maybe a five-minute walk to the restaurant, so stop stalling. I want to hear every detail. What do you know about Vanessa Gallo's virginity?"

I smile wide. God, I love Lacey. I love how she knows who she is and accepts it. She's the exact opposite of Vanessa Gallo. Graham's story about taking Vanessa's virginity is exactly the kind of juicy gossip that would delight her, and I wish I could indulge her, but unfortunately, I was sworn to secrecy.

"I don't know anything specific," I say. "It's just the vibe I get from her videos."

"Oh my God." Lacey scowls, and it makes me smile. "That's the biggest letdown. I thought you were going to say you've had sex with her and were going to tell me all about it. God, you're a disappointment. No wonder your grandparents hate you."

I bark out a laugh. "You're going to feel really bad when you see that they really do."

She scoffs as she takes off her seatbelt and adjusts her tight dress. It's perfect. She's going to look like a harlot to my grand-parents.

"You have a trust fund," she says. "If my grandparents gave me that kind of money, I'd look the other way if they were serial killers burying people in their backyard."

I plant a kiss on her cheek before stepping out of the car. When we walk inside the restaurant, we're directed to the edge of the back patio. There's an expansive view of the ocean. No doubt my grandma insisted on having the best table in the whole restau-rant when she made her reservation.

My grandma's gaze falls directly on Lacey's long legs, and I resist the urge to smile. "Grandma and Grandpa, this is Lacey. She's a *close* friend."

My grandpa only nods, but my grandma gives Lacey a small smile. "Nice to meet you."

"Carter has told me so much about you." Lacey rushes over to my grandma and wraps her arms around her shoulders. Grandma stiffens at first, but then her smile grows. "Oh, you're a hugger."

"Yes." Lacey sits next to my grandma. "We're all very huggy in my family. Carter isn't very touchy, so I'm guessing the rest of the Blake family isn't."

My grandma's smile falters. She shoots me an accusatory look, probably because she's annoyed that Lacey's words imply inti-macy between us.

Everything is about appearance with my grandparents. They claim to be against sex outside of marriage for moral reasons, but the truth is they really don't care that I've had sex with Lacey. They only care that she'd talk about it publicly.

They want me to find a sweet, prim little girl. Someone who will sit with her hands in her lap and shyly tuck her hair behind her ears. Someone who will call my grandpa Mr. Blake and ask them where they go to church as if it's a given. They don't care if I fuck the brains out of this prim, sweet girl behind closed doors, as long as I can present her like a prize on my arm in front of their rich religious friends.

"So, Lacey," my grandma says, "are you also a UC Santa Barbara student?"

When Lacey shakes her head, I glance down at my menu to hide my smile. She's about to give them a straight answer, because she doesn't have any shame. My grandparents' wealth and name mean nothing to her.

"I was until I got kicked out." She giggles. "I partied a little too hard in my sorority, and my grades were horrible."

"That's unfortunate," Grandpa says, still not looking up from his menu.

"That's exactly what my dad said," Lacey says. "Except he had a few swear words peppered in there."

I chuckle as I reach out and set my hand on Lacey's knee. Grandma's gaze follows my hand. "She's really smart," I say. "She just has ADHD, so focusing is hard for her."

"Oh." Grandma frowns at Lacey. "Well, I hope you can get that figured out."

"Oh, man." Lacey sets her menu down on the table. "I just realized I forgot to take my Adderall today." She turns to me. "It's in my purse, and I left it in your car. Can I have your keys?"

"Do you need me to go with you?" I ask.

"Nah, I'm good." When she stands up, her short dress is riding up her thighs, making it look like a bathing suit.

Perfect.

As she walks away, I make a point to stare directly at her ass.

"How do you know Lacey?" Grandpa asks, not even trying to hide his disdain.

I smile lazily as I turn to him. "She lives in the sorority next door to our frat house."

Grandma's brows lift. "She's still in the sorority even though she was kicked out of UCSB?"

"Technically, no." I grab the bottle of wine at the center of the table and pour myself a glass. "But the girls love her, so she still has a room there."

Grandpa sets down his menu. "While she's out taking her... medication, your grandma and I have something to talk to you about."

"Okay," I say, "but I have something to ask you first."

Grandma frowns. "Is everything okay?"

"Yeah, it's nothing huge. One of our washers broke at the frat house. I was hoping you'd be okay with me buying a super nice one. The kind that has a handwash setting that actually works."

Grandpa waves a hand. "You don't have to tell us how you spend your trust fund."

I want to laugh. He says that every time I ask to buy something big, but he certainly looks at my purchases. I once made a huge transfer to my mom and forgot to send it to my personal account first. He had a stern talk with me about how I can't let my mom's "entitled" attitude make me feel guilty when she's mishandled her money.

Her heart would break if she heard some of the things he's said about her over the years.

In the end, I told him I'd only transferred her the money so she could buy kegs for our fraternity winter formal because I wasn't twenty-one yet. He smiled and said he would have done the same thing when he was my age.

Hypocrite.

"You're not going to have to worry about big purchases soon," Grandpa says. "I have big news for you tonight. News to celebrate. Your grandma and I were hoping we would have time with just us as a family, but you seem to always need a girl with you."

"Dan, we don't mind if he—"

"I've got this." Grandpa lifts a hand to silence her, and I can't help but grimace. God, they have the strangest relationship. He treats her like a dog, using hand signals to make her halt.

"He's a grown man." Grandpa turns to me, his lips quirking. "He knows what he's doing. I had my fun before I met you."

"Dan." Grandma frowns, but my grandpa doesn't glance her way.

He shoots me a lazy smile. "Carter knows the difference between the type of woman you marry and the type of woman you have fun with."

"Dan!" Grandma's glaring daggers at him now. "What would Jesus say if he were sitting here with us?"

"I don't think any of us are under the illusion that Carter is following Christ right now." Grandpa's smile looks a little smug as he stares at me. "But he will. After he's sowed his wild oats and is ready to settle down."

Heat washes over my skin, and I grimace. "Grandpa, this conversation is getting real weird."

God, he's such an antiquated old man. Our dinners always go this way, although he's getting weird a bit early. Usually, he needs a few whiskeys before I start feeling like I've stepped into the old West. Like he's going to dismiss Grandma for the night and have whores sent out for our masculine entertainment.

"I want to talk about your future," Grandpa says. "The woman you settle down with will be a huge part of our lives."

I grit my teeth. Because of the company. Everything always comes back to that goddamn company. It's the only reason I'm even in their lives in the first place having these weekly dinner dates. After kicking my mom out of their mansion for getting pregnant with me at fifteen, they didn't even meet me until I was ten.

My grandpa still hardly speaks to my mom. All communication has gone through Grandma.

What a fucking misogynist hypocrite. Here he is talking about me "sowing my wild oats" when he still won't even speak to my mom for doing the same thing twenty-one years ago.

Grandma sets her hand on Grandpa's shoulder. "Lacey will probably be back soon. Maybe this conversation can wait."

Grandpa's smile is almost a sneer. "Carter isn't going to want to wait a second longer to hear our news."

A prickle runs over my skin. He's been hinting over the last few months that we're going to have a "discussion" soon after Beach Burger goes public, but that's not for another month.

I frown. "News?"

He grins. "I want to start by saying how proud your grandma and I are about how good your grades have been these last several quarters, especially considering how much partying we know you do. Don't think your grandma doesn't look at your Instagram."

"Oh, stop it," Grandma says. "I'm too old for Instagram. I only see the stuff that shows up on Facebook."

"I've been thinking a lot about the future of the company," Grandpa says. "I'm not getting any younger, and as much as we have a strong team, it's always been a dream of mine to pass on this company to family. You're a Blake through and through. Smart as a whip, and you have your grandma's good looks.

When I grimace, Grandpa laughs. "I digress. I want to talk about your future. I know you've worked on that little ovulation tracking app with your frat buddy, but we have a space for you at the company that'll take your career to a level you won't get anywhere else."

His satisfied smile makes me want to roll my eyes. He doesn't know that I've already taken the "little" job with OvuTrac and that I'll be making enough to take care of both me and my mom even if he cuts off my trust fund.

I don't want anything to do with Beach Burger. My grandpa has branded himself as a Christian CEO. The company does extremely well with the church crowd because he pretends to embrace "traditional Christian values" in company policy. I'll do a lot of things for money, but pretending to be religious is not one of them.

And anyway, there's no way I'd live under his thumb. I don't care what kind of job he's about to offer me or how many zeroes I'll have in my salary.

"I want to announce you as my new chief of staff shortly after we go public," Grandpa says. "What that means is that you'll be my right-hand man for the next few years, so that when I'm ready to retire—"

"Grandpa, I don't really have any interest in fast food, so—"

He holds up a hand. Fuck, now I'm his dog.

"I didn't have any interest in it either. It was your great-grandpa's passion. It's not about fast food. It's about business. And family. You're my grandson."

"Yeah, but I don't—"

"I'm not talking about you working for Beach Burger. I'm talking about you becoming the CEO. When I retire."

His smile is triumphant now, and I sigh heavily. He's not going to listen to me no matter what I say, so there's no point in arguing. Even if I tell him my new job comes with a ten percent stake, he'll shrug it off like he has every time I've tried to talk about it. He considers it a pet project, not a real company.

"You don't have to make a decision right now," Grandma says.

"It's not a decision." My grandpa waves a hand without looking in my grandma's direction. "It's a no-brainer."

Grandma frowns. "Lacey is probably going to be back any second now. Let's save this conversation for—"

"That reminds me," Grandpa says. "Before she gets back, there's one more thing I want to bring up with you."

Grandma winces. "This can definitely wait—"

Grandpa holds up a hand to silence Grandma. "I need to say this quickly, because I don't want Lacey to hear. This is going to be a very public role. You'll be coming to events with me. You're going to be attending all of the senior meetings, so your image and reputation need to be aligned with our company values."

"Dan, we don't know anything about his rel—"

"You can't bring a girl like Lacey to any of our events." Grandpa pins me with a hard stare. "Find yourself a quality girl."

The rage starts as a prickling heat over my skin. I'm familiar with it because he always brings my mom up eventually. It's rarely direct. Most often it's just an off-hand misogynistic comment, but it holds an entire world of meaning about her. The woman he threw out of his life.

She's not a quality human being, is what he means.

Because she humiliated him.

Fuck, I should take this opportunity to humiliate him. I should bring "a girl like Lacey" to one of the Beach Burger public events and fuck her on the dining room table in front of all of his rich friends.

"Ultimately," Grandma says, "we want you to find a woman of God. For your own sake. Your grandpa's making it sound like it's only about appearances."

"I'm not asking you to get married to anyone soon." My grandpa's voice booms over my grandma's. "It won't be hard for you to find a quality woman. You're a very good-looking kid. You always have the church girls giggling over you. You haven't come with us in a while. We have some very good-looking young women..."

My grandpa keeps talking, and I find that all I can do is retreat into my head to keep the rage from bubbling out. I have to keep my head right now. My grandparents pay my tuition and all of my bills. They bail my mom out of her financial struggles without even knowing it. I can't tell him to shove his archaic worldview up his ass, but oh God, he always makes it so difficult. Here he is, talking about the young women at his church like they're prize hogs for me to choose from, without even thinking twice about his own daughter. The person who should be the future CEO of

Beach Burger, if only she'd been given the same opportunities I was.

* * *

I'm buzzing on the drive home.

I have to use this rage to my advantage. This could be a golden opportunity to humiliate Grandpa. There's no need to tell him to shove this chief of staff position up his ass. I can play along with him and pretend I'm taking the position and go to public events with him.

I'll be starting with OvuTrac in six weeks, and I'll no longer need his money to fund my life. Or my mom's.

I can't just simply cut him off. It'll sting his pride for sure, but he deserves so much more after the pain he's inflicted on my mom for twenty-one years.

My revenge needs to be big and spectacular.

When I pull up to the frat house, I turn to Lacey. "You want to come hang out? There's probably a game of beer pong going on."

She wrinkles her nose. "Nah, I have kitchen duty tonight, but I might meander over later and crawl into bed with you."

I lean in and plant a kiss on her cheek. "You're always welcome."

After we step out of the car, she blows me a kiss before sauntering in the direction of her sorority house. Lacey is the perfect fuck-buddy because she's wired exactly like I am. We're both incapable of developing deeper feelings.

When I walk into the house, a group of guys is standing around the couch with their heads bent. As I get closer, I see that Armaan is sitting on the couch with his phone in his hand, and everyone is staring at the screen. A moment later, I hear her speak.

Ah, that sweet, mellifluous voice.

Vanessa Gallo.

"I need someone who makes me comfortable, because I'm

hoping whoever I choose will want to go live with me on here after we...do the deed."

A tingle ripples over my skin. What the hell is she talking about?

I look at Armaan. "Choose who?"

A slow smile spreads over his face. "The guy to take her virginity. She's made it official. She's losing it in the next thirty days."

Holy fuck. So that's what Lacey was talking about. My pulse races.

"Alright." Dominic, our fraternity president, claps his hands twice. "We've got to work as a team on this. It's going to be someone in our frat taking the Vanessa V-Card Championship belt. I'll have failed you all if I can't make it happen."

As a mixture of cheers and laughter breaks out, I roll my eyes. If anyone had the gall to film some of the shit the guys in our house say, our fraternity chapter would shut us down in a heartbeat. Hell, if anyone knew that Sigma Theta Epsilon actually bought a championship belt with a big "V" in the center, all of their future careers would be over.

"What do you think, Carter?" Dom says. "Do you think you can win?"

I grimace. "I think you all should be forced to register as sex offenders. It's so fucking weird that you even want to win that plastic belt."

"It's not about the belt," Beckett says. "It's about our frat becoming legendary."

I snort, shaking my head. "She's not even a virgin. She's manipulating all of you. You do realize that, right?"

The whole room grows quiet.

"Dude!" Armaan scowls. "Don't call my girl a liar."

"Oh, that's right!" When Dom pats Armaan's back, beer spills out of the red cup in his hand. "Your sister is her bestie, right?"

"Yep." Armaan takes a sip of his beer. "And roommate. Vanessa's a sweetheart. She's got a little bit of a stick up her ass, but she's solid. I trust her even more than I trust my own sister. There's no way she's lying about being a virgin."

He's obviously never heard Graham's story.

"You really think she just announced on her TikTok that she's losing it in thirty days with no clue that half the guys on campus would go crazy? She's a con artist. A good one."

"I don't care what she is," Dom says. "I want someone in our frat to win that belt. Alright, Armaan, I want you to get her to our party tomorrow night."

Armaan frowns. "Fuck no. Then my sister will come. I don't trust any of you around my sister. Or Vanessa, for that matter."

"Goddammit." Dominic lifts both hands in the air. "Think of the greater good. I'll make sure no one goes near Saanvi, but Vanessa is fair game."

Armaan shakes his head. "The only way I'm getting her to come to the party is if you give me a thousand from the pool."

Dominic scowls. "Your parents are hella rich. Why do you need the money?"

Armaan shrugs. "My parents don't give me shit."

"Alright, fine." Dom groans. "But you're only getting the money after you get her here." He turns to me. "Carter, you need to take it from there. You have a near-perfect track record with women."

I shake my head. "I have no interest in Vanessa Gallo."

It isn't the truth. My whole body is on fire. Blood is sizzling through my veins at the thought of fucking that girl.

Why?

I want to wipe that insincere smile off her face—the way she widens her eyes and pouts her lips sweetly. I want to see those eyes glazed over in ecstasy. I want her to scream my name.

"Think of the greater good!" Dom says. "And it's just one night. Think of all your brothers." When he gestures around the couch, chuckles break out.

"It's not just one night," Ethan says. "Whoever she picks is going to have to go live on TikTok with her too."

My mouth drops open. "Wait, what?"

"Yep." He grins. "How fucking crazy is that?"

"That's the best part," Dom says. "She'll be making it public. There will be no denying the winner. Come on, Carter. Do it for me. Do it for your brothers. Do it for the legend of Alpha Lambda Xi. Take Vanessa Gallo's virginity, and let the world know."

Distantly, I hear the murmur of laughter. Holy shit, Dom might really be on to something.

What better way to humiliate Grandpa? What would he do if I took the "virginity" of a good Christian girl and spoke about it on social media? My God, this type of thing will probably get media coverage given the subject matter. Vanessa's purity-culture TikTok is famous on the UC Santa Barbara campus. A Live about her losing her virginity has the potential to get national attention, as I'm sure she knows.

If I announce that I'm the grandson of Dan Blake—the CEO of Beach Burger—it certainly would.

It's almost poetic.

"I'll do it," I mutter.

"Yes!" Dom shouts. "I knew you would come around."

I have. I've fully come around.

I'm going to take Vanessa Gallo's fake virginity.

anessa

"You look gorgeous," Saanvi says. "Armaan's creepy frat brothers are going to be drooling over you."

I shift my hips from side to side as I stare at my burgundy dress in the mirror.

Why don't I enjoy my body? Objectively, I find it quite lovely. When I see a woman on campus with a figure like mine, my gaze will often drop to her butt as she walks, and I'll admire it without this uncomfortable stirring in my gut. Sometimes I'll even envy her, and why should I? I have a pretty body.

I hate purity culture.

Saanvi reaches out and brushes her fingers through my hair, and I lean into her touch. "That feels good," I say.

Her brow furrows as she stares at a strand of hair in her hand. "The curls have kept well, considering I did them two hours ago."

I shake my head slowly, letting my dark tresses drift over my shoulder. At least I can enjoy my long, beautiful hair, thank Jesus.

"Nothing can get a curl out of my hair," I say, "not even beach fog."

"I just hope you don't get the drunken sweats." She brushes her fingers through the hair around my temple. "These tiny strands will get frizzy."

I smile. "I don't care. They all just want to take my virginity for clout anyway. I don't think I'll be picking anyone tonight."

She winces. "We don't have to go. I can just get a thousand from my parents and give it to Armaan."

"Your family dynamics are so twisted."

She rolls her eyes. "It's all Armaan. Well, my mom can be kind of a bitch too. But he's not trustworthy. He's a schemer."

I purse my lips as I stare into the mirror, running my hand through my hair one last time. "I feel kind of bad for him. He seems like the family's dirty secret, and why? Because he's a fifth-year senior? He's at UC Santa Barbara, for crying out loud."

"Trust me, he doesn't care. He's never cared, as long as he gets what he wants. In high school, he almost got expelled from our *prep* school—which means my parents were paying them an ungodly amount of money—because he was selling his Adderall on campus for a hundred bucks a pill."

I snort out a laugh, unable to help myself. "At least he's fun."

Saanvi grins. "He *is* fun. And so is his buddy Carter."

Heat ripples over my skin. I almost forgot Carter Blake was in Armaan's frat. He's well known at UC Santa Barbara as "the player." He owns his sexuality like a badge, oozing physicality and confidence whenever I've seen him on campus. He's the complete opposite of me.

"I've heard he's even worse than Armaan," Saanvi says.

My gaze shoots to her face as she applies a layer of buttery gloss on her lips.

"What have you heard?"

Her eyes light up as she rubs her lips together and makes a kiss face in the mirror. "I've heard *so* many stories from Armaan.

Carter's a no-feelings guy. He can only have sex with someone once." She pauses for drama. "And then he drops them."

When I stick my finger in my mouth and pretend to gag, Saanvi giggles. "I know. They're all so predictable. A bunch of horny dumbasses. I swear, their frat would make the best reality TV show."

"I'll need to stay away from Carter. His experience makes me nervous, like he'd constantly be comparing me to all the partners that came before me."

Saanvi's eyes widen. "Oh, I wouldn't rule him out. He might be able to make it worth your while. I've heard he has a magic penis."

I slam my hand over my mouth as I burst into giggles, and she laughs with me.

An hour later, Saanvi and I are standing in a line waiting to get into the frat. Saanvi pulls out her phone. "Should I text Armaan so we don't have to wait?"

I wince. "I don't know. I'd rather not draw attention to myself, given everything..."

Saanvi lifts her hand high in the air, and when I turn around, Armaan is striding in our direction. When he gets close, he frowns at Saanvi. "I'm not letting you in unless you promise to stick to a three-drink minimum."

Saanvi scowls and opens her mouth to speak, but I step forward. "I'll keep an eye on her."

When his dark eyes shift to my face, he smiles. "Well, if it isn't my favorite virgin." He reaches out and pulls me into a tight hug. "Let me know if you're ready to lose it tonight, Gallo. I'd be happy to help."

The words are ridiculous, but his tone is full of warmth, and I can't help but smile.

"Eew," Saanvi says. "Stop touching her. Ness, you'll probably get an STD in your ear from him whispering in it."

Armaan steps back, scowling. "Do you want to be let in or not? I could literally have you banned from all of our parties."

Saanvi rolls her eyes. "Then I wouldn't ever help you get money from Mom and Dad again."

He snorts, shaking his head as he looks at me. "Do you hear her? How do you trust this mercenary?"

I lift a brow. "You're the one who sold me to your frat for a thousand dollars."

"You're an angel for helping me, which is why you'll be treated like a VIP tonight. I'm going to make sure you always have a drink in your hand. Whatever you want. Oh, and none of them are touching you. I already have someone lined up to take you both home later ton—"

"No." Saanvi shakes her head sharply. "I'm crashing here tonight. You're giving me your bed."

He scowls. "The fuck I am."

"I'll tell Mom and Dad you cheated on Brenna, and that's the real reason she broke up with you."

He clenches his jaw. "Alright fine. Get the fuck inside."

The floor is vibrating from the blasting bass when we step into the frat house, and I try to retreat into my head. I hate parties. I've only started drinking at them in the last year, but even that hasn't made them fun.

It's so pathetic that they make me yearn for my youth group days, when I would walk into a "party" and find my friends surrounding a coffee table with a board game on it.

But if I want to lose my virginity, this is where I need to go. This is where the sexually confident people gather.

I wish I were one of them.

Saanvi and I push through the crowd of bodies until we make it to the kitchen. She heads straight for the keg and grabs a red cup. "Do you want one?"

My nose wrinkles. I still can't stand beer, even after a year of trying to acquire a taste for it. "Do you think we can do shots?"

Saanvi opens her mouth and closes it when a tall form steps behind me, casting a long shadow over me. A lovely musky scent hits my nose, sending a tingle down my spine.

25

"Oh, we can do shots, for sure," a deep voice says.

Carter.

I'd recognize that voice anywhere. It's deep and dark but has a hint of playfulness. I school a blank mask over my face as I turn around, but I'm probably going to be unable to keep myself from reacting.

My God. He's a sight.

He's built like a lumberjack with his huge, muscular shoulders and chest, but he has the face of an angel. He has plump lips and thick eyelashes that frame those pale-blue eyes. And those dimples...

My God, those dimples.

His smile is famous on campus. I once overheard a girl say, "Carter Blake's dimples make me want to sit on his face," and I understood in my gut what she meant even when I was still ingrained in purity culture and knew nothing about sex. His smile does something primitive to the body, something that not even heavy brainwashing can override.

Why does he have to intimidate me so much? He'd be a perfect candidate otherwise. Saanvi's right that he's probably really good at sex. If I could only get over this self-consciousness...

No. I need someone who can make me feel completely at ease. Someone who isn't a sex god. It doesn't matter how skilled Carter is with his "magic penis." If I'm feeling self-conscious, I'll be in danger of having another humiliating panic attack like I did with Graham.

I can flirt with Carter, but I need to resist any temptation to choose him as my guy.

Carter

She turns around, and my breath hitches.

Her wide brown eyes meet mine before dropping to my

mouth, making my dick twitch. Fuck, why is she looking at my mouth?

Oh. Probably because it's hanging open.

Holy fuck, I didn't expect her to be this beautiful. I've seen her face dozens of times in her videos, but I've never stood this close to her. She has an objectively gorgeous face—perfect for an influencer. Big, expressive eyes, pretty skin, and shiny hair that looks soft to the touch. She has that special sparkle that makes it look like she has some kind of internal light.

I've seen so many beautiful women. I've fucked so many beautiful women.

What is this ache in my chest, like a quiet voice whispering that she's dangerous—that I'll follow her to my peril?

This must be her magic. This is why she has the whole campus in her thrall.

"Do you have vodka?" she asks, thankfully pulling me out of my head so I can stop staring at her.

Fuck, where is my game? I'm lucky Armaan already assigned me to take her home in exactly two hours from now. If not, I'd be in danger of losing her to someone else.

I smile, and her eyes widen as her gaze drops to my cheeks.

Perfect.

My smile always seems to do something for women. It's my dimples, my mom tells me. Women love my dimples. They make me seem non-threatening.

Eat them up, baby girl. Revel in them so I can lure you into trusting me.

"Vanessa Gallo likes vodka?" I ask.

She shrugs. "I don't like beer."

I take a step closer to her. I'm about to speak when her scent washes over me, and I'm momentarily stunned. What is that? Like I'm in a garden, but also somewhere safe and familiar. It's her perfume mixed with whatever scent is uniquely her, and oh God, I really like it. I want to maul her.

This has happened to me before. I didn't find a woman attractive until she stood close to me, and then I wanted to lick her everywhere. I've never felt it this strong before. Vanessa Gallo's prim personality is irritating in her videos. What does it say that I'm already starting to think she's more interesting, without her saying beyond ten words to me?

I need to be careful with this one. She seems to have something secret just for me.

Still, revenge is going to be that much sweeter. Fucking this one will be lovely, and thankfully this annoying power she has over my senses will vanish as soon as it's over. It always does.

In a way, this curse of needing constant novelty in my sexual partners serves me well. When people command your emotions, that gives them power, and not everyone can be trusted with that power. I'll never be in danger of getting my heart broken.

"What if I made you a drink?" I ask Vanessa.

She smiles, and something twinges in my chest. She has so much more warmth in person.

"What could you possibly make?" She leans against the kitchen counter. "I have top-shelf taste in cocktails, and any mixed drink I've ever had at a frat party usually had the cheapest ingredients."

I step closer and loom over her, and her gaze falls to my pecs. I have to keep myself from smiling. She's not even trying to hide the fact that she's checking me out. "You have top-shelf taste, huh? From all those years of abstaining? I watched your TikTok about alcohol and the church. I heard you say you only had your first drink last year. Now you have no tolerance for anything but the good stuff?"

She purses her lips primly. "I would have been this way even if I hadn't been deprived until last year. I'm a sucker for ambiance. I want my drink to take me somewhere. I want it to be an experience. When I order a mai tai, I want it to make me feel like I'm watching the sunset in Hawaii after spending the day surfing. When I have wine, I want to feel like I'm sipping something ancient with my nonna, overlooking the countryside in Assisi."

I grin. "So you're a sucker for bullshit is what you mean? Advertising must work really well on you."

She grins back, and my breath catches.

My God. When she smiles, it's like a bright light has turned on, and the warmth of it radiates all around. I want to drown in her...

What the fuck is going on? Why am I so affected by this girl?

I'm never drawn to fake people. Their bullshit doesn't work on me, probably because I'm the biggest bullshitter I know. Every trick in the book is too familiar to be alluring. Why is hers seeming to work right now?

Maybe she's not quite as insincere as I thought. Maybe she's only fake in her videos.

"Yes," she says. "I'm totally the type of person who can be sold on the packaging and not the product itself."

I grin. "So does that mean you don't actually surf? You just like to feel like you've been surfing when you're sipping a mai tai?"

She purses her lips to the side, like she's giving earnest thought to the question. "I guess I am technically a surfer, because I do have my own surfboard and take it out once every few months. But to be honest, I'd prefer sipping a mai tai and feeling like I've been surfing to actually surfing."

I bark out a laugh. "So you're not a very good surfer is what you're trying to say?"

She shrugs. "That's a matter of opinion."

I shake my head sharply. "It's not, actually. It's very much a measurable skill. Tell me where you surf, and I'll know exactly how good a surfer you are."

She smiles sheepishly. "Leadbetter is my favorite spot."

"Ah, baby waves. I know everything I need to know about you, Gallo, and I'm sorry to say I won't be taking you surfing anytime soon."

She pouts her lips dramatically, and I have to keep my jaw from dropping open. This look is so unpracticed—almost awkward—

like she doesn't know how to flirt, and yet it takes everything within me to keep myself from grabbing her by the face and kissing her.

I'm startled when Parker appears at her side. "What do you want, beautiful?"

I roll my eyes. "I'm getting her a drink. Go away."

Parker doesn't even look my way. Typical. Most of the guys here tonight are trying to win her at all costs. Thank God Armaan basically gave me dibs on her. No matter how much the guys interrupt our conversations tonight, I'll at least have her all to myself on the drive home.

"What do good Christian girls drink?" Parker asks. "Wine probably, huh? Didn't Jesus turn it into water?"

Vanessa sucks in her lips, as if she's fighting a smile. "Other way around."

"Dumbass." I glare at him. "She wants me to make her a cocktail. And she wants you to go away."

Vanessa narrows her eyes—holding my gaze—and I smile innocently back. Just as she opens her mouth to speak, another guy appears at her side. As soon as I see who it is, I can't stop my eyes from rolling.

Derek.

Our one church-attending brother.

Goddamn him. Of course he would try with her.

"I watched your video this morning," he says after introducing himself. "I thought it was really brave."

Her expression softens. She smiles at him, but it's a different smile from the ones she's been giving me. The smile she gave me was flirtatious. This one is something else...

It's one of mutual understanding.

I can't let this go on. He's going to steal her from me before I've even gotten started.

Vanessa

. . .

30

Something loosens inside of me. It feels so good to hear someone call me brave.

Who is this guy?

I scan his face. He's not as beautiful as Carter, but he's very good-looking with his symmetrical features and kind brown eyes. I feel safe with him, and I'm not sure why. I don't even know this man.

"I've gotten used to being vulnerable on camera," I tell him. "I've shared enough embarrassing things since I started my TikTok. What I did this morning wasn't so different."

A notch forms between his brows. "Don't downplay it. What you're planning to do is hard. I know it's hard because I was raised Catholic. I went through a lot of the same stuff."

"Derek, you've had sex with like half of AOPi." It's Carter's deep voice, and he sounds exasperated. "I don't think you can relate to Vanessa's virginity show."

A smile tugs at my lips. When I meet Derek's eyes, he seems to share my amusement. "My 'virginity show,'" I say. "It sounds so salacious."

His slight smile lifts into a full grin. "Can you imagine what you would have thought in junior high youth group if someone had told you that you'd someday have a virginity show?"

Our gazes hold. "I probably wouldn't have thought it was that weird. I'd have assumed it was a show about the benefits of staying pure until marriage. It would have seemed perfectly logical back then."

Derek's smile remains, though his brow furrows. "Damn, you're right. I almost forgot what it was like. There was so much talk about sex in youth group, considering we weren't planning on having it anytime soon."

"It's really twisted how much church leadership talks about sex with kids that young. It's probably why I'm so comfortable talking about it now, even though I'm not even slightly comfortable having it."

The compassion that fills Derek's eyes tugs at something deep inside. This man understands. I feel it. Our shared background means that nothing I'm saying is weird to him, which is liberating.

"It's not impossible to overcome," he says. "In fact..." He smiles mischievously. "Breaking out of it can be fun. Try not to intellectualize it. Try to let your body do the work for you."

"Fuck," Parker says. "This conversation is too deep for me, and I'm too drunk." With that, he staggers off in the direction of the keg.

I almost forgot that Parker and Carter were still around. The depth of this conversation pulled me into a private space with just Derek. When I turn to Carter to offer a polite apology, I'm momentarily arrested. What is that look he's giving me? His smile is bland, but there's something brewing behind his eyes. Something almost angry...

Good Lord, could he be jealous?

Why does it fill me with this hot, liquid delight? I know Carter is just like all the other frat guys. He wants to take my virginity to prove something. He's interested in me as a conquest, not a person.

Still, the idea of Carter Blake wanting me does strange things to my insides.

"We don't need to talk about this here if it makes you uncomfortable," Derek says. "A frat party is kind of an awkward place to be discussing our religious trauma."

I shake my head. "Not at all. It's the most appropriate place for me. My religious trauma makes frat parties hard to enjoy. As a matter of fact, this is the most fun I've had at a frat party. Ever. And it's because I found someone like you to talk to. Someone who shares my religious trauma."

Derek shoots me another smile, and it makes all the tension leave my shoulders. This ease I feel with him is a good sign. Maybe he's a good candidate to take my virginity.

He's perfect in so many ways. He's handsome, but not in an intimidating way like Carter. Most importantly, he understands.

He understands in a way that most people don't. If I had a panic attack, he wouldn't freak out the way Graham did.

I'm startled when a red cup is set in my hand. I glance up to see Carter's blue eyes boring into me. "I made that for you."

I stare down at the pinkish-orange drink. "I didn't even realize you left to make it."

When he doesn't say anything, my gaze roams his face, and now I have no doubt that he's angry, and it makes my stomach do a little turn.

I take a tiny sip out of the red cup. Something sweet, warm, and tropical bursts on my tongue, and I hum in delight. "What is this?"

"A Bahama Mama," Carter says. "Sort of. We didn't have grenadine or coconut rum, so I had to improvise."

I smile at Derek. "I wouldn't know they were missing if he hadn't said it."

As Derek opens his mouth to speak, I'm bumped in the shoulder. A moment later, cold wetness seeps into the bodice of my dress, and I shriek. When I glance up, Parker is staring down at my boobs with a baffled expression. "Holy shit, I'm so sorry." He looks around the area. "Someone pushed me... Fuck."

"Nice job, dumbass." Carter sounds irritated.

I grit my teeth to fight the cold. "Would you mind..." I shoot pleading eyes at Derek, and he nods and walks away before I get the chance to speak. He knows I need a towel without me having to say it, and it's a momentary relief. Then a burst of cool air from the wide-open front door makes my nipples harden, and a ball of icy shame forms in my stomach.

I hate this. I hate this so much.

I hate this visceral disgust mixed with sadness that overtakes me every time I become aware of my body. Any attention or stimulation on my breasts sends a wash of self-loathing over my skin.

I hate that. I hate that I can't make that feeling go away through rationalization. There's no reason to hide my body. I have lovely breasts and pretty skin. No one is disgusted looking at me right now. No one else even cares.

Only me.

"Come on." Carter grabs my forearm and tugs me away. I keep my head down as he guides me through the crowd. Before I know it, he's opening a door, and we're in an empty bedroom. I exhale a shaky breath.

He leaves me in the center of the large room and walks to what looks like a bathroom. When I look up at the big window, I catch sight of the moon's silver reflection sparkling on the ocean.

"Oh my God," I mutter. "Is this your room?"

"Yep." He emerges through the doorway with a towel in hand. "I have the biggest one in the house."

I glance at the blood-red cloth he hands me. "Your family must be wealthy."

When he chuckles, I inwardly wince at my rudeness. I press the towel firmly against my chest. The ball of ice in my stomach melts away like I've stepped into a hot bath.

"Sorry," I say. "It's hard for me to think when I'm soaked."

"It's okay." His voice is gentle.

I start to speak, but when I look up at him, all traces of what I was about to say vanishes from my head. Heat fills my gut, and my skin starts to tingle.

In a good way this time.

Oh Jesus, he's beautiful.

This is different from how I felt standing in front of Derek. My attraction to Carter is in my body rather than my mind. Theoretically, I know we aren't a good pairing. Everything Saanvi's told me about him confirms he's exactly the stereotypical frat boy he looks like. He's the type of guy who dumps people after they "catch feelings," for crying out loud. His primary interests probably include lifting and going to the gym, as if those are two separate things.

"Do you want me to get you something to change into?" he asks. "I can throw your dress in the dryer."

"Yeah, a T-shirt and shorts would be nice."

A grin spreads over his face, and my stomach does a little turn. He walks over to his dresser and opens the bottom drawer. After rummaging a little, he glances back at me. "Do you want Metallica or Beach Burger?"

I grin. "I forgot your family owns Beach Burger. I'll take that one."

He snorts. "This T-shirt actually has a taco on it." He stands up and lets the T-shirt unfold. It's aqua blue with a taco resting on a beach and a sunset in the background. "Something they tried about five years ago. They were...disgusting."

I grab the T-shirt. "I tried them. I didn't think they were disgusting. They certainly didn't taste like a real taco, but they were their own thing. They were solid for ninety-nine cents."

His smile holds, though his brow knits. "They were kind of their own thing, huh?"

I nod. "They had ground beef instead of carne asada, but it didn't taste like Taco Bell either. It tasted kind of like...a burger. They should have called them burger tacos or something."

Carter's smile grows, his eyes crinkling at the corners. God, why am I rambling about tacos?

"You're very analytical about...marketing, I guess."

"I'm very analytical about everything."

That smile holds. "Are you a business major?"

I wrinkle my nose. "Oh, no. I have no interest in business. I already sort of run a business with my TikTok, and I hate the financial aspect of it. I'd rather have a steady income." I glance at the bathroom. "Can you get me some shorts so I can change?"

His gaze is fixed on my face for a moment, and I can see thoughts racing behind his eyes. Maybe he isn't quite as brainless as I thought. As if coming to some conclusion, he snaps out of his daze. "Sure."

After changing out of my dress, I emerge from his bathroom.

His gaze is fixed on me as I walk toward him, and something flashes in his eyes. Something that sends a little jolt between my legs. He stares at my bare thighs, and for the first time in my life, I don't have the urge to cover myself.

What is this? Why do I like it when he looks at my body?

"You don't even need the shorts," he says. "That shirt is a dress on you."

I frown. "How tall are you?"

"Six-three. You?"

"I'm five foot one."

His jaw drops. "What? You look way taller than that. It isn't possible."

He moves toward me and stands so close I can feel the heat of his body, and it makes liquid heat pool in my belly. My God, I like the scent of him. He smells a little musky, probably after being in that muggy room surrounded by a crowd of bodies. I catch the spice of his cologne, but that's not what makes me wish I could bury my head into his chest. I just like the smell of *him*.

Scent seems to be the root of all human attraction. The fact that I like the smell of him so much means something.

"People always think I'm taller," I say. "It's because I have long legs."

"No." His voice is husky, and it makes my stomach flip. "It's not your legs. It's you. I don't know what it is about you, but you somehow have a tall personality. You take up a whole room with it."

The heat in my belly cools, and I snort. He frowns at me.

"I liked you until you said that," I say.

His confusion seems to grow. Does he think I'm not onto him?

"I do not have a big personality. Nor do I want one. I don't want to light up a room at a party. I want to find my closest friends and pull them to a corner where we can have our own party. I don't want to be charming, because I don't like charming people—generally speaking, of course. Charming people are often fake and empty. At least, in my experience."

He looks utterly baffled, and it fills me with hot satisfaction. I can't help but smile, probably a little smugly.

Try to convince me I'm charming after that, Carter Blake. Then I'll know you're a liar.

"If you prefer one-on-one conversations, how about I take you somewhere?" he asks. "Away from this party. We can go take a hike on Inspiration Point and watch the sunrise."

I wrinkle my nose. "Are you being serious?"

That baffled look holds. "Yeah, why not?"

"I don't even know you. You might take me on a hike to murder me." I shake my head. "I'm actually over this party. The spilled drink killed it for me, and I have to work early tomorrow. I'm going to order an Uber."

Just as I turn towards the door, he grabs my arm. "I'll take you home."

I whip back around. "You've had a few drinks. I'd feel safer calling an Uber."

"No, I haven't had a single drink. Armaan enlisted me to get you and Saanvi home, but I guess Saanvi's staying here."

"What?" I frown. "He did?"

"Yeah. He doesn't trust the guys when they get too drunk. He's afraid they're going to get too...assertive, I guess, after your virginity proposition."

I stare at him for a long moment, trying to put the pieces of the puzzle together. "And he trusts you?"

He smiles lazily. "Yep. I'm probably the only guy he really trusts besides De—" His mouth closes, his eyes widening. "No. Actually, I'm probably the only one he really trusts."

Was he about to say Derek? Why did he change his mind?

Carter

. . .

I like her.

Goddamn it, I like her a lot.

What does this mean? My attraction to her will disappear after I fuck her. My desire to lean forward and kiss her nose when she speaks with almost scholarly seriousness about Beach Burger tacos will fade away once I have her beneath me.

But I'll probably still like her, and I'm not sure what to do about it. The publicity of her TikTok is a golden opportunity to get the ultimate revenge on my grandparents, but would it bother her if she knew that's the reason I'm pursuing her so hard?

I can't think about that now. Not when I haven't won her yet.

When I glance to my right, she's sitting with that plastic bag holding her dress clutched tightly in her lap. She's hardly spoken at all since we left the frat house.

She's shy.

She really is just as prim as she seems in her TikTok videos, though she has bursts of being a little more playful in person. She smiles more and even flirts in her own earnest way. Was I crazy for finding her annoying? Maybe she only seemed insincere in her videos because she's so shy.

If so, I'm going to have to change my tactics with her. I'll have to mirror her earnestness. If I'm too flirtatious, I might scare her away.

I have to hand it to Derek. He really knew how to get through to her tonight. Then again, he might actually want her beyond the whole virginity proposition. He's a sap when it comes to women like her. As much as he's broken away from his church background, he always seems to prefer the sweet, demure ones like Vanessa.

But he's not going to win her. He's a boy scout. Not nearly as ruthless as I am, and he doesn't have a fraction of my charm. He'd never pay someone a hundred bucks to spill a drink on her and still be able to hold her gaze with a smile afterwards.

It's time to dial my ruthless charm up to a thousand so that I can lock her in for a date tomorrow, before Derek gets the chance to steal her from me.

"Is this it right here?" I gesture my head to the apartment complex on my left.

She nods. "You can turn in here so I can use the side gate."

I nod as I pull into a tiny parking lot. "I'll walk you to your apartment."

She laughs, and the musical sound of it drifts over my body like warm water. Fuck, she really is charming, despite what she says. Just the way she moves and talks has me enthralled.

Or maybe it's just that she seems to be made for me.

"No need. I live here. I'm not going to get kidnapped in the hundred-foot walk to my front door."

I unbuckle my seatbelt. "Well, I'm doing it, so deal with it."

"I actually had some fun tonight, and I wasn't expecting it," she says while we step out of the car. "I really liked Derek."

My stomach roils. Fuck Derek. I'll never be able to compete when it comes to Christianity. I can fake a lot of things, but I'd rather be punched in the balls than pretend to embrace my grand-parents' religion.

"Yeah, he liked you too," I say. "He was trying pretty hard tonight. Working the whole Christian angle with you."

"You're so simple," she says. "It's almost refreshing."

I frown as I turn to her. "What do you mean?"

"It's so clear what you want."

I grab her by the arm. "What do I want?"

She stares down at my hand, as if she's affected by my touch. I'm affected by hers too. Her skin is so warm and soft that I want to press my mouth against it. I bet she tastes delicious.

"You're like all the other guys in your frat, except maybe Derek. You just want to take my virginity."

I let out a laugh. "Oh, honey. If I wanted sex, I could literally pull out my phone and pick from hundreds of different women. Your virginity means nothing to me."

"Maybe not my virginity itself, but I think the competition

does something for you. I know your frat has a bet going, and I bet you would just love the bragging rights. I mean, look what you just did." She gestures at me. "You just bragged about having your pick of a hundred women."

I stare at her, my head swimming. My God, she's much more honest than I thought she would be. I never thought she'd mention the bet. I always imagined her playing the sweet, innocent card and pretending to be appalled by it.

She really thinks I want to win it, as if I give a shit about the clout I'd get for it. She seems to think I'm simple and stupid, and something about that exhilarates me. My deviousness hasn't been obvious to her at all.

How far can I take this?

"Okay, yeah." I shrug. "I do kind of... I don't know... It's been kind of a competition for a long time. The bet started out as a joke, but when your purity culture TikTok really started taking off—"

She lifts a hand. "You really don't have to explain yourself. The bets are gross, but so is purity culture. I prefer that you're straightforward with me rather than pretending to really like me like all your brothers. Honesty is really important to me, even when it hurts my feelings."

I nod once. "Alright. How about from now on, I'll be brutally honest with you?"

She crosses her arms. "Go for it."

I stare at her for a long moment. There's a challenge in her expression, as if she doesn't really believe I'd be honest enough to risk losing the bet.

What if I was? It's a gamble, but hurting her feelings right now might be worth gaining her trust in the long run.

"I have no interest in dating you long term. I want to win this bet. Not because I need the money, but because I want to go live with you and announce that I took your virginity. I'd be a celebrity on campus—more so than I already am. I'm vain, I guess." I shrug. "Sorry."

Under the blue light of the lantern, I see her cheeks darken. Still, she holds my gaze. "I appreciate that you admitted it."

There's something in her voice... Is it admiration? Either way, I can hear in her tone that she really means it.

Victory.

"I won't be picking you, but I really do appreciate your honesty, especially admitting that you're vain." She smiles. "How embarrassing."

I grin back at her, and her eyes widen minutely before drifting to my mouth. Heat pools in my stomach.

You won't be picking me yet, baby girl, because I haven't worked my magic. Yet.

"Exactly," I say. "You should feel sorry for me."

Her smile grows. "I would if you weren't so..."

I quirk a brow. "So what?"

She narrows her eyes on my face before turning around and walking toward the concrete staircase.

"So we've established that I'm not going to lie to you to sleep with you," I say as I catch up to her. "But if honesty matters that much to you, you should be careful with the other guys. I'm not saying they're bad guys. But they'll probably tell you just about anything to sleep with you."

"I figured."

I grab her arm and halt her step. "Even Derek."

She turns to me, her gaze locking on my face. "You're saying Derek would lie?"

The dismay in those big brown eyes sends a prickling heat through my veins. Fuck, am I jealous?

"He might," I say. "He was the most vocal of our group about wanting to win the bet."

She jerks back as if I hit her, and my stomach sinks. Fuck, I don't like it when she looks at me like this. I wish I could take her into my arms and kiss that expression off her face.

"That doesn't sound like him at all." Her voice is slightly breathless.

She's right. It doesn't sound like him. Maybe I should have been a little less heavy-handed. I could have still won her without lying so thoroughly. Derek's a great guy, and I've probably permanently ruined his chances with her.

Why don't I feel guilty? I must be a selfish bastard, because exhilaration pumps through my veins at the thought of keeping him away from her.

"He was telling me about his past," she mutters, her dark eyes growing unfocused. "His own experiences being raised in purity culture. He'd have to be a sociopath to lie about it."

"He just wants to win the bet. Everyone in my frat does."

Her eyes widen. "He seemed so sincere."

"I don't think he was totally lying. He was just using his religion as an in with you."

She shakes her head slowly, her eyes narrowed as if in deep concentration. "I hate him for it."

I frown. "Hate is a little strong."

Her eyes remain unfocused. "I hate him for tricking me. For making me think we had a real connection. What a creepy thing to do."

"If you think that's creepy, you should be a fly on the wall at one of our meetings."

Her gaze snaps to my face. "Why are you even in this fraternity?"

"Because it's fun. They're my brothers, and I love them. I'm an idiot just like them."

"You at least have a little more self-awareness. And honesty."

I grin. "I'm glad you see that. Anyway, choose Derek at your own peril, but I think you should choose me."

"Obviously you do. You're desperate to win the bet. You've fully admitted it."

"So is everyone. You have the whole campus chasing after you. Do you not understand that? Anyone who approaches you in the next thirty days is probably doing it because of your announcement. And if they aren't, how will you know? That's the disadvantage of going about it the way you are."

"I knew it would be. I'm not sure if I really care. I'm not looking for a long-term partner. In fact, I want this to be only about sex. Their intentions don't matter if it's purely physical."

Damn. This girl is far more pragmatic than I thought she was.

"That's the spirit," I say. "Pick me. Let me take you out to dinner tomorrow night."

She frowns. Her gaze roams my face for almost a full thirty seconds, and inexplicably, I find myself holding my breath, waiting for her answer.

Yet, there's also a mixture of dread. If she agrees to this, we're on the path to this chase being over, and there's something I enjoy about sparring with Vanessa. She's a worthy opponent. Her pragmatism makes her strangely unpredictable.

I almost dread thinking about this spark fading after I fuck her.

"No."

I blink once. "No?"

"No, I don't want to go out with you. I think I'm done with your fraternity. I don't like being tricked. If I pick you, I might run into Derek again."

With that, she turns around and walks away, and I find myself so stunned I can't even think of a way to get her back over here.

Fuck.

* * *

As soon as I walk inside the house, Dom and Ethan appear in front of me. "Dude! You took her home? What the fuck?"

I roll my eyes as I walk in the direction of my bedroom. I'm in no mood to rejoin the party after tonight's failure. It's time to pass out so I can regroup tomorrow. I have to think of another plan.

"She wanted to leave," I say. "Parker's drunk ass spilled beer all over her dress."

Dom scowls. "Goddammit! This was our one opportunity, and Parker fucked it over. I should have assigned some of the pledges to keep an eye on her."

I whip around. "No, you should not have done that. She already feels like we're creeping on her. In fact, she said she's done with our fraternity."

Dom's mouth drops open. "Fuck."

"I already have a plan," Ethan says.

Their reactions grate on my nerves. No wonder Vanessa is weirded out. This is all so out of hand. They're all treating her like she's a beer pong tournament.

I scowl at Ethan. "A plan for what?"

"She can say she's done with our fraternity, but what if she's forced to be around us?" He grins.

"That sounds creepy," I say.

"What is your plan?" Dom asks as if he didn't even hear me. God, how are these people my friends?

"She works at the Gospel House Crisis Center. It's like a shelter thing, kind of. Anyway, my friend Landon is her boss. His dad owns it. He says they're always taking volunteers, so I'll be there bright and early tomorrow morning."

"Damn." Dom pats Ethan's back. "Nice work."

Ethan's dumb, satisfied grin is the outside of enough. I turn around and march to my bedroom. "At this point," I call out, "I'm almost worried I'm going to find her head in our freezer."

"You're just jealous you didn't think of it," Ethan shouts back.

He's totally wrong. I'm happy he did the work for me. At least ten of them are going to show up at her shelter now, which means I'll be able to look that much less creepy. Plus, I'll be able to show my "honesty" by admitting I'm just there to win her, while the others will pretend like they really care about the shelter.

Looks like I have plans tomorrow.

Chapter Four

anessa

"I promised I'd tell you the story of my first—absolutely embarrassing—attempt at getting over my sexual shame."

I take a sip of my tea before cradling it against my chest. Why did I decide to do this now? I'm in a terrible mood. I'll need to go on a run after this to clear my head and give me some endorphins.

I woke up this morning with a gut feeling that I'd have an email from Rachel Moore, only to be disappointed.

Rachel has her own purity culture show on Instagram, and she was instrumental in helping me break away from it all. I emailed her three weeks ago asking for an interview, and I still haven't heard back.

It's disheartening. I know she must be extremely busy, but this is so important. A superstitious part of me believes that her lack of response is a bad omen for the next thirty days.

I know it's silly, but in my fragile state of mind, I can't shake the prickle of foreboding at the back of my mind.

The whole ordeal with Derek last night isn't helping. How could he have done that to me? How could he have used our shared background to manipulate me? It's such a low move for someone who was raised to follow Jesus.

Then again, Carter could be lying. I really don't think so, though. It doesn't seem like there's enough going on behind those pretty blue eyes of his for him to be that calculated. Besides, there's something about him that seems trustworthy and honest. My gut says he's telling the truth, and Derek is the manipulative one.

I take a deep breath before pressing the red button on my screen. "In my last video, I told you about how I had a bad sexual experience. This is my story of what happened.

"About a year ago, shortly after I created my TikTok account, I was just starting to get to know a guy I really liked. I'm not going to say his name, because he didn't do anything wrong..."

Just as I expected, that sick shame grows like cancer in my gut. I hate telling this story, but I need to do it so that my followers can understand the significance of my announcement two days ago.

"He was really cute and easygoing, and we got along right away. Because we connected, I trusted him. I confided in him. I told him how hard it was for me to enjoy my body. I even told him how hard it was to feel pleasure from touching myself." I smile. "Pardon the euphemism. This is TikTok. Anyway, when I shared those things with him, he was very accepting, nonjudgmental, and encouraging. This made me feel like... Like I could probably..."

I shake my head and take a sip of my tea. Normally, I stop the video when I lose my train of thought, but it might be good for my followers to see how much telling this story unsettles me. If they share my struggles, they might feel less alone—the way that Rachel Moore made me feel.

"Anyway, we kissed a few times, and it wasn't...terrible. God —" I wince "—I really hope he doesn't watch this and think I'm blaming him in any way. That's not what I'm doing. All the problems were in my body."

My vision grows a little fuzzy. Just talking about that day resurrects that cold, stirring sickness in my stomach.

"Eventually, I let him...touch me. I'm sure you can imagine which part of my body I'm talking about. Anyway, I ended up... having a panic attack. It's so embarrassing. I was half-naked and pacing his room, trying to catch my breath. He was understandably weirded out. After that, I never heard from him again, which made me feel..."

When my throat grows tight, I glance at the time. God, this video is getting way too long.

"Gross," I say before turning off the record button.

* * *

I roll down the window, letting ocean wind brush over my hot cheeks during the last few minutes of the drive. When my phone rings, I glance at the screen of my car's center console, and my stomach plummets.

Livvy.

I squeeze the steering wheel as it continues to ring, hating myself as the phone goes silent when I pull into the parking lot. I haven't spoken to my sister since she and Cole came over on Wednesday night and announced their engagement. We typically text each other at least once a day. She must know something is up.

I can't talk to her right now. Not when my nerves are so raw after the video I made this morning. I won't be able to hide the fact that her engagement has thrown me into a funk. She'll think that I'm not happy for her and Cole, and that will dampen her own happiness. I'll call her after I've had more time to process everything, maybe even after my shift this evening.

I'm so thankful I have a job like this. Assuming my boss isn't here, and he usually isn't early on Saturdays, today is going to be peaceful but distracting enough to get my mind off the Graham incident.

I hate that talking about it has resurrected all of the old feelings.

After stepping out of my car, I walk along the back of the brick building. When I make it around the corner, my stomach flips over. Why are there so many people waiting outside? And why are they all...

College students.

Male college students.

I sigh heavily. I should have predicted this. Gospel House has a contract with UC Santa Barbara, making it one of the easiest non-profits to volunteer at when students need to accrue volunteer hours.

Or try to seduce the charity's virgin intern.

Jesus, why is this happening today when I'm in such a low mood?

Then again, maybe this will be cathartic. I'll be their boss. They won't be able to interact with the residents anyway—not without training—so I can give them all of the worst tasks. All of the things that have been on my to-do list for months.

When I march forward, a bunch of heads whip around. Smiles spread across their strong jaws. Why do all frat guys look vaguely similar? They all have square faces and dumb half-smiles.

I wave shyly, and their grins get bigger. Maybe if I act like the girl in their gross virgin fantasy, they'll work even harder today.

"Are you guys here to volunteer?" I ask, trying to infuse as much innocence into my tone as I can. As if it isn't brazenly obvious why they're all here.

While several of them state their agreement, one guy steps forward. As soon as his familiar face comes into view, laughter bubbles from my chest.

Armaan.

Oh my God, of course. Of course it's the Alpha Lambda Xi guys. They probably all feel cheated out of their chance because I took off early last night, especially after paying Armaan a thousand bucks.

I can't believe they're up this early. This bet clearly means a lot to all of them.

"Hey there, Ness." Armaan's voice has an affected smoothness, like he's trying to sound smarmy. "So I'm not sure if you know this, but I'm in a fraternity called Alpha Lambda Xi—"

"You're such an idiot," I interrupt, my voice choked with laughter.

His grin grows. "Probably, but I'm an idiot who wants to make the world a better place, which is why we're all here." He gestures to the guys behind him. "We all love to do charity work in our spare time."

"I'm sure you do. That sounds so like you. I'm sure Saanvi would agree."

His smile falters. "Can you keep this between us?"

"Um..." I frown. "Why?"

He sighs heavily. "She'll know what I'm doing. She'll probably tell our older brother, who will tell my parents."

My frown grows. "Why would your parents have a problem with you volunteering at a crisis center?"

His jaw hardens. "They'll assume it's not sincere. They always think I'm up to no good, even when I'm doing charity shit."

I stare at his face for a moment. "Why are you doing it? I mean—" I lower my voice to just above a whisper "—I get why those boneheads are doing it, but you know this won't impress me, even if you were trying to win me over. And it seems like you'd have a million other ways to entertain yourself."

He lifts his hand and scratches the back of his head. "I don't know... Being a fifth-year senior fucking sucks. My mom's the CEO of a multi-million dollar company, and she wouldn't even give me a job as the coffee bitch if I asked her. I have to figure out what I'm going to do with my life. I'm just kind of...trying shit out, I guess."

Wow, I've never seen this side of him before. I almost wish he would let me tell Saanvi about this. Maybe she wouldn't be so hard on him.

I make it a point to smile warmly. "You're the only one I trust out of all these boneheads. I wish I could tell them all to go away."

"Don't worry." He lifts a brow. "I'll keep them in line."

I sigh. "They won't all be welcome. We can only take five volunteers a day. Two of them will have to go home."

His smile grows lazy. "I already know the two I want to eliminate."

I giggle. "You're a—"

"You're going to have to eliminate three now."

Heat rushes through my body at the sound of Carter's deep voice.

Of course.

Of course he would come.

I shouldn't feel this rush of exhilaration flushing through my veins. His persistence has nothing to do with me. It's about the bet. But damn. He's so attractive. Would it really be so bad if I gave in to this attraction?

Yes.

It would be.

My self-consciousness might dissipate when we're close, but it would come back in full swing once I'm naked in front of him and thinking about all the sex he's had and how unimaginably awkward I must seem in comparison.

When I turn around to face him, those blue eyes brighten. "Hey, Gallo."

I cross my arms over my chest. "I didn't know you volunteered at non-profits in your spare time."

His grin grows, his eyes crinkling at the corners. "Oh, yeah. All the time. I love volunteering at..." He glances up at the brick building. "Homeless shelters."

I snort. "It's not a homeless shelter. It's a crisis center. We work with teens at risk for homelessness. You won't even be seeing them, because you have to be trained. You'll be doing—" I smile "—household chores."

He takes a step in my direction, and his proximity alone

makes heat curl in my belly. "You think I'm not up for a little bitch work?" He smiles lazily. "Especially when you're in charge of me?"

I lift a brow. "I know your frat has a housecleaner and a chef."

"Ah, so you think I don't know how to use a stove or clean a dish. I didn't have those luxuries before college, but the other guys did. You're going to have your work cut out for you with them."

"Armaan said he'll keep them in line."

Carter snorts. "Armaan's going to smoke weed in the bathroom and get tired and leave."

"No way," Armaan says, his gaze fixed on his phone. "Weed makes me focus better. I'm really good at fixing shit. Tell me what's broken, and I'll get to work."

I beam at him. "That's perfect. One of our faucets is leaking. Can you take a look at it?"

He nods once. "I'm on it."

"Perfect. Carter, do you want to help him?"

He scowls. "Fuck, no. I'm going to be wherever you are."

"Looks like I'm finally going to get around to painting the pantry."

He narrows his eyes on my face, his lips quirking at the corners. "Is that supposed to scare me, Gallo?"

My stomach flips over at that smile of his. My God, those dimples.

"I think you're going to find that today's going to be a lot more work than you anticipated."

He leans forward. "I think I'm going to enjoy it."

Carter

After pouring the last bit of plaster powder into the metal bucket, I glance in her direction. An involuntary smile tugs at my lips.

Goddamn it, she's cute. Her little brow is furrowed while she explains to Ethan how to stack the plates in the dishwasher and where to put the detergent. There's not even an ounce of judgment in her tone. She's using her typical prim schoolteacher voice, even though she must internally be rolling her eyes at him for having the audacity to volunteer at this shelter.

God, he's a fucking idiot. How did he think he could score points with her when he doesn't even know how to do something as basic as running a dishwasher? Everyone in my frat is a rich kid. We're well known as the trust-fund frat, because our house is an old Victorian mansion that overlooks the ocean.

I didn't have my trust fund until I was fifteen, which gives me an in with her. She's clearly not rich herself. My humble beginnings will upend her expectations. She probably thinks I'm just as inept as the rest of them.

If only Armaan weren't here. He's probably the most handy out of all of us, and not because he grew up doing any of this shit, but because he actually enjoys fixing things.

I'm startled when her face is suddenly in my vision. "How's the plaster coming along?" she asks, her expression tight.

Damn, she's exhausted. Why do I have the strange urge to reach out and hold her and tell her she can relax against me?

My body is so drawn to hers, the desire to touch her feels like an instinct. It's going to be heaven when I'm finally able to fuck her.

"Fine," I say. "It needs to set a bit before I can start stirring."

Her eyes widen, and a pleasant tingle runs over my skin. It's working. She's impressed.

"Where did you learn how to do this?"

"Um..." I smile. "Where did I learn how to mix plaster?"

"Yeah."

I chuckle. "It doesn't take a genius to mix water with powder. I think I watched my dad do it once, and I figured it out."

And I also googled the instructions when she wasn't looking.

Her brow furrows, and she stares at my face for a long moment. My stomach turns into knots. I love this look of hers.

This earnest, puzzled look. She seems to be always assessing and analyzing.

"I know it's rude to ask about money," she says, "but I'm going to do it, anyway. I figure it can't be any worse than you admitting you want to take my virginity to win a betting pool you don't even need."

That involuntary smile tugs at my mouth again. My God, this woman makes me grin like an idiot. I love how direct she is. "Ask away."

"Exactly how wealthy are your grandparents?"

I snort as I pick up the trowel and start stirring the plaster. "Very wealthy."

There's that intense gaze of hers again. God, I love it. It turns me on.

I'm going to make her look at my face when I finally fuck her.

"You say that kind of resentfully. I caught the same vibe when you gave me the Beach Burger T-shirt."

Ah, she is perceptive.

"I have a complicated relationship with my grandparents."

Out of the corner of my eye, I see her nod. "Money usually makes family relationships complicated. I'm almost grateful my parents don't have a ton of it. My dad can be overbearing enough."

"Overbearing is an understatement when it comes to my grandpa."

"I can see that. I'm always a little wary of people who make their faith a big part of their business."

I whip around to face her. "You do?"

She looks surprised by my strong reaction. "I don't think Jesus would want his name used to promote a business. I'm not saying your grandpa is doing it on purpose. He probably thinks making his faith public is the right thing to do."

"No. He's absolutely using it to promote the business. He wants the church crowd. He wants the people who believe eating at Beach Burger is a way to embrace traditional Christian values.

He can say it's about his faith all day, but it's not. It's about money."

Vanessa winces. "I'm sorry. I feel like I'm bringing up family drama."

"I could talk shit about my grandpa all day, but I have to say... I'm kind of surprised you of all people would say that. About combining faith with business, I mean."

A knowing smile overtakes her face. "Because of my TikTok."

"I mean..." I turn back to the bucket of plaster and give it a perfunctory stir. "You are making money off of it, right?"

"I do have sponsors, yes, but I think that's different. My TikTok is about me. It's about my struggles and my joys. My faith is a big part of it, because my faith is a big part of who I am. I don't see it as monetizing my faith, but monetizing *me*."

Something cold settles in my gut, and it takes me a moment to figure out where it's coming from.

She's different from what I thought she was. Maybe she's aware that she's taunting creepy college guys with her fake virginity, but it doesn't seem to be her intention. Her religion and all of this purity-culture stuff seem to really mean something to her.

Can I really go through with this? Can I use her TikTok to humiliate my grandpa?

Yes.

It's worth it, and in the end, I'm not really doing anything to harm her. What does she care if I name my grandpa on her TikTok? The rest of it is all her. I'm not forcing her to talk about sex. That's her brand.

Besides, for all her sincerity, she's still lying about being a virgin.

"My sister's fiancé comes from a really wealthy family, too."

I frown. Why is she telling me this? When I turn toward her, she's staring down at the kitchen counter with a troubled expression.

"Are they assholes or something?" I ask.

She glances up suddenly, as if caught off guard. "No... I've just learned a lot about the complexity of money over the past few years. Through her experiences."

There's still something in her tone. Something I don't quite get. It's wistful and melancholy. She brought this up for a reason. Something is bothering her.

"How long has she been engaged?" I ask.

She bites her bottom lip. "Just a few days."

Bingo.

"You seem kind of bummed. Do you like not like him or something?"

"No." Her voice is soft. "He's perfect."

My stomach plummets to the floor. Holy fuck. She's in love with him. That must be it. Why else would she seem so dejected? Why else would she call him "perfect"? An uncomfortable heat claws at my insides. "Then why do you seem upset?"

When she flinches, I realize that my tone is much more biting than I meant. Holy shit, why does it bother me so much that she's in love with him? She still wants to lose her fake virginity in thirty days. I'll still get to go live with her and make my announcement. It will have no effect on me.

"Wow," she mutters.

"What?"

She shakes her head slowly, and I feel like I'm being turned inside out waiting for her to respond.

"It's really good that you said that. I didn't realize how obvious it was."

My heart jumps into my throat. Oh my God. She just admitted it. A raging heat pulses through my veins. Fucking hell, I want to kill this guy. I take a deep breath through my nose. "Obvious that you're in love with him?"

She stares at me for a long moment before chuckling. "God, no. He's like a big brother."

I exhale a long breath, almost dizzy with relief.

What's wrong with me? Why am I so damn upset?

This woman is making me crazy.

"But I have been…struggling a little since she got engaged."

Something in her expression makes me want to lift my hand and stroke my fingers over her cheek. It's a strange urge. I'm not usually one for non-sexual affection.

Something about Vanessa Gallo commands my whole body, as if she's pulling me toward her by an invisible force.

"How so?" I ask.

She purses her lips to the side as she grabs the trowel. Her gaze is fixed on the bucket as she stirs slowly. "I don't even know really, but her engagement feels like it's throwing off my whole life. I'm so happy for her—" She shuts her eyes. "It sounds fake when I say it, but it really is true. I am happy for her. I love her more than anything, so I'm happy she's happy."

"I believe you."

When she glances up at me, that melancholy expression has returned. "I've just always wanted—"

"Vanessa."

Her gaze darts to the door, and a forced smile spreads over her face. "What's up, Landon?"

When I turn around, a blond guy is standing in the doorway. This must be Ethan's friend, the guy whose dad owns this place.

"How's everything going with the volunteers?" Landon asks.

"I'm putting them to work." Vanessa's eyes narrow as she smiles—making her look almost flirtatious—and it makes something unpleasant stir in my gut.

"Yep." Ethan raises his voice from across the kitchen. "She's a drill sergeant."

Landon smiles at Vanessa, and it makes my jaw clench. There's something in that smile I don't like… Possessiveness, I think. "That's my girl," he says before walking away.

My jaw drops. When Landon's footsteps fade away, I scowl at Vanessa. "What the fuck was that? Isn't he your boss?"

She shrugs, not looking at all affected. "Yeah, but the roles are pretty relaxed here."

My scowl grows. "He should get written up for sexual harassment."

She snorts, waving her hand in my direction. "When you're a woman, you learn you can't be too—"

"Hey, I think I got the dishwasher running."

She jerks back at the sound of Ethan's voice, and I can't stop myself from glaring at him. I wasn't done with the conversation, especially if she was about to brush off sexual harassment like it's just part of being a woman.

What makes me so protective of her?

"Nice work," Vanessa says. "Did you fill it up completely?"

Ethan grins. "Oh, hell yeah. That thing is jam-packed."

I roll my eyes. "Great job, Ethan. We're both proud of you. Here—" I grab the plaster bucket and hand it to him. "Finish stirring this. It's a really difficult and important job. Vanessa will love you for it."

Vanessa shoots me an exasperated smile as she reaches out and grabs the bucket from Ethan's hands. "There's no need for that. Carter was just about to get started on covering the holes in the pantry. Another very difficult and important job."

I smile at her. "Which is why I need you to keep me company while I do it."

"Naw, man." Ethan steps forward. "You've been hogging her. It's my turn."

"There's actually a sign-up sheet in the front office." I gesture at the door. "I get Vanessa for the next hour. If you want a turn, you have to go sign up."

Ethan's brow furrows. "Are you serious?"

"Absolutely. You'd better hurry. I bet you Beckett already booked himself three slots in a row with her, greedy bastard."

Vanessa smiles, rolling her eyes. "He's messing with you."

Ethan chuckles. "Aww, man. I was thinking it was, like... You know... For the shelter. Teaching volunteers what to do."

"No, you weren't," I say. "You were thinking Vanessa has a sign-up sheet for guys competing to win her virginity."

"Enough, Carter." Vanessa's tone is scolding, though she's still smiling. "A sign-up sheet would actually be a better system for how we train our volunteers. In fact, I can help you find another task, since Carter is all set with his."

She shoots me a challenging look, and fuck, I want to kiss her. I love how she flirts. Like a prim little school teacher putting me in my place. God, this girl and I could have some fun in the bedroom.

"How about this..." Ethan smiles at her. "How about I save you the time by finding my own task, and you let me take you out to dinner instead."

Vanessa's eyes grow huge, and hot irritation pumps through my veins. I scowl at Ethan, but he doesn't see me. His gaze is fixed on Vanessa.

"Sorry, if that was really forward," he says. "I just couldn't miss the opportunity."

"Yeah, Ethan." I can't keep the bite out of my voice. "It does seem really forward, and you're embarrassing me. Go away."

"Where did you have in mind?" Vanessa asks Ethan.

What the fuck? Heat washes over my skin. Is she really considering taking him up on his clumsy request for a date?

Ethan's eyes fill with confusion for a minute, and I could almost laugh. He never expected her to say yes. He's shooting his shot with reckless abandon, because he doesn't think he has a prayer of winning her if I'm around.

Unfortunately, she's not as predictable as I expected.

"Um..." A faint smile rises to his mouth. "Somewhere super delicious. Bouchon, maybe?"

Vanessa's adorable little nose scrunches. "That's way too fancy for me. Why don't we get taco-truck burritos and have a little picnic on the beach?"

Glee overcomes Ethan's face, and I really could punch him. A beach picnic with her sounds like heaven. We could go surfing early in the day. Afterwards, she could rest against me, using my body heat to keep her warm while she dries. She's probably a spectacular sight in a bikini—all that pretty skin exposed for my eyes and my hands...

"That sounds awesome!" Ethan grins. "I love picnics."

I roll my eyes. This date will be completely wasted on him. He has the conversation skills of a nine-year-old.

Which could play to my advantage...

I'll look that much better to her in comparison to Ethan, especially if we're side by side.

Looks like I'll be going for an afternoon walk on the beach.

"So should I pick you up at, say, six?" Ethan asks.

Vanessa tucks a thick strand of hair behind her ear. "That's perfect. That gives us time to catch the sunset."

Ethan's jaw drops into an open-mouthed grin. "Damn! The sunset. This is going to be awesome."

My eyelids flutter. He's incapable of playing it cool. He can barely even contain his excitement over his good fortune.

After they exchange contact info, Ethan heads out of the kitchen in search of the other guys.

"He's an idiot," I say. "You're going to realize that on the two-minute drive to the beach, and you're going to hate yourself for committing to this."

"Sex doesn't require intelligence. Besides, I've always wanted to have sex on the beach."

My jaw drops open, and a chill runs down my spine. I turn around slowly, lowering my chin as her gaze meets mine. "Are you really going to fuck him on your first date?"

Her shrug is jerky. "I want to get rid of my virginity as soon as possible."

It takes everything within me to keep from laughing. Virginity, my ass. God, I almost wish I could tell her I'm friends with Graham. I want to see how she would handle it. She seems so sincere, but she'd have to lie. Too much rides on this lie. She has hundreds of thousands of people who follow her just to listen to her talk about purity culture.

"You should pick a guy who could actually make it good for you."

Her eyes narrow. "Are you implying that you could? With all that practice, you think you're some kind of sex god?"

I smirk. "I've picked up on a thing or two."

"Well, everyone's body is different."

I allow my gaze to sweep over her curves, slow and intentional. The effect on her is immediate. Her cheeks redden, and she licks her bottom lip.

I take a step closer. "Yeah, like a puzzle. I like puzzles. Especially when the goal is figuring out all the ways I could make you come."

Her eyes turn to saucers.

You have no idea who you're dealing with, little Vanessa.

There. Now she'll be thinking about me all throughout her date. She'll be excited to see me when I finally join them.

Chapter Five

V anessa

As I unfold the blanket, a gust of ocean wind billows it upward like a hot-air balloon. When the wind settles, I lay it out on the sand and glance at Ethan.

"You're so cute," he says.

I manage a smile, though I'm sure it looks forced.

Not that he would notice.

It's probably the tenth time he's called me cute in the last hour for doing the most basic tasks. I was cute when I ran back inside my apartment to grab this blanket and when I asked for extra napkins at the taco truck. He seems to have a broad definition of "cute."

"How so?" I ask, because I can no longer hold back. If he's going to call me cute for doing something mundane, he needs to justify himself.

Out of the corner of my eye, I see him shrug. "Just all of it. Having a picnic on the beach. Bringing a blanket."

"Do you not usually bring a blanket to the beach?"

His grin falters. "No, I do."

"Then why is it cute when I do it?"

"Probably because *you're* cute." That statement is followed by a satisfied smile, and I turn around and grab our burritos so that I can roll my eyes without him seeing.

Why am I here? Ethan doesn't interest me even slightly. Why did I let my irritation with Carter get the better of me?

There was a moment at the center when I almost liked Carter, but then he switched into his competitive mode—mocking Ethan and trying to get more alone time with me. I was reminded of why he's spending time with me in the first place. I'm only a competition to Carter, and that makes him dangerous.

Because I'm kind of starting to like him.

Carter doesn't try to hide the fact that he's only trying to win the bet. He doesn't feign interest in me to win me over. His sincerity makes him much more stimulating to talk to than the other frat guys who pretend like I've suddenly become the most interesting person in the world to them. How stupid do they think I am?

Carter is the only one who's even mentioned my video announcement. Well, besides Derek.

I still can't believe how devious he was. What kind of person uses his religious trauma to hit on a girl? It's gross.

I plop down on the blanket and reach into the bag. As I pull out my burrito, the foil shimmers under the evening sun. It's a gorgeous day. Why the hell am I here with this bonehead?

"I love that you ordered a burrito," Ethan says, his voice holding a smile.

It takes everything within me to keep myself from saying something rude. *You're in college, Ethan. How do you have nothing to talk about but what is happening right in front of us?*

"Why do you love that I ordered a burrito?" My mouth is tight. I couldn't force a smile if I tried. What a completely inane thing to say on a date.

"I don't know." He shrugs. "You seem like a salad type of girl."

"Taco trucks don't usually have salads."

"I know. I love that you wanted taco-truck burritos."

I huff out an almost hysterical laugh. "You just love everything about me, don't you?"

A large shadow casts over our blanket. "How could he not?"

Carter's deep, smooth voice makes my stomach jolt. When I twist around, his broad form hovers over me. He looks like such a fuckboy with that side-smirk and hooded eyelids. Why am I so happy to see him?

Probably because I know the evening is going to be substantially more interesting now that he's here. Despite my reservations, I can't help but love his confidence and transparency. He's so certain he can win me. He's not even trying to hide the fact that he's here to sabotage my date.

He's brutally honest. Sometimes even unkindly honest, like when he told me he just wanted to win the bet, but that makes me feel safe with him.

An idea sprouts, shooting arrows of heat throughout my insides. Maybe he would be a good choice to take my virginity. At the very least, I can trust his intentions.

No.

The simple truth is that I like Carter, and that makes him a terrible choice. Sex wouldn't be about cleansing my body of shame but growing intimate with him. I can't have that right now. It would give me performance anxiety. I'd want to be good at sex, especially given his extensive experience. I might even have another panic attack.

The incident with Graham made me feel like a failure. Not only could I not enjoy sex, but I also drove away a guy I liked because of it. No amount of rationalizing—telling myself it wasn't my fault or that Graham was too insensitive—could make it go away.

Shame is a primitive emotion. It doesn't listen to reason, which is why I need to fight it in a primitive way.

Through meaningless sex.

Carter sits down next to me and shoots me a lazy smile. Those dimples do strange things to my insides, so I force myself to look away.

Ethan narrows his eyes at him. "I thought you had a midterm tomorrow."

"I'm taking a walk to process everything I've studied."

Ethan snorts. "Don't listen to him, Vanessa. He never takes walks on the beach, at least not without a girl. He's trying to steal you from me. He doesn't know that you'd never date a trust-fund bro."

I laugh. Out of the corner of my eye, I see Carter whip his head in my direction. "Did you really say that?"

I roll my eyes. "That's not exactly what I said. I'd just rather date someone in my social class."

Carter frowns. For the first time, he seems genuinely upset. Why? It's not like he wants to date me. "That's kind of classist," he mutters.

I repress a smile. "I don't think it works in that direction. It's really just a preference. I wouldn't let it sway me entirely. But I'd rather not be dating someone who always wants to do expensive things, like going to fancy restaurants. Things I can't afford with my—"

"I'd pay for everything we did." When he leans forward, and his gaze grows hooded, heat curls through my insides. Why is he getting so intense about this? "You'd never have to spend a dime. And anyway, I'm not really a trust-fund kid because I didn't grow up with money."

"Dude," Ethan says. "It still counts. It doesn't matter when you got the money. You have more of it than anyone else in the frat."

I smile at Ethan in an attempt to compose myself. "I agree."

Carter rolls his eyes. "You live in a house on the beach too, Ethan."

Ethan shrugs. "Yeah, my parents have money. But they don't own a giant fast-food chain like your grandparents."

"You didn't know how to run a dishwasher until this morning. That's about as trust-fund kid as it gets."

I giggle. "I can't believe you guys are fighting over who is the poorest. I haven't even gotten an opportunity to chime in and say that I win."

Ethan grins at me. "You misunderstood. I fucking love money. I wish my parents had way more of it. I just want Carter to own up."

Delight spreads through my belly, and I laugh again. Ethan is so right. Carter dismisses his wealth like it's an embarrassment. What a rich person thing to do.

My laughter catches in my throat when I glance at Carter's face. My Lord, why is he looking so intense again?

Carter

My God, she's so beautiful when she genuinely laughs. Those shining eyes and that toothy smile pull at something deep inside, resurrecting a feeling as ancient as the earth. It's safe and warm and peaceful, and I want to live in it forever.

What is this damn feeling? Why is it Vanessa Gallo of all people that pulls it out, even when her delight isn't for me?

Fuck Ethan. He made me look like a whiney prick, and now she's laughing with him. Where is my game? He was supposed to make me look better by sharp contrast.

It's time to fight a little dirty.

"So, Ethan..." I shoot him a lazy smile. "Lacey asked me where I was headed when I left the frat, and I told her you had a date with Vanessa. She didn't seem very happy."

Ethan's eyes flash, and something that looks like triumph fills them.

I knew it.

I knew he was mostly using Vanessa to make Lacey jealous. What a dumbass. Lacey doesn't give a fuck what he does—he's far too boring for her—and what a shitty thing to do to Vanessa.

When I glance at her, those brown eyes are fixed on Ethan's face. She's watchful, this girl, always analyzing her surroundings. You can see it in those huge, expressive eyes.

It's fucking adorable.

Ethan huffs. "It's none of her business. She's not my girlfriend."

I shrug. "Maybe she wants to be."

"She's fucking you too, so it's not like she's—" He winces and turns to Vanessa. "Sorry. We can talk about something else."

"No, it's okay." There's not even a hint of disappointment in Vanessa's voice, and it's a relief. If anything, she sounds almost intrigued. "If you have something going on with another girl, I don't want to get in the way."

He waves a hand. "It's not like that. She and I have just... You know..."

Vanessa nods. "Fucked."

Ethan grins. "I like your style, Vanessa. You just straight up say it."

Vanessa beams back at him, like she's proud of herself, and my chest twinges. She says swear words with such emphasis, like she's practicing a foreign language. Why do I find it so cute? Why does everything about her make me want to kiss her?

"Anyway," Ethan says. "She's not exclusive to me. She's also fucking Carter and basically any other guy or girl who flirts with her when she's drunk. She's as big of a ho as Carter. That's probably why he's her favorite fuck-buddy."

"Not anymore," I say. "She says she's done being my fuck-buddy."

Ethan's eyes grow wide, and his posture shifts toward me. "When did she say this?"

"A couple of days ago. She said she's done with her 'ho phase.'"

"Was it Thursday?" Ethan asks.

There's so much urgency in his voice, I want to laugh. This is even easier than I thought it would be. I assumed I'd have to make up a much more complicated story than this. I was prepared to drop heavy hints that Lacey wants to settle down with Ethan.

As if she ever would. Lacey is wired exactly like me. She loses all romantic interest after one fuck. It makes her the perfect fuck-buddy. I've never had to worry about her catching feelings.

"Yeah," I say, since Ethan is obviously inferring some kind of significance into Thursday. My guess is they probably fucked the night before. "Thursday night, when we went out to dinner, she didn't want to…" I glance at Vanessa to make sure she's okay with me talking about this, and she's smiling mischievously. Is she onto me? Does she like that I'm manipulating Ethan? "She didn't want to have sex when we came back. It seemed weird."

"And she texted me to come over that night," Ethan nearly shouts. "But I was trying to play it cool, so I said no." He shakes his head, his eyes growing unfocused, as if he's putting all the pieces together in his head.

All of the fabricated pieces.

Vanessa smiles at Ethan. "It sounds like you and Lacey need to have a talk."

His head whips in Vanessa's direction, like he forgot she was even there. What is wrong with him? This girl is perfect, and he's willing to throw her away for Lacey, who's told him again and again that she has no serious interest in him outside of sex.

"Yeah," Ethan says. "I think… We had a really good night Wednesday. I wonder if she thought so, too."

A pang of guilt shoots into my gut. Damn. I thought this would be a harmless lie, but it seems like he's more into Lacey than I thought.

She's going to kill me when this gets back to her.

Oh, well. Ethan needs to learn. When someone says "I just want a casual fling" in the future, he should believe them. Here he is using Vanessa—potentially toying with her feelings—when she never did anything to deserve it.

You're using her too, Carter.

Fuck. Am I growing a conscience?

There's no reason why I should be bothered by my plan, even if I do like Vanessa more than I thought I would. The difference between me and Ethan is that I'll be able to make up for using her. I'll give her fantastic sex.

"Maybe you should go talk to her now." Vanessa sets her hand on Ethan's shoulder. "You wouldn't want her getting any more upset about our date."

"Damn." Ethan stands up and pats sand from his thighs, not wasting a moment.

What a dick. Thank God Vanessa doesn't seem to mind. On the contrary, she seems almost eager to make him leave.

She must have been ready to die of boredom, just like I'd warned her she would be.

"I'm going to head to Lacey's sorority," Ethan says. "Vanessa, I hope you don't..." He shrugs awkwardly.

Vanessa waves a hand, smiling wide. "Don't worry about me. I have a replacement date."

Ethan nods and glances at me. "Make sure you..." He scratches the back of his head.

"Make up for you being a shitty date and for the fact that you're ditching her right now?"

He winces. "Yeah, I guess."

"No problem. Thanks for being such a shitty date and making me look better."

Ethan smiles sheepishly as he runs off, and Vanessa turns to me. "I didn't realize you're a matchmaker."

I stare at her for a long moment, her words not computing at first.

Oh, damn. She didn't fully understand what I just did there. She thought everything I said to Ethan was true.

That cute little mischievous smile came from the fact that she thought I was matchmaking. As if I would ever take the time. Oh God, I could squeeze her to death. She's so sweet. Here I thought she was just as devious as I am, using her TikTok to taunt horny bastards by pretending to be a fantasy of virginal innocence.

Maybe there's only one lie with her. Maybe it's just the Graham thing.

I shrug. "I just didn't want him using you to make her jealous."

She cocks a brow, something I've seen her do in videos, and it always stirs something within me. For someone so serious, this expression is feisty and playful. "Yeah, right. You're just using me to win the bet."

I lean toward her and smile, tightening the muscles in my cheeks to make my dimples more prominent. Her gaze falls to my mouth, making my gut clench.

"Do you really think that's all I want?" I keep my voice low.

Her swallow is audible, and she averts her gaze from mine. "Maybe you think I'm pretty—"

"Gorgeous."

"Fine, gorgeous. But I've seen you around plenty of gorgeous girls. I'm only a means to an end."

"That doesn't mean I won't enjoy the means...immensely. When you pick me, I mean."

Her smile returns, but she keeps her eyes fixed on the blanket. "I never thought I would find cockiness charming, but—"

"But you find it charming on me, because you should pick me."

"Why?"

"Because the chemistry we both feel every time we're together means we'll have good sex."

Those dark eyes bore into mine. "Is that a real thing? Can you really tell if you'll enjoy having sex with someone just by being near them?"

I frown. Her tone is so earnest, and I was mostly talking out of my ass.

"Yeah, it's real. I should know. I have a lot of experience with it."

She nods profusely. "Being as big a player as you are would give you a lot of data."

A chuckle erupts from my chest. "I mean... Yeah, I guess so. I don't have a spreadsheet to show you or anything."

Her eyes crinkle at the corners. Fuck, I want to kiss her when she smiles like that.

"I wish you did. You'd be a great case study, since I've heard you rarely have sex with the same person more than once. That Lacey girl seems to be an exception."

I grimace. "You heard that? That's definitely not something I brag about."

She shoots me a skeptical look. "You brag about never catching feelings, which is just as insufferable."

My mouth drops open. Damn, this girl is bold. "I've never once said that."

She cocks her brow again, and this time, it takes everything within me not to lean forward and press a kiss against her mouth. It's not the right moment.

Soon.

"What is it like having sex with so many partners?"

The question catches me off guard, and I blink. "Um...what do you mean?"

"Was it always easy to do? It seems like it would be awkward to be that intimate with a stranger."

I narrow my eyes at her. "That's what you're doing with your whole thirty-day thing."

"Yeah, but I'm doing it knowing it will be awkward. You do it for fun. Was it always fun?"

I snort. "It's sex. It's generally fun for people."

"Then why not just choose a good fuck-buddy like Lacey if you want sex and no relationship?"

"You ask a lot of questions."

"I'm intrigued."

Warmth washes over me. She really is intrigued, and it's so obvious in her expression. Her posture is turned toward me, and those beautiful eyes are fixed on my face. A notch is pulled between her brows like she's trying to figure out a puzzle.

I love this expression of hers. I love that she's so serious and inquisitive all the time.

"Having lots of partners is its own unique fun," I say. "There's something exhilarating about having sex with someone new."

"And it's never awkward?"

I shrug. "I don't know anything else."

Her eyes grow wide. "That must be the key."

"Um..." I frown. "I'm not totally sure what you mean."

"You're immune to sexual shame because you've done your own form of desensitization."

Coldness settles in my gut. So that's why she's so intrigued. She's comparing me to herself.

Why does it make me sad? Why do I want to pull her into my arms and tell her there's nothing wrong with her? She doesn't need desensitization.

She just needs someone who's better at sex than Graham.

"I don't think you need to be like me to get over your issues. I think you just need to have good sex, even if it's only with one partner."

She shakes her head. "I won't know if I'm over it until I've had sex with multiple partners. I've been taught since I was a child that I can only have good sex with my husband. I'll be in danger of falling in love with the guy I choose if I'm not careful about how I approach this."

He'd be a lucky bastard.

What the fuck? Am I out of my mind? The last thing in the

world I need is for Vanessa Gallo to fall in love with me. Then I'd really have to think twice about using her to humiliate my grandpa.

Eyes on the prize, Carter.

"If the chemistry thing is really true," she says, "then you probably would be a good choice."

My body grows still. Did she really say what I think she said? "A good choice for...taking your virginity?"

"Yes."

The euphoria that sizzles through my veins makes me almost dizzy. Oh my God, I did it.

I keep my body very, very still, as if it might spook her into changing her mind if I make a quick movement.

"My only reservation," she says, "is that I'll feel self-conscious with you. You make it seem like you're a connoisseur of sex. I'd be afraid you'd compare me to all your other partners."

"I would never compare you to anyone else. I never think about anyone but the person I'm with."

"Of course you would say that." Her voice is faint.

"It's the truth."

She smiles. "You are certainly truthful. Sometimes to a fault."

Goddamn. *Truthful to a fault.* I should be delighted that she thinks so, but instead, a heaviness settles in my chest.

I don't want to hurt this girl.

I have to make it up to her. I have to give her the best sex of her life. I'll read her every expression and moan and let them teach me how to give her exactly what she wants. Those big brown eyes already tell me so much.

I can already imagine what they look like when she comes. They probably grow really wide and glassy, and those eyelids probably flutter closed.

But I won't let them. I'll grab her by the chin and make her look at me. Make those glazed brown eyes fix on my face to thank me for making her feel so good.

Jesus Christ, it's going to be heaven fucking her.

"Do you think we could..." She takes a hand and lifts it to her hair, tucking a strand behind her ear. "Hang out for a bit? Maybe get to know each other first. Before we...you know. Have sex."

I smile. "I'd love that." My voice has a husky quality. "Let me pick you up tomorrow morning. Why don't we go surfing, and then I'll take you to lunch."

She wrinkles her nose. "I have church tomorrow morning."

"I'll pick you up afterwards."

"I have a paper to write." She stares at me for a moment, her smile growing lazy. "You can come to church with me."

My face falls. "No way."

"I guess I'll see you at the shelter on Monday."

Her mischievous smile tells me she knows how badly I want this getting-to-know-you period over so that I can finally get my hands on her skin. "Fine," I say. "I'll go to your goddamn church."

She grins. "I can't wait."

Strangely, I can't either. It might be a drag to be in church, unable to touch her or flirt with her, but I'll still be with *her*.

I love being around her.

Should I be worried about this? I'm not sure that I've ever been this intensely attracted to a woman in my life. These feelings for her... This ache in my chest... It feels kind of like falling in love.

It will go away after I fuck her. It always does, but my affinity for her won't. I like this girl. I think she might actually be a good person.

Which is why I need to get in and out quickly. Only one fuck. Then we'll go live on her TikTok, I can make my announcement, and we'll part ways. If I let it drag on any longer, I'll be in danger of hurting her.

I don't want to do that. Somehow, in the span of two days, she's become almost...

Precious.

Chapter Six

V anessa

My stomach churns as I pull into the church parking lot. This will be my first time seeing Livvy in over a week. I've given only brief responses to her texts, and I know she senses I'm distant. I told her I've been extremely busy this week, and I hope she bought it.

She's worried about me after my TikTok announcement. While that isn't a surprise—I've talked to her more than once about giving myself a virginity-loss deadline, the way she did years ago—it upset her that I didn't tell her before I made the video. I told her that I didn't want to steal her thunder after she announced her engagement, but she seemed skeptical.

My sister is extremely sensitive, and she's always been in tune with my emotions.

God, why do I have to be so petty? Livvy is the kindest person in the world. If anyone deserved to get over their sexual shame quickly, it was her. Her journey has nothing to do with mine.

I say this to myself over and over again, and it doesn't make a difference. I still feel this clawing jealousy, and it's made me avoid her. She doesn't even know that Carter's planning to join us at church this morning.

As I walk up to the church entrance, I catch sight of Livvy, Cole, and her best friend, Mariana, standing near a large pillar, each with a coffee cup in their hands. Cole has his hand on my sister's lower back, and I clench my jaw.

He's extremely touchy with her, and she's totally at ease with it, even in public. They were best friends for years before they got together. During that time, he barely touched her at all, probably because he was afraid it would make him want her too much. He's certainly making up for lost time.

I shouldn't be jealous. Someday I'll have someone whose touch comforts me. My body is not damaged.

"A podcast?" I hear Mariana ask Cole as I get closer. "Is that really what you do when you come to church?"

Cole nods. "On the rare times I come. Livvy doesn't mind."

"I just think it's sweet that he comes with me," Livvy says.

Mariana shakes her head. "How can anyone listen to a podcast when Pastor Brandon is speaking?"

My sister giggles. "Right? He has the voice of an angel."

"I don't know if I like that," Cole says.

I smile as I walk up to them. "Now you know how everyone feels when you call my sister an angel."

Livvy beams at me, probably because she's relieved at the lightness in my mood.

Good. That means I pulled it off.

"She's right, Cole." Mari gives me a quick side hug. "It makes us all feel like we're in the room with you while you're having sex."

Cole smiles down at my sister. "I only use it in the bedroom when she's a good girl."

"Yuck!" I punch him in the shoulder. "You seem to get especially gross when you're at church."

Cole sets his arm around Livvy's shoulder as we walk inside

the lobby. "Probably because she and Mari are always drooling over the pastor," he says. "I'm a simple dude. I got to assert my dominance when I can."

I snort. He certainly is a simple guy. Maybe that's why he's so perfect for my sister. In many ways, he's the type of guy we grew up with in the church. He just has a little more self-awareness, and he adores my sister enough to let her assert her own dominance, since he doesn't consider dominion over her his God-given right.

I wouldn't be happy with a simple man like Cole. I wouldn't be happy if it turned out a man was the key to fixing my body—like Cole was for Livvy—so I shouldn't be jealous that I haven't found my own Cole.

"Oh, hush!" my sister says. "I'll have none of your toxic masculinity when I'm at church."

"Besides, Cole," Mari says. "I think Pastor Brandon could take you in a fight." She makes a little grunting sound. "And I'd love to see him do it."

"Mari!" Livvy whisper-shouts. "He's right over there."

Just then, pastor Brandon's head jerks in our direction, and his eyes lock on Mariana. Why is he always looking at her? He starts walking in our direction, and this time he almost seems like he's actively trying to *not* look at her.

If I didn't have the utmost respect for him as my pastor, I'd think he has a boyish crush.

"Vanessa," he says with a big smile. "How did your finals go?"

I'm always struck by his attractiveness when he's this close. He's so tall, and his voice is especially deep. The type of voice that makes him sound like he's talking dirty, even when he says something mundane.

"Pretty good," I say. "I don't think I'll get straight As this quarter, but I'm not going to cry about it."

"Straight As," he says, turning to Livvy. Pointedly not Mariana—even though she's standing right in front of him. "I was happy with straight Cs in college."

"Weren't you kind of a..." My sister lowers her voice, "*partier*?"

Cole laughs. "I don't think you need to whisper it, angel."

Brandon's eyes grow wide. "Angel? I feel like I'm interrupting an intimate moment here." There's laughter in his voice.

Mariana lifts her chin. "Cole's just asserting his dominance over you so you don't get any ideas about his fiancé. He's very jealous."

"Mari!" Livvy scolds.

Mari doesn't look Livvy's way. Her gaze stays fixed on Pastor Brandon. They stare at each other for a moment, and something electric passes through the air between them.

"I think Cole knows he doesn't have anything to fear from me."

"I don't know, Pastor." Mari smiles. *Pastor*. She always calls him that, while the rest of us just call him Brandon. "You've got some guns." She points to one of his forearms. "Cole might be huge, but I think you could take him in a fight."

Brandon's gaze holds hers, his smile fading. Why does he always look like he wants to scold her for being audacious? Or spank her? Sometimes I almost want to cover my eyes when they're around each other. It feels like we're all interrupting *their* intimate moment.

I glance at Livvy and Cole to see if they're picking up on it too, but Cole is looking at his phone and my sister is...

Damn. She's looking at me.

She glances away quickly, probably trying to hide her expression, but I caught it. I'm as in tune with her emotions as she is with mine. She's worried about me. If I know her, she's worried about our relationship.

I'm going to have to talk to her soon—maybe even after church—and I'm not ready. I don't want her to see how much I'm struggling with her engagement.

Thankfully, as soon as Brandon walks away, Mariana distracts my sister by shooting her a big, mischievous grin. "It's too easy with him," she says. "He can't hide the fact that he used to be kinky, and he's trying to wash the kink away with the blood of Jesus."

Livvy giggles. "You definitely aren't helping his cause by always flirting with him."

When we make it to our seats, Livvy sits down next to me. Hoping to avoid a confrontation, I pretend to be busy by looking at my TikTok notifications.

It doesn't work.

"So..." She exhales a long breath. "How has the...man hunt gone?"

I school a light smile as I turn to her. "I love your word choice. Unfortunately, I've been the hunted one."

Her brow furrows. "Have a lot of guys been bugging you?"

"I wouldn't say 'bugging' necessarily. As a matter of fact—"

"Vanessa Gallo."

I shut my eyes at the sound of Carter's deep voice. Damn. Now my sister really will be worried. Why didn't I tell her he was coming?

Why did I think inviting him was a good idea? Sunday service is my favorite time of the week. The only time I'm relaxed and forget about my day-to-day worries. Inviting Carter is going to remind me of the fact that I promised to lose my virginity in twenty-seven days from now.

I school a smile on my face before turning to Carter. "Hey, heathen."

He glances at my sister, who is staring at him in shock. "Did you forget to tell your friends we have a date?" he asks.

I don't need to look at my sister to know her eyes are huge. Mariana is probably fighting a smile. She texted me earlier this week with four words: "Get some dick, girl." This isn't nearly as emotional for her as it is for Livvy, even though she's known me since we were children and she's practically a big sister, too. Hopefully, some of her lightness will rub off on Livvy.

"I wasn't sure if you'd come," I say to Carter.

He grins devilishly. "How could I not come after *you* invited me?"

The way he lowers his voice and lets his lips caress the word "you" sends heat into my gut. This man is sexual all the time, even in church.

When he sits down next to me, his thigh brushes up against mine. He's so big and muscular everywhere. What would his body feel like on top of mine? It seems like it would crush me, and for some reason, that makes my belly flutter.

"Ness," Cole says. "Don't be rude. Introduce us to your date."

The word "date" sends a prickle of nervousness over my skin. I knew Cole and Mari would make a big deal out of this. I knew my sister would try to be casual, but sensitive as she is, she wouldn't be able to hide her alarm. I force a smile, though my lips are tight. "This is Carter. He's a volunteer at Gospel House."

Mariana eyes him up and down. "I think Carter wants to be much more than a...volunteer at Gospel House. Am I right, Carter?"

"You're damn right about that." I hear a smile in his voice. "Oops. I guess I shouldn't swear here, huh?"

I turn to him. "It's fine. This is a more...progressive church than the one your grandparents go to."

His gaze stays fixed on my face, but his eyes narrow. "You know what church they go to?"

"Everyone knows. Coastal Outreach is a megachurch. All the famous people in Santa Barbara go there."

His eyes grow hooded. "You should be there. The Santa Barbara virgin."

Something about the way he says "virgin" sends a wash of hot irritation over my body. Almost like it's a badge. Something I use to boost my fame.

As if I wouldn't give up my small-time celebrity in a heartbeat if it meant being able to have sex like a normal person.

I grit my teeth. "I don't like megachurches. I need a smaller community to feel safe."

He frowns, staring at me for a long moment. "It's weird that you share so much on TikTok. That you feel safe doing that."

That prickle of irritation spreads like fire over my skin. He sounds just like Graham. Just before I took off my shirt, baring my bare skin for the first time for a man, he said something similar.

"It's weird that you're uncomfortable with me when you share so much on your TikTok."

I stare at Carter for a long moment, and his lazy smile doesn't falter. He knows he's upset me, and he doesn't care. This is the consequence of his devil-may-care attitude.

I was wrong thinking that he could be a good choice for me. If this is who he is, I'll never be comfortable with him. It doesn't matter if we have off-the-charts chemistry. It doesn't matter how good he can make my body feel.

This was a mistake.

My pulse throbs at my temples. I lean forward and give him a hard stare. "My TikTok allows me to be deeply vulnerable about my struggles in a way I'm not able to in public. Have you ever even watched my videos? It's all about sexual shame. Do you think that's easy to talk about in a large group of people? With people looking at me and..." I shake my head, memories of that night with Graham flooding through my senses in a rush.

Graham's hungry eyes fixed on my nipples. The air in the room made them tingle, and I felt unaccountably sad. Sadness that no amount of arousal could overcome. My breathing started growing shallow, and I...

Fuck. My breathing is shallow now.

"Do you think I don't..."

My voice sounds far away to my own ears, and my head grows heavy. I see myself, for a moment—my shoulders and dark hair. Then I see Carter again.

Fuck. I have to get out of here.

I'm having a panic attack.

A firm hand touches my shoulder. "Are you okay?"

It's Carter's voice. Though it's distant, it holds much more warmth than it did a moment ago.

I nod quickly and stand. Though I glance in the direction of the others, I hardly see them. All of their faces are fuzzy. "I'm going to get a drink of water."

I plow through the lobby, past the drinking fountains, and out into the cool air. When I inhale, the salty, briny scent of ocean hits my nostrils, and my body is pulled deeper into the present, but the relief is short-lived.

How am I ever going to have sex? How am I ever going to get over this if this is how strongly my body reacts to just a memory?

A strong hand grabs my arm. "I'm really sorry." It's Carter's deep, smooth voice.

I shut my eyes. Why did I let him see that? Why couldn't I have just kept my shit together?

"Your sister was worried when you ran out," he says, "but I told her it was my fault, and I would check on you."

Heat washes over my face, and I jerk from his hold. "It's not a big deal. I get panic attacks sometimes."

When I feel shame the deepest.

Even with the words not said, they hover in the air, like he can see my shame branded on me. He's thinking about how awkward and uptight I am, and how I would be so bad at sex...

I need to stop. Self-pity will get me nowhere.

Carter is silent for a long moment, so I walk to the edge of the concrete. A gust of wind brushes over me, cooling my body.

His big footsteps sound behind me. "You get panic attacks from...talking about your purity-culture stuff?"

The disbelief in his voice makes my eyes roll of their own will. Thankfully, he can't see me, because he sounds as kind and soft as he's ever been. I hate that he finds my struggles silly.

I twirl around and lift my chin to look in his eyes head-on. "Talking about my...limited experience resurrects certain feelings.

This isn't something I can control. If I could, I would have gotten over it a year ago when I finally decided saving myself for marriage was toxic for me. This is the problem with being taught that wanting sex is bad. The bad feelings become tied to wanting sex. Sexual desire is primal, and primal thoughts aren't rational. You can't tell your body to stop feeling something."

He stares at me for a long moment. "That makes sense."

The gentleness in his voice caresses me like a blanket. It's too much for me to bear in my fragile mood, and my eyes start to prickle.

Oh, no.

Jesus, why are you letting me cry in front of him? I turn around quickly and cover my face. My skin crumples against my hand. My chest is heaving, but I'm able to stay silent as I cry. Until he wraps his arms around my shoulders, and then the sob comes out of its own will.

"Oh, baby girl. Please."

Please. It's such a gentle word coming from his lips, and it makes the tightness in my chest ease.

"I don't know why I'm crying right now," I choke out.

His hand grazes my back. "It's okay. Cry all you want."

"You just caught me in a vulnerable moment." My sentence is barely audible.

"You're at church. This is where you go to feel safe. I shouldn't have..." He swallows. "I should have been more respectful. I shouldn't have brought up stuff that..."

His gentle voice draws me toward him. I burrow my head into his chest, and he wraps his arms around me. It feels so natural, as if he's been holding me and only me for years. His hand brushes up my back and settles at my nape. The touch sends a tingle down my spine that settles in my groin.

Jesus, what is happening?

Why does his touch feel so good? For the first time since I signed that purity contract, I don't feel sinful for being touched by a man.

. . .

Carter

Oh Christ, she's heaven to hold.

I never thought a woman's warmth and scent could make me feel this way. I let my mouth graze her head and relish the softness of her hair. She has those fuzzy little strands that stick out at the edges.

I want to eat them.

I want to eat her.

She has that special secret something just for me. Having her this close is overwhelming. She's like a drug.

God, I need to fuck her soon, before I become addicted to her.

I trail my lips along her skin until I reach the tip of her nose and press a little kiss on it. A deep, distant part of me recognizes that I'm being a little too touchy considering she's crying about her body shame, but it's so hard to stop. Especially when she's letting her body weight sink into mine.

"Is this okay?" I ask, my lips brushing against her cheek.

"Yeah," she whispers.

My mouth seeks hers as if it has a will of its own. Now is not the appropriate time to kiss her, but she has me under some kind of spell.

The first touch of her lips sends an electric current into my core, and I take in a sharp breath. Her body grows limp in my arms, so I slip my hands to her hips and pull her tightly against my thighs. I slip my tongue into her mouth, and everything around me fades.

The whole world is heat and skin and that heavenly scent. Her gasps and moans mingle with mine. Her small hips twist under my grip, brushing lightly against my cock, and my body catches fire.

Holy fuck. Kissing someone has never felt this good before.

"Baby girl." The voice is my own, but it sounds like it came from outside my body.

She hums. "I really like this."

My mouth trails down the soft skin of her neck. "Of course you do. Your body was made for me."

When she jerks away from me, the world is fuzzy for a moment. I blink several times before emerging from my daze.

"What do you mean?" she asks.

"Sorry." I can only manage a whisper. "I was just talking. It doesn't mean anything."

She stares at me for a long moment, and I find myself searching her face to see if that kiss impacted her as much as me. Her eyes are a little glazed and dreamy, but does she also feel this faint sense of panic?

How could a kiss be that good? I've kissed hundreds of people, and I've never lost my head like that. Is she some kind of witch?

"I've kissed three guys," she says.

And she fucked one of them. My jaw clenches. How was I able to sit there and listen while Graham described what it was like?

Just thinking about it now makes me want to kill him.

"It always made me feel kind of...gross." A notch forms between her brows. "But kissing you makes me forget about everything. I *really* like kissing you."

A triumphant thrill courses through my body.

That's right, baby girl. I'm the only one who makes you feel good.

I reach forward to pull her back into my arms, but she halts me with her hands. "No, not right now," she says. "We need to go back inside soon, but I want to figure this out. I think we really do have some kind of animal chemistry that pulls me out of my head. This is something we can talk about on our Live."

Her words don't compute at first, but when they do, a coldness washes over me. It will all be over after that Live. Even before then. I'll fuck her first—probably soon judging from that kiss—and all of these magical feelings will fade away.

What does it mean that I'm dreading that?

"Do you think it's the key?" she asks.

"Um... What?"

Her eyes are earnest and probing, and there's that inquisitive expression that I've grown to love. "Do you think maybe I chose the wrong guys before?"

"Fuck yeah," I say, though I'm still not entirely sure what she's talking about.

"I think so, too." She nods slowly, her eyes growing unfocused. "I think animal chemistry might be the key."

After staring into space for a moment, her gaze snaps into focus. "This is hopeful. Thank you."

I laugh. "Any time."

She rolls her eyes. "I mean, for helping me come to this conclusion, not for kissing me."

"Good to know. Now I won't get my heart set on being thanked after fucking you."

"I will thank you if you can keep me out of my head the whole time. That'll mean that I can use kissing as a sort of litmus test."

"What do you mean?"

"I mean, I'll kiss the next guy as a test to see if he's a good candidate."

"A good candidate for what?"

When she blinks once, I realize I raised my voice louder than I intended.

"For sex," she says, and my whole body grows cold. "Alright, we need to get back inside before my sister comes out looking for us."

When she turns around and walks away, I linger behind for a moment, my pulse racing.

I shouldn't be nervous. This will all be over soon. Sure, I've never felt this possessiveness before—the desire to lock her up and keep her away from all these guys she's planning on kissing and fucking after me—but that doesn't mean that there's anything special about Vanessa Gallo. She's probably right. It's some kind of potent animal chemistry.

Still, it's strange that I've fucked hundreds of people and never felt it before.

 anessa

Nervousness flutters in my stomach as I stir creamer into my coffee, turning it from black to a creamy brown.

I ought to be relieved after yesterday. Carter's kiss taught me that there's more to this journey of getting over my sexual shame than I thought.

Instead, I can't shake this fear. What if chemistry isn't the key? What if the key is Carter?

That's crazy.

One person can't hold that kind of power over someone's body, no matter how fucked up it is from purity culture. Carter just happens to be crazy hot and exceptionally good at kissing. My body is telling me there's something unique about him because I was taught at a young age that I was only meant to be physically intimate with one man.

I need to have sex with someone else right after him, or else I'll be in danger of falling for him.

He'd probably pity me if I did. The sweet, pathetic virgin who thinks she's in love with the campus player.

Just the thought of it makes my stomach roil.

There's a knock on my front door, and I jump. Can that be him already? I set my mug on the table and walk into the living room. When I open the front door, I'm startled to see my sister standing on the welcome mat with a coffee cup in each hand. Her nose is pink from the cold air.

I frown. "What are you doing here?"

"I brought you coffee." As she walks through the front door, she hands me the heavy paper cup. "It's a Mexican Mocha."

I shut my eyes tightly. It isn't good that she showed up like this. I must not have done a good job of pretending that everything was normal yesterday at church.

My sister plows over to the living room couch and sits down. She cradles her cup against her chest and looks at me expectantly.

I sigh. "I have work. Carter's going to be picking me up in fifteen minutes."

"I know." She takes a sip of her coffee. "I heard you guys talking about it before he left church. You seem to have gotten close pretty fast."

I walk over to the chair across from the couch and sit down. "Are you worried about me?"

She frowns. "No, just...intrigued, I guess. He seems to really like you."

I snort. "No. He's in Alpha Lambda Xi. He's one of the guys trying to win a big betting pool."

My sister's eyes grow huge. "How do you know?"

When I take a sip of coffee, I release an involuntary hum at the nutmeg on my tongue. "Nice and spicy," I mutter. "He told me. He's extremely honest, which I think is why I feel safe with him. All the other guys are pretending to want to date me, but Carter straight up told me he has no interest in me outside of the bet."

Her expression grows incredulous. "You're a gorgeous girl. You don't need a guy who only wants you to win a stupid bet."

I shrug. "The way I went about this complicates everything. My video made losing my virginity sort of a challenge. There's no way I'll be able to trust anyone's intentions in the next twenty-something days, especially if they pretend to really like me."

My sister stares at me for a moment before dropping her gaze to her coffee. "Why did you do it then?"

"I don't know. It was an impulsive decision."

Livvy rotates her coffee cup in circles, trailing her thumb along the cardboard sleeve. "That doesn't sound like you. You're usually very thoughtful when it comes to big decisions, especially about this."

My skin prickles. Is she hinting at the significance of the day I posted my video? My sister's far too perceptive for it to have been lost on her.

I force a little laugh. "I don't know if you remember how much wine I had that night. My head was about to split open from my headache the next morning. I wasn't thinking."

Her smile is tight. "Why didn't you talk to me about it?"

I sigh. "I'm talking to you about it now."

She frowns and sets her coffee on the table in front of her. "I feel like you must be mad at me about something. This is a momentous time in your life. We should be having coffee dates or slumber parties where you tell me every detail about all the guys who have hit on you and why you picked Carter. Was I..." She purses her lips for a moment. "Was I really insufferable when Cole and I announced our engagement?"

A pang shoots into my chest, and I let out a small grunt. My sweet sister. Of course she would think it's all her fault. My disgusting selfishness would never cross her mind because she would never feel this way in my shoes. "Of course not."

"I was being kind of braggadocios about my ring." She touches the big stone with her index finger. "I kept talking about how much I love it."

I smile sadly. "Of course you were. You'd just gotten engaged, for crying out loud. And it's a gorgeous ring. In fact, I want you to let me wear it for a bit the next time we have a slumber party."

Her expression grows skeptical. Does she think I only said that to appease her?

She's right. I don't want to wear her ring, even though wearing her clothes and jewelry is something that I've always done to feel close to her, and she's probably the only big sister in the world who never minded when I did.

But I don't want to wear her ring. It's the symbol of how far she's come. She and I both used to wear purity rings. She took hers off a week before she was cured of her sexual shame, and I took mine off a year ago.

God, I'm the worst.

Why can't I be happy for her?

"You've been ignoring me," she says, confirming my suspicion, "and it doesn't make any sense. I went through exactly what you're going through. I even set a deadline to lose my virginity. Of everyone in your life, you should want to talk to me the most."

"And I do. I've honestly just been really busy. I know that sounds like a lame excuse."

"It is a lame excuse." My sister's eyes are so full of concern, I can't even be annoyed that she's calling me out on my bullshit. "You are mad at me, Vanessa Faith Gallo. I feel it. Don't lie to me."

"No, I'm not, Livvy. It's just hard in general to talk about—"

There's a loud knock on the door, and my mouth closes.

My sister's whole demeanor changes. A curious expression overtakes her face, and it makes the tension leave my shoulders.

"That's him!" she whispers. "Okay, I'm going to sit back so he doesn't see me. I want to know what he's like when you two are alone."

I laugh as I walk toward the door. "He's exactly the same."

But it turns out I'm wrong. As soon as I open the front door, Carter's hungry gaze locks on my face, and I know what's coming. Sure enough, he sets his hands on my shoulders and pulls my body forward. When his lips touch mine, my belly catches fire. My God, it's wonderful being kissed like this, like it's just how we greet one another.

Still, my sister is watching. Just as he starts to nibble at my bottom lip, I set my hands on his shoulders and push him back. "My sister's here," I whisper.

He frowns. "This early?"

I shoot him a somewhat exasperated look. "She stopped by to bring me coffee."

"Ah." His eyes widen. "She caught a vibe from you."

"What do you mean?"

"I mean..." He glances over my shoulder before lowering his voice. "Everything you told me at the shelter."

My skin grows hot. I almost forgot how much I shared with him that day in the kitchen. God, this man is a good listener. I'm not used to it with college boys.

When Carter walks inside, he heads straight for the couch, smiling at my sister. "Did you come here to make sure I don't get too handsy with your sister?"

Livvy grins. "I think she's only hanging out with you right now because she's hoping you'll get extra handsy with her sometime in the next thirty days."

Carter's mouth drops open. "Damn! She tells you all this stuff?"

Livvy waves a hand. "Of course. I watch every single video she posts. What kind of big sister do you think I am?"

Carter shakes his head. "I misjudged you Gallo women. I thought you were all good Christians. Turns out you're both freaks."

Livvy giggles, seeming genuinely charmed by Carter.

This is good. This will diffuse the tension between us.

For now.

"I've only become a freak after lots of training from my fiancé," she says. "I'd probably be super vanilla right now if not for him." She lifts a brow. "I hope you're nice and freaky. If he's not, Ness, I think he needs to be nixed."

Carter chuckles. "This should be the most uncomfortable conversation, and yet somehow it feels totally normal, like we're talking about the weather."

I smile. "Livvy has that effect on people. She's very prim and proper when she talks about anything, even sex."

"You're that way too." He smiles as he reaches out his hand and touches the tip of my nose. "I love that about you."

The room goes quiet. My sister is probably just as aware of the sexual energy as I am, but Carter seems completely unaffected. He just stares at me steadily.

He's so comfortable in his skin. He's so comfortable being sexual.

Hopefully, some of it will rub off on me.

"Well." I turn to Livvy. "We really need to head to the center. Do you want to walk us out?"

She glances at Carter and then back at me, and something sparks in her eyes. "No, I think I'll stay until Saanvi wakes up so I can catch up with her."

My sister's lighter mood is such a dizzying relief that it takes me a few moments to notice Carter's big hand on my lower back as we walk to his car.

What will it feel like between my legs?

"Why are you smiling?" he asks as he guides me over to his car, and I'm thankful for the excuse to change the subject.

"Oh my God," I mutter. "Is this really your car?"

He chuckles. "Isn't it insane? I never thought I'd own a Tesla. It was my Christmas present this year."

"Why didn't you drive it a few nights ago?"

"That was the frat's car. For designated drivers."

I laugh almost hysterically as I open the door and step inside. The new-car leather smell floods my senses. "I can't believe you guys have your own car. Damn, I'd love to be rich."

Carter chuckles as he turns on the ignition. "It's not quite as fun when you have an old man who makes you perform like a circus monkey when you need cash."

I snort. "I'd perform like a monkey on TikTok for this car. And 'need' is a matter of opinion. I didn't even have a car for my first two years at UCSB. You certainly don't need a Tesla."

His expression grows somber. "I wasn't talking about this car. My mom needs money from time to time, and I'm the only person who can make sure gets it."

"I'm sorry, what? Are you saying you have to get money from your grandparents for your mom?"

He laughs humorlessly. "It's fucking ridiculous. My grandparents cut her off when she got pregnant with me. My grandpa still hardly speaks to her."

My mouth drops open. "Carter, oh my God. You weren't kidding that your grandpa's an asshole."

His smile grows lazy as he removes a hand from the steering wheel and sets it on my thigh. "I love you for that."

My stomach flutters at his use of the word "love."

Jesus, help me. I can't start thinking this way. Carter drops girls for catching feelings, and we haven't even had sex yet.

"He is a major asshole," Carter says. "My mom has never really been able to get on her feet ever since. My dad helped a little with child support, but she was mostly on her own. She's never had a high-paying job, and she's always hustling, trying to find new ways of making money. I can't even tell you how many jewelry or clothing party things she's done over the years."

I wince. "Pyramid schemes, you mean?"

He smiles warmly. "I always tell her that, and every time, she insists it's the next big thing. She doesn't really have a head for business, but it shouldn't matter. She's good at other things. She's crazy good with people. She would have been great in HR or something. My grandpa could have easily found a place for her within the company, and he wouldn't."

"All because..." I close my mouth, wondering if I should say more or if I'm prying too much.

"Yep," Carter says, as if reading my mind. "All because she got pregnant. You know how ridiculous he is about 'traditional' values—not that he gives a shit about them behind closed doors, but her pregnancy was a public humiliation, especially way back then."

I nod. I know just how judgmental Christians can be sometimes. At least all the ones I know are sincere. It sounds like Carter's grandfather is what I've always suspected. He uses Christianity to sell his business.

"That's really awful. I'm sorry."

"Yeah, they suck. Which is why you should come to my weekly dinner with them tonight."

My gaze jerks to his face, and he has that signature lazy smirk.

"You want me to come out to dinner with you and your grandparents?"

He flips on the turn signal and glances over his shoulder. "Yep."

"Why would you want me to do that?"

A dinner with his family seems oddly intimate. More intimate than sex, somehow. Especially with someone like Carter, who only does one-night stands. Meeting his grandparents seems like something he would do with a girlfriend.

I need to be careful doing intimate things with him. I already like him a lot, and I need to work hard to separate my feelings from sexual pleasure.

"Because I absolutely hate it," he says. "It's a weekly thing they make me do, and I always dread it." He squeezes my thigh. "Having you there will make it actually enjoyable."

His words make my stomach flip over, but I can't let him see my giddiness. With effort, I shoot him a saucy smile. "It sounds terrible. Why would I want to go?"

That smirk grows, revealing those adorable dimples. Jesus, help me. I'd lean over and kiss him if I had the courage. "Lots of reasons."

"We only have two minutes before we get to Gospel House. I'll give you that amount of time to make your case."

"Okay. Three reasons. Number one, and this is the most important, so pay attention. I'll be there. You love being around me."

I snort. "Do I?"

"Absolutely."

"I'll take your word for it. What's the second reason?"

"I'm so glad you asked." His big fingers start trailing up my thigh, moving with tormenting slowness. "I hate going. Did I mention that?"

"You did." My voice is husky from the heat curling in my belly. "I don't see how that's a reason for me to go."

His fingers halt their slow trail. He frowns at me in mock seriousness. "I thought you were a charitable person, Gallo. In fact, I think we're driving to a charity right now."

"Yep. We'll be there in thirty seconds, and you still haven't convinced me."

He squeezes my thigh again. This time, he's so close to my groin that I take a sharp breath. He must notice my arousal, because that smirk returns. "Reason number three, I'll reward you afterward. But only if you're a good girl."

My stomach jolts. "How will you reward me?"

After pulling into a parking space and putting the car in park, he leans toward me, stopping within an inch of my face. His warm breath brushes over my skin, sending the faint scent of mint into my nose. "However you want."

I swallow. "You're talking to a girl who's unable to enjoy sex."

"You don't know you're unable to enjoy sex with me. I think you just haven't been with the right guy. Me." He presses a hard kiss against my cheek before opening the driver's side door. "How about you let me know at the end of our shift if you want to come to dinner?"

I take my time unbuckling my seatbelt and stepping out of the car, trying to calm the whirling of my nerves.

What will happen if I really do catch feelings? I don't think I could stand it if I scared another guy away. It was hard enough with Graham. It would be so much worse with Carter.

Because I'm really starting to like him.

Carter

She kneads the flour into the meat with her gloved hands. Good God, this woman is beautiful doing anything. She even cooks with grace.

I love being around her.

All morning, I've been telling myself that I only invited her to dinner tonight so my grandparents could meet her before I use her to humiliate them. It would be sweeter if they got to know and like her before I make my announcement on the Live. My grandpa will be enraged if he endorses her as good for my public image, only to find out later that she talks about sex on TikTok.

That's not really why I asked her, though.

I want her with me because I really do dread these dinners. I'll dread this one much less if she's there.

This is different than having Lacey there, or any number of girls I've brought over the years. I don't want a distraction or someone to annoy them and entertain me as a result.

I want someone to center me. I want to feel at ease during a time that generally puts me on edge.

Fuck, these feelings for her are getting uncomfortably tender. I don't think I've ever liked anyone as much as I like her.

It will all go away. It has to go away. I can't give her power over my emotions. When people have power, they wield it. They manipulate you because they can. Because you need them. Even good people like Vanessa are capable of it.

God, I just need to fuck her. I'll feel so much better once it's over, and I realize that I was freaking out for nothing.

The sight of her wrinkled brow pulls me out of my head. She stares at the ball of meat she's kneading with a concentrated expression, and a smile rises to my lips. I love that look of hers.

"So it's your job to prep the food," I say, "even though you have a chef?"

She laughs. "Chef. That's such a rich-person word. Our cook only comes three nights a week, so the rest of us have to pick up the slack. I usually prep the food because Landon isn't much of a cook. Plus, I like doing it. I find it relaxing."

My skin heats at her mention of Landon. That prick.

"Here." She hands me a spoon. "Start scooping the meat and forming it into balls."

I grab a clump of meat from the bowl. "Landon was eye fucking you when we all came in. I really think he's a creep."

She scowls, shushing me. "He could be anywhere. I don't want to get fired."

"Fired? Isn't this an unpaid position?"

"That doesn't mean they can't terminate my internship. And I might want to work here after college. Here." She grabs the ball of meat from my hand and sets it on a plate. "You don't have to make them that perfect. We're going to have to make about a hundred. We need to get moving."

"Why would you want to work here if the director's a..." I lower my voice, "weirdo?"

She rolls her eyes. "He's not a weirdo. He's just a guy who has a little bit of a crush on me, and that makes you feel threatened. You're afraid I might choose him over you, and you'll lose the bet."

My mouth drops open. "I'm sorry, what? You're really considering choosing that guy?"

"Well, no..." She glances down at the bowl of meat. "I couldn't choose him because he's my boss."

"And I'd fucking kill him if he creeped on you like that, so you'd be sentencing him to death."

When she snorts out a laugh, I lift my hand high in the air and bring it down crisply on her ass. The cracking sound sends a jolt to my dick.

She whips around with a scowl on her face. "Carter Blake, we are at my place of work, and you're making food for our residents. Save your silly toxic masculinity for your frat house. Keep your hands off my body parts. And go wash your hands."

Laughter erupts from my chest as I turn on the sink. "God, you're cute. You sound like a kindergarten teacher."

She huffs as she grabs a small chunk of meat and rolls it between her palms in one smooth motion. "Very sexy."

I pump soap onto my hands and bump her lightly with my hips. "It is sexy. Sometimes I think about you dressing like a librarian and telling me to keep my mouth shut."

She turns to me, looking so adorably wide-eyed I want to kiss her. "Do you really think about that?"

"I think about a lot of things." My voice is husky.

She shakes her head slowly, looking dazed. "My fantasies are so tame compared to that."

I snort. "A sexy librarian is also a pretty tame fantasy, Ness."

Her brow knits. "No, I mean much tamer. The kinkiest I get is imagining doing it on the beach."

My chest clenches. She's so much more innocent than I thought. Graham must have exaggerated the number of times he had sex with her. There's no way she could be this good of an actress.

I'll have to be very slow and sweet with her, which won't be difficult. She pulls out something soft within me that I didn't even know was there.

"Doing what on the beach?" A deep voice drifts in from the entrance of the kitchen.

I grit my teeth as Landon walks into the room. I knew he would wear my nerves thin today. Aside from devouring Vanessa with his eyes, he also gives me the look of death. I could laugh.

Vanessa is mine.

Landon walks over to the counter and leans against it. His gaze drifts down Vanessa's body, and I want to kill him.

"We were just talking purity-culture stuff," Vanessa says sweetly. "Carter comes from a religious family, so he understands a lot of my trauma."

Landon reaches out and sets his hand on her shoulder, and Vanessa immediately stiffens. She doesn't like being touched by him. An electric pain shoots into my jaw, probably from clenching it so hard.

Don't lose your shit. She can handle herself.

"I'm here anytime you need me," Landon says. "I didn't grow up that way, but I minored in religious studies. American culture is so steeped with Christianity, I feel like I had to know it well just to navigate the world."

With effort, I keep myself from laughing humorlessly. "Yeah, I bet your minor gave you everything you need to understand Vanessa's trauma."

Vanessa's eyes are huge when she turns to me. Fuck, why did I let jealousy make me so snarky? I told myself to let her handle this. It's not like I can be her bodyguard every hour of the day, as much as I might want to.

Landon frowns at me before turning to Vanessa. His eyes soften. "I didn't mean to imply that I understand. Only that I'd be happy to be a listening ear if you need one."

She looks up at him from under her lashes. "I'd like that."

It takes all of my effort to keep from scowling. What is she doing? Why does she look so meek and submissive? If I said I could be a listening ear for her, she'd roll her eyes at me.

I don't like this insincere side of her. I don't like it at all.

His gaze grows hooded as he stares down at her. "Do you want to get coffee after your shift?"

Oh. Fuck. No.

I really might kill him.

Vanessa lifts a hand and tucks a strand of hair behind her ear. "Oh, you know—"

"We have plans," I say, grabbing Vanessa by the waist and pulling her little form against me. "But I appreciate that you want to be a listening ear for her."

When Vanessa pulls away from me as if my body is burning her, my stomach sinks. Fuck, why did I do that? I'm not usually this impulsive.

She glares at me. "Can I talk to you for a second?"

With effort, I smile. "Always."

My levity seems to incense her even more. That adorable little nose wrinkles in a scowl. She grabs me by the arm and yanks me out of the kitchen and into what looks like a storage room.

"What do you think you're doing?" she asks as soon as she closes the door.

My lips quirk. "What do you mean?"

"Why did you fondle me in front of my boss? What was that about?"

I laugh. "You call that fondling?"

Her scowl grows. "Stop dismissing it. I know what you're about. You just want to compare dick sizes, and I don't have time for it. This is my job. That was completely inappropriate."

I snort, though an uncomfortable heat pulses through my veins. "Ness, I—"

"Don't call me Ness." She crosses her arms. "That's my family's name for me. I hardly know you."

That simmering heat turns to coldness in my gut. I don't like her dismissing our intimacy. I'm not a stranger.

I'm the only guy whose touch makes her comfortable.

"*Vanessa*," I enunciate. "You already said that things are laid-back here, and there aren't the same repercussions for these school internships. They don't hold students to the same—"

"I don't give a shit."

My eyes widen at her use of a curse word.

"It's not for you to decide how professionally I behave at my job. This is my career path. These internships mean nothing to trust-fund kids like you because you already have a career path ready to be handed to you when you graduate."

My nostrils flare. "You know nothing about my plans after I graduate."

Her eyes roll dramatically. "Your plans. Who cares? You have options. If your plans don't work out, you have a hundred-million-dollar company waiting for you."

I open my mouth to protest, but my retort dies on my lips. She's right. Even in the aftermath of what I'm planning, Beach Burger will still be around. If things got bad enough—if OvuTrac fails in its first five years—my grandpa would probably enjoy watching me beg for another chance to become his chief of staff.

I've always known this. No matter what I do, no matter how much I disappoint him, I could never drop to my mom's level in his eyes.

I'm a man, and to someone with his antiquated views, I'm automatically of more value to him. My moral choices won't make or break me, because my virtue doesn't determine my worth.

Not that I ever would beg him for a job, but that will sound like lip service to Vanessa. She doesn't know what I had to see growing up. She wasn't there when my mom picked me up from my weekends with my grandparents while my grandma stood on the porch, watching me walk to the car. Not even giving my mom a wave. She didn't see my mom's lips twitching and face grimacing as she tried not to cry in front of me.

"I don't have what you have," she says, "and I like Gospel House. I may even want to work here after I graduate."

Jealousy flares through my veins at the thought of her remaining close to that prick. "Why would you want to work with Landon? There are dozens of nonprofits in Santa Barbara."

She waves a hand. "And most of them are probably run by men, statistically speaking. Who's to say they won't have a director who wants to have sex with me? At least Landon listens to me." She smiles slightly. "Even more so when I flirt with him a little."

Holy fuck, is she really saying what I think she's saying? A fire roars through my body. I take a step in her direction and stare down at her. "Are you telling me you flirt with him to get what you want?"

She shrugs. "I do what works to get things done. That's why I'd be good at running a non-profit. I'm very practical."

I huff. "And here I thought you were working here out of the goodness of your heart."

She snorts, and it startles me. I don't know what I was expecting. Perhaps to offend her.

"No one does anything purely out of the goodness of their heart," she says. "I don't think humans are wired that way. Helping people makes me feel good. I can tell myself all day that I do this work because Jesus calls me to be charitable, but it's probably much more primitive than that. I get a rush of dopamine knowing that we've served a hundred more teens since I started working here."

Her words are like a bucket of ice water over my hot rage. Damn. How could I let jealousy make me so selfish and dismissive of her career? Maybe I really have become a rich prick in these years that I've had my trust fund.

Her fierce practicality is one of my favorite things about her.

I swallow. "That's a really good perspective. Healthy, I think. I can't stand people who humble brag about wanting to help people."

When her expression softens, I reach out and stroke her cheek. "I want us to be friends. Even after...we have sex and do our Live."

Fuck, why does that suggestion make the hair on my neck stand up? I really do like her, but for some reason, being around her long-term seems dangerous.

Maybe I'm worried that she'll get attached to me. But as long as I'm clear about the boundaries of our relationship, her feelings shouldn't matter. I've had one-night stands get attached to me before, and I never blamed myself.

I like her too much. It's starting to feel...uncomfortable.

Vanessa sighs. "Can we go back in there now and be normal for the rest of the day?"

I nod. "I promise I won't fondle you until later. When I reward you for coming to my horrible dinner date."

She smiles. "And you won't be rude to Landon?"

"I'll play nice."

"Thank you."

My eyelids grow lazy as I grab her by the waist and yank her against my body. I press a hard kiss on her mouth before walking towards the door. "I won't kiss you in front of him, either."

"Thank you." Her footsteps sound behind me. "I'll schedule a coffee date with him this weekend. That way he won't—"

I whip around to face her. "Date?"

When she flinches, I realize I nearly shouted at her, and I don't care.

She crosses her arms. "I need to do it. He's been asking to hang out for a while, and there are only so many times I can—"

"You say no," I grit out. "It's fucking ridiculous that you would have to say yes just because he can't take no for an answer."

Her eyelids flutter. "We just went over this. I've learned how to finesse this man. One coffee date could do a lot for this shelter. I've been wanting to stock up on socks, and he tends to be stingy—"

"You shouldn't have to whore yourself for socks."

She rolls her eyes. "One date isn't whoring myself. He's actually a pretty smart guy, and I like the challenge of—"

"You shouldn't like it. I don't care if it's a challenge. It's morally and ethically wrong. My grandpa would even be creeped out if he knew women in his company had to go on dates to get basic business necessities. And that's a very, very low bar."

Her raised-brow look is a little smug, and I don't like it. As if I'm missing something that's obvious to her.

"Your grandpa wouldn't even know about it. Most men are completely oblivious. In fact, Landon probably doesn't even know he's doing it. It's all subconscious. This is just how things are." She laughs humorlessly. "It's how the world works."

"You shouldn't accept how the world works."

I know I sound petulant, and I don't care. The idea of her going on a date with this man, speaking with that earnest frown of hers as she talks about her social work major and how rewarding she finds this work... Fuck, I want to go out there and pummel Landon.

"I don't accept it," she says. "At least, I don't accept it in my heart. That's why I talk about my struggles publicly. I want to influence people, but I can't change everything. I have to pick my battles, and..." She glances at my shoulders and then back to my face. "Stop looming over me like you have a right to be angry. You're acting like a jealous boyfriend."

Her eyes grow huge as I grab her by the waist. "Yes, I am. I want you all to myself."

When I crash my mouth against hers, she gasps. I trail kisses down her jaw. "You're mine," I say between kisses. "I won't share you with anyone else."

She stiffens. "I shouldn't be doing this at work."

I slip my hand under her shirt, relishing the softness of the skin on her tight stomach. "Do you want me to stop?"

"I don't know."

I fight the smile rising to my lips. Her voice is both husky and shy.

"You can do it," I say. "I'll go slow. You'll be nice and quiet, like the good girl you are."

She gasps when I slip my hand under her bra, cupping that delicious squishy mound. "And you'll stop if I ask?"

"Of course."

"Okay."

The word is faint, but it lights a fire in me.

. . .

Vanessa

His teeth sink into my neck, sending a jolt into my belly. "Carter," I gasp.

He slips his hand into my pants and trails it downward. When his fingers reach the band of my underwear, my whole stomach grows taut.

Why do I feel only heat? Where is the cold, sick shame?

What if this man really is my antidote? What if there's something about our sexual chemistry that unlocks my body, freeing my mind of high-level concerns and unleashing primitive desires from deep within?

If he's the key, I'm in trouble.

He's the campus player. The man who discards women for feeling the normal attachment that comes from sexual intimacy.

I have to fight this.

My mind goes blank when his fingers settle on my clit. He rubs in a circle, and my legs turn to jelly.

"Is this okay, baby?"

"I don't know." My voice is breathy. "I like it, but I'm scared."

"No one is going to know." He presses a kiss on my head. "My beautiful girl. I'll make sure no one comes in. And if you get too loud, I'll cover your mouth."

His words send fire into my belly. The idea of him covering my mouth pulls a whimper from my throat.

"Tell me how you like it," he whispers.

I thrust my hips forward. "A little faster."

He groans. "What a good girl you are. Telling me exactly how to make you come."

Wetness trickles into my underwear. Oh my God, am I really turned on by 'good girl'? I used to be so grossed out by pet names.

Carter could say and do anything, and it would turn me on. What is it about this man? That deep voice and those dimples and his musky scent. It feels like he was designed for me.

Maybe he has a purpose.

Maybe Jesus sent him as a first step to healing my body.

If so, I have to remind myself that he's only a first step. As much as I might love being around him and as delicious as his fingers feel on my clit right now, he's only temporary. I won't know if I'm really healed until I've had multiple partners.

One finger dips lower and swirls around a bit in the slipperiness between my pussy lips. His hand grows still. "Oh fuck, you're so wet."

My lips twitch. "Why do I not feel embarrassed?"

I gasp when two fingers enter me roughly. He grabs the back of my ponytail and yanks my head back.

"Because your body belongs to me."

I whimper. "Carter."

"Say my name again."

He rubs my clit, his touch deft and gentle. I grit my teeth, feeling like I might die from the pleasure.

"Say it again." The words are delivered through clenched teeth.

"Carter!"

"Aww, what a good girl you are." He kisses me on the cheek and slips one hand under my shirt and my bra. When he pinches my nipple, I gasp.

"Perfect," he says. "You're a dream fuck, aren't you? I'm dying to get my cock in this tight pussy."

"Yes!" I whimper. "Oh, please."

"Please what?"

That husky voice pulls every muscle in my body taut. I'm ready to explode.

"Please... Make me come."

He hums. "Say you'll come to dinner tonight."

A deep, distant part of me wants to laugh at him for his shamelessness, but I'm too lost in the haze to muster anything more than a tiny shake of my head.

His fingers grow still. "Say it."

Hot, tingling frustration rushes through my body, coiling my already taut muscles. "Fuck, I hate you!"

He chuckles darkly. "I know you do. Give me what I want, my sweet girl."

My hips start to jerk of their own will, but he steadies me with his arm.

"Carter, I'm going to..."

He presses a hard kiss against my mouth. "It's okay. Let go. You can do it. Be my good girl and come for me."

I whimper as heat shoots into my core. "I don't want..." I grimace. "I don't want to be loud."

"I'll cover your mouth. Do you want Daddy to do that for you?"

I nod frantically, and he immediately puts his palm across my lips. Being held this tight and close makes something unlock inside of me. It only takes a few more brushes of his fingers before pleasure crashes through my whole body, and the world starts to grow misty and warm.

"That's my girl." His voice is encouraging. "Come for Daddy."

I sob into his hand as the last spasms of pleasure shoot through my veins. My hips flail every which way before everything grows quiet.

A moment later, the world comes into focus. My limp body is held tightly against Carter, and he's gently caressing the back of my neck.

"Oh Jesus," I mutter.

Did I really just do that? Did I really just let him finger me in the storage closet of Gospel House?

I push away from him, hating the loss of his warmth. "Congratulations," I say. "You're the first man to make me come."

"Really?"

There's so much delight in his voice, I can't help but smile as I pull my pants back up. "And you made me forget that I'm at work. You should get extra points for that."

"I know what you like." He smiles smugly. "You can't resist me."

I shake my head. "I can't believe you tried to manipulate me by fingering me at my place of work."

"I don't consider it manipulation. It was an audition. For tonight, when I'll reward you in the bathroom of the restaurant. We'll make public places our kink."

Unable to help myself, I snort out a laugh.

"Did I get the part?" he asks.

"Yes, I'll come to dinner with you."

He beams at me, and something loosens in my chest. He really wants me to come tonight. It's clear from the expression on his face.

Why? Why is my attending a dinner with his grandparents so important to him?

Chapter Eight

C arter

"So, Vanessa..." Grandma swirls the wine in her glass. "You go to New Morning Church, you said?"

Vanessa smiles brightly as she nods. I've come to know it as her public smile. It's nothing like the crinkly eyed grins or bubbling laughter she gives me when it's just the two of us. This smile is sweeter but doesn't sparkle as much, like a part of her can't break the surface if the chemistry is wrong. She's not fully at ease with my grandparents, and the change in her is obvious.

The fact that she's at ease with me makes me feel like a king.

I can't believe I used to think she was fake. My girl is just a little shy.

"My pastor was the worship leader at my old church," Vanessa answers. "I left when he left."

I whip my head in her direction. "You've known your pastor that long?"

A notch forms between her brows, probably because I reacted so strongly. Am I really jealous of her goddamn pastor?

This woman is making me crazy.

"He led the church college group back then," she says, "and I always appreciated his teaching style. He's actually educated in Biblical history. A lot of pastors aren't."

Grandpa smiles at her—an enamored, indulgent smile—and it makes my stomach roil. On the outside, Vanessa is the exact type of girl he'd choose to help me with my public image. She's beautiful, sweet, and deeply involved in her church. He's probably already imagining what everyone will think of her at the next company party.

Thank God my grandparents are too old for TikTok.

Why do I even care? They'll still be just as horrified and humiliated when I go live with her, even if they find out what she does sooner.

It's almost as if a part of me doesn't want them to hate her.

"I know exactly what you mean," Grandpa says to Vanessa. "There are so many pastors with no credentials. I think there ought to be some kind of certification."

Grandma frowns at him. "That's not how God works."

Vanessa's brows draw together as she purses her lips. It's her thoughtful expression, and it makes me want to lean in and kiss her nose. God, she's so cute. How did I never see it until I met her in person?

"Though I see your point, I think I mostly agree with Nancy on this," Vanessa says. "I don't like the fact that anyone can claim they were called by God without knowing a thing about the Bible. On the other hand, it's dangerous to gatekeep our religion. That's the type of thing that happened in the Middle Ages when literacy was used as a barrier to keep people ignorant about the Catholic church."

Again, that satisfied smile spreads over Grandpa's face. "You know your church history."

I can't even stop myself from frowning at him—not that he

notices, because he only has eyes for Vanessa. He's probably thinking how she'd be the exact type of wife he would have chosen years ago. He might even be comparing her to Grandma, thinking how she has more fire. She's willing to disagree with him and meet his eyes when she does it.

He'd only tolerate it so far, though. Vanessa's audacity still fits in with his antiquated ideas about a woman's role. She's still sweet and prim when she disagrees with him.

If he knew she talks explicitly about sex on TikTok, he'd think she's a whore.

"I actually don't really know much about church history." Vanessa smiles shyly, smoothing her palms over the napkin in her lap. "Most of what I do know, I learned after starting at UC Santa Barbara. It's amazing how little actual history we're taught in Sunday school."

She turns to me, smiling, as if she's expecting me to agree with her.

"I didn't go to church growing up," I say. "My grandparents disowned my mom, and she was done with Christians after that."

"Carter." My grandma's voice is stern.

"It's alright," Vanessa says. "He told me a little bit about what happened, so we don't need to go into it." She turns to me, shooting me a stern look that makes my chest squeeze. She's able to say so much with those expressive eyes. Right now, they're telling me not to embarrass her, that she's already nervous enough.

Fuck, I don't want her to be nervous. I set my hand on hers. "I won't bring up any more family drama."

"Carter loves ruffling our feathers," Grandpa says. "A trait he gets from his mom, though the comparison stops there, thankfully."

Hot rage flares suddenly, making my jaw snap shut. How dare he insult my mom in front of me. In front of Vanessa. Just as I open my mouth to tell him to shut his fucking mouth, Vanessa speaks.

"It seems you like ruffling feathers, too, Dan." She stares at him steadily. Good God, did she really just use his first name? "I haven't known Carter for very long," she continues, "but it's already very clear to me how much his mom means to him. I'd be so hurt if my papa ever talked about my mom the way you just did about Carter's."

My grandpa's lips close, and he blinks once. He looks stunned. "I'm sorry," he mumbles, removing an elbow from the table and sliding side to side in his chair.

Holy shit. What just happened? I don't even think my great uncle—the CFO of Beach Burger—is brave enough to talk to my grandpa like that. I've certainly never seen my grandpa shift in his seat.

She was defending me, because she knows how much it hurts to hear him dismiss my mom like that, as if she means nothing to him.

A strange tug pulls at my chest—an ache, almost. *This is what it feels like to be cared for,* a voice says. *This is what you've always wanted.*

No.

I can't think that way. My relationship with Vanessa is only temporary, and what an insult to my mom for me to say I've never been cared for. She'd be heartbroken if she knew I had such disloyal thoughts.

"Thank you, Vanessa," Grandma says, puncturing through my dreamy daze. "I promise you my husband and grandson aren't normally this rude in front of guests."

Grandpa huffs as he takes a sip of his whiskey.

Vanessa smiles back at my grandma before turning to me. "I'm going to use the ladies' room."

I swallow and nod, still too dazed to think of a response. She gets up and walks away, and another blanket of warmth washes over me.

This feels like love. It's so overwhelming and tender. So big and soft, like I could stroke it with my fingers. I want to pull her back over here and squeeze her tightly, never let go until she becomes part of me.

This is madness.

I need to fuck her soon. I need to get her out of my system before I lose my mind entirely.

"What a quality girl."

My head jerks up at the sound of my grandpa's voice. When the meaning of his words registers, a raging heat pulses through my veins. "She's not a leather couch."

"Good Lord." Grandma sets down her wineglass. "Why are you so sensitive about everything your grandpa says? He just meant she's a smart and interesting girl."

Damn, she's right. I'm not usually quite so edgy when I'm around them.

I'm itching for something, and I think I know what it is.

I exhale a shaky breath. "I'll be right back."

As I walk away, Grandma asks where I'm going, but I'm too in my head to answer her. My urgency is unnecessary, and yet it's like I'm being pulled toward my girl by an invisible string. As soon as I make it to the bathroom hallway, she emerges from the door. Her eyes widen as I wrap my arms around her.

As our lips touch, I disappear into her. My world is just softness and warmth. I could live here.

A part of me must be mindful of my sappiness, because I'm able to pull away, but I can't stop myself from pressing my forehead against hers. "You slayed over there," I say. "I don't think my grandpa has ever been put in his place like that."

She's quiet for a moment. "Is that why you came over here to kiss me, because I put your grandpa in his place?"

I pull away and search her eyes. How much can I tell her?

I hate that I feel so much so soon. I hate that I'm not sure if I'll feel anything at all after I fuck her.

Or that I'll feel too much.

Somehow, I'm able to manage a smirk. "You've got balls, Gallo."

She wrinkles her nose. "I've got ovaries."

My smile softens against my will. "You've got big ovaries."

When she smiles back, I press a kiss against her nose.

Our food has arrived by the time we make it back to the table, thankfully diffusing the tension by giving us all something to do for a bit instead of talk.

"So, Vanessa," Grandma says later that evening. "Do you ever dog sit?"

Vanessa's brows pull together. "Actually, yes. I've been doing it for people at my church since I was a teenager. Why do you ask?"

"Dan and I are going out of town for the next few days. Our dog sitter came down with a fever last night, and we're scrambling to find someone. I just thought I'd try."

Vanessa glances at me. "Carter can't do it?"

Grandma chuckles. "Carter threw a party the last time he dog sat. He's been banned ever since."

I roll my eyes. "I had a few people over."

Grandpa takes a sip of his whiskey before setting it down on the table. "One of your *few people* threw up on the kitchen balcony."

"If I had seen it, I would have cleaned it up."

"Boys, stop arguing." Grandma's tone is scolding, though she has a smile on her face. "What do you think, Vanessa?"

Vanessa frowns at me, as if expecting me to object. As if she's thinking I'll be offended that my grandparents trust her more than they trust me.

I smile at her. "They pay well, and I'd love to come by and visit you."

When her gaze grows molten, my stomach flips over. Holy fuck, is this an invitation? Am I finally going to get what I've been waiting for?

"I'd love to," she says, and a wash of exhilarated heat pumps through my veins.

But then it cools.

It will all be over tomorrow. Once I've been inside her, this magical connection to her will sever, like it has with every other person I've fucked.

* * *

My somber mood hasn't lifted on my way home from dropping off Vanessa.

When I walk inside the house, a bunch of the guys are playing beer pong in the living room. I head straight toward my bedroom, resolving to get out of this funk by putting my hand on my cock and letting memories of Vanessa's sweet moans, soft skin, and face scrunched in ecstasy flood through my senses.

"The manwhore is back," Dom shouts. "And judging by the look on his face, I don't think he took any virginities today."

"Yeah, but he will," Beckett grumbles. "He's so lucky, and he doesn't even appreciate it. Vanessa's so fucking hot. I'd give up my trust fund just to stick my dick—"

"Shut your fucking mouth," I say, and the whole room grows quiet.

Hot rage singes my skin. I know after it cools, I'll regret that I've become unhinged over what was just an offhand comment made by someone who's most likely drunk. All the guys will probably give me shit for weeks about it. They'll tell me I've finally fallen in love.

I don't care.

Somehow, I don't care.

How dare they all talk about her like this, like she's a fucking Ferrari instead of a human being.

I clench my jaw. "Keep Vanessa's name out of your mouth, Beckett."

His eyes grow wide as they avert from mine. "Technically, I didn't say her na—"

"Nope." I cross my arms over my chest. "Don't do that. You

115

know what I meant. Don't even mention her. You lost that privilege. We clear?"

He exhales and then nods. "Yep."

"Good." Just as I start to turn around, a thought occurs to me, and I widen my stance as I let my gaze drift over all of their surprised faces. "It should go without saying that none of you are allowed to talk about Vanessa Gallo's virginity ever again. I don't care about the stupid plastic belt or that goddamn money. If I ever hear you mention it, I'll make you regret it."

"Damn," Dom mutters, his eyes huge. "Carter's about to throw hands."

"I don't want to hear any more of your sex-offender talk," I say. "It was gross to me before, but now it's just straight unacceptable. She's mine. It's official." I smirk. "And you will catch these hands if any of you even mention her virginity again."

As I turn around and head into the hall, the quiet room erupts into noise—a mixture of cheers, laughter, and "oh damns" —but I don't wait around to enjoy it.

I don't even care about them.

Somehow, all I care about is her.

Chapter Nine

V anessa

"I think I'm going to try the bright-pink blush." Saanvi reaches into the metal makeup case and grabs a large brush. "I want to give you a just-after-sex look."

I wrinkle my nose. "Pink always looks unnatural under the ring light."

She shakes her head as she swirls the brush around in a circular pink palette. "I think you should position yourself in front of that window." She gestures with her head as she pats my cheek lightly with the brush. "Use natural light and stay in your PJs. Or, better yet, put on a sexier PJ shirt. One that hangs off your shoulder."

I snort out a laugh. "Wouldn't it be better if I looked this way on our Live?"

"I'm not thinking about your followers. I'm thinking of Carter. I want him to watch this and go crazy with anticipation.

Okay, look down so I can apply a light layer of mascara. We want it to look natural."

I lower my gaze to my lap. "Carter's not even going to see it. He's probably never even seen a single one of my videos."

"You know that's not true." Her tone is matter-of-fact.

"He straight up told me he has no real interest in me. This is all about the bet."

In my periphery, I see Saanvi shake her head. "Armaan told me he doesn't even care about the bet that much. At least not compared to the others." She sets her hand under my chin and guides my face upward. Her lips purse as her gaze roams my face. "He's lying to you. His family is wealthy, so he obviously doesn't care about the money."

"He says he'll be a legend on campus."

Saanvi snorts. "No way. He's the campus player. He's already a legend. My theory is he saw you at that party and fell madly in love. He's just using the bet as an excuse."

My stomach flutters, and I wish it wouldn't. I know Carter isn't madly in love with me. He's so blunt he'd have told me the second he felt anything beyond lust.

It's silly that I want it to be true. If he really liked me, I'd be tempted to start a relationship with him, and I can't do that right now. I need to have meaningless sex with multiple partners first. I need to purge my body of shame before I can even consider settling down with someone.

Besides, if I fell for Carter, I'd be uplifting the values of my upbringing. I'd be reinforcing the belief that sex, love, and commitment are inextricably linked.

"I can't think this way," I say as I stand up from my seat and walk over to my tripod. "I'm already prone to falling for whoever I lose my virginity to because of the way I was raised. I need to try my hardest to separate sex from feelings."

While I sit down in front of the window, Saanvi walks over and starts playing with my hair. Judging from her movements, she's trying to make it look a little messy. "I hate to tell you this, but people like you and me weren't built that way."

I frown. "What do you mean?"

"We think too much. Everything we do has meaning, even sex. Carter's going to make you feel so good that your brain is going to look for a reason why. You're going to end up thinking your way into having feelings for him. It's just how you're built."

I examine myself through my front-facing camera, trying to wipe the frown from my face so that I can look relaxed while I make my video announcement. "Then I'll just have to think my way out of those feelings."

"Good luck with that." She plops back onto my bed. "I say just let yourself feel what you feel. I'm pretty sure I'm right about Carter."

I take a deep, steadying breath, trying to let all thoughts of Carter's feelings for me vanish on exhale.

"I'm planning to lose my virginity tomorrow night," I say to the camera, immediately pressing the record button afterwards to stop filming. I smile at Saanvi. "How's that for an opening line?"

She laughs. "The city will be flooded by the tears of UCSB frat boys."

"Except for one frat boy." I turn back to the camera. "Alright, try not to make me laugh for the rest of this video."

"I'll cover my face with a pillow."

Carter

"I'm not going to lie," she says with that plastic smile. "I'm more than a little nervous. This will be a first in so many different ways."

My lips quirk. My sweet, shy girl.

I can't believe I used to think she was insincere. One little lie about losing her virginity to a prick like Graham doesn't mean that she'd scam all of her followers. Her TikTok platform means something to her.

How could I have been so stupid?

"I'm not going to reveal the identity of the guy I've chosen," she says, "but a lot of you will probably recognize him when we go live. He's sort of famous on campus."

She glances away from the camera for a second with a small smile, and even though it's just the slightest quirk of her lips, my chest seizes with this familiar ache.

I should be exhilarated. This blood pumping through my veins and tightening of my muscles should be from the anticipation of finally getting my cock inside her.

I shouldn't be panicking.

Vanessa

"You don't seem very impressed by my grandparents' house," Carter says with that adorable smirk. "You've bragged a few times about being a poor girl. I thought you'd be dazzled."

I scoff as I slide open the door to the kitchen balcony. The dark-gray ocean expands in each direction. I probably would be dazzled by a view like this any other time. But all I've been able to think about is what I'll be doing with Carter tonight.

"I've never bragged about being poor," I say. "You were trying to deny your wealth."

"I really wasn't. I know I'm lucky to have a trust fund, but I think they'll probably take it away soon. Neither of them will really give a shit about me if I'm not useful to them, and I don't plan on working for Beach Burger."

I whip around. "Are you being serious?"

He frowns. "About working for Beach Burger?"

"No. About your grandparents not giving a shit about you."

He shrugs. "I think my grandma kind of loves me. As much as

she's capable, but is it really love if she's not willing to stand up to my grandpa when it counts? I know she'd let him disown me the same way he disowned my mom."

I walk over to the counter and grab the bottle of wine Carter took from the basement cellar. As I pour myself a glass, the crystal wine tumbler sparkles from the evening sunlight. He's so lucky he gets to enjoy this kind of luxury on a regular basis, though I think I'm starting to see why he fights it so hard.

"Not everyone is good at love." I take a sip of the wine, and I'm struck by how smooth it is. Damn. I guess there really is a difference between cheap and expensive wine. "Some people love in really shitty ways, but it doesn't mean their love isn't real, or isn't as strong as love in a healthy relationship. Your grandparents definitely love you, even if they're bad at it."

He walks over to the counter and pours himself a glass, and just his proximity makes my body warm. My gaze falls to those big hands as they grip the bottle.

Those hands will be all over me tonight.

"What did they do last night to make you think they love me?" he asks, thankfully distracting me from my horny thoughts. "I literally can't think of one thing."

"Are you kidding me?" I lift a hand in the air. "You have a weekly dinner date with them, and you made it sound like they lose their minds if you try and cancel."

He shakes his head before taking a sip of his wine. "That's just so they can keep tabs on me. On how I spend their money."

"They could keep tabs much more easily by checking your purchases on their banking app. Time is money for someone like your grandpa, and he devotes a couple of hours every week to his grandson."

His brow knits. "Why are you defending my grandparents?"

His walls are rising, and I can feel the growing distance between us. He's skeptical of me. Is it because his grandparents and I share a religion?

I turn around and walk to the edge of the kitchen, pretending to look at the ocean but really trying to give him space. "I'm not defending them. I'm trying to help you."

"How is this helpful?"

"You're obviously deeply hurt by them, and that makes you cynical. I'm trying to give you a different perspective."

"I'm not hurt in the way you think. I barely even know these people. They were strangers to me until I was ten years old, and after that they were still distant. They bought me nice presents and took me to Disney World, but they always had a nanny helping them. A *nanny*. They brought a nanny on every vacation until I was fourteen years old and perfectly able to take care of myself. That's how little they knew me."

I lift my hands in the air. "Do you hear yourself? You *are* hurt. Things like that bother you because it makes you feel like they don't really want to be around you."

"I'm not hurt for myself." His jaw tightens, and there's a fire burning under those icy-blue eyes. "Those people disowned my mom. They cut her out entirely—took away her inheritance and didn't speak to her until they wanted to see me. That's not love. Shitty love isn't love."

I shake my head. "I disagree. Love isn't a static thing. It's not all or nothing. I think love is an action. A skill, even. Something you can learn to be good at with practice."

He wrinkles his nose. "That's therapy talk, and I don't buy it. I think love is much simpler than that. It's like an instinct. My grandparents don't have it for their own daughter, and I don't have it for anyone except my mom. My family's fucked up. I seriously think we're broken somehow, like a genetic thing or something. I don't even think I really love my dad. Not in the way I love my mom."

I set my hand on his forearm, and he glances down at it. "Is that why you don't get romantically attached to people?"

He sets his hand on mine. "I think so." His voice is just above a whisper. "My mom has always needed me. She's sort of...fragile, I guess. In an emotional way. Getting disowned was really hard for her. She lost everything. Her parents. Her whole community, really. We were it for each other growing up. I didn't spend much time with my dad when I was really little. I think maybe...by the time I got to a certain age, there was no room for anyone else but her."

"That's not how love works."

"Not for everyone, but maybe that's the way it works for me. Maybe some of us only have a certain amount of love to give, and mine is capped out."

"Or maybe you're afraid to let yourself love anyone else with your whole heart. Maybe your mom's experiences have made you scared of loss."

"Ness." His voice is just above a whisper, but I hear a hint of pity. "I don't want you to think—"

"Don't worry," I say quickly. "I'm not catching feelings."

He flinches. "I don't want to sound like an asshole. I just—"

"I know. You only do one-night stands."

He smiles. "But I make sure everyone has a good time. A *really* good time."

His words are so dark that a hot pressure builds in my belly. Oh God, it's really going to happen. I'm finally going to lose my virginity.

Jesus, please keep the shame out of my body tonight.

And don't let it be replaced by feelings for Carter.

Carter

Goddamn it, I don't want to hurt her.

She licks her lips, looking so shy and sweet I want to take her into my arms and tell her I'm sorry that my love is capped out. I can't help that I lose interest after sex. If I could love anyone, it would be her.

That must be where this panic is coming from. That must be

why my heart is pounding and my hands are shaking. My nerves are probably every bit as raw as hers.

I'm afraid I'm going to hurt her because I like her so much. In probably less than an hour from now, I'll be thoroughly relaxed after an amazing fuck, but the novelty luster of her will be gone. I'll still like her, but not with the same intensity, and those watchful eyes of hers will see it.

Or maybe the luster won't be gone. Maybe she'll shine even brighter.

Fuck, that can't be why I'm scared. I'm not capable of loving anyone other than my mom. I meant everything I said to her a moment ago.

"Carter," she whispers, pulling me out of my head.

"What, baby girl?" When I lean in and press a soft kiss on her nose, she takes in a sharp breath.

"I hate saying this, because it sounds so cliche and stupid, but I'm kind of nervous."

My throat grows tight. "We don't have to do anything you aren't ready for."

"I know. But I want to do everything tonight. I want to get it over with."

I can't help but chuckle, and it's a relief in my current turmoil. "That's very flattering."

"You know what I mean."

I do. I'm only her second sexual partner, and I have that stupid reputation as the campus player. She's nervous I'll be comparing her to everyone that came before.

As if I could. How could I think about anyone else when I'm inside Vanessa Gallo?

"Can we go outside?" she asks. "Maybe go for a walk on the beach before we...do more?"

Oh God, she's precious.

"Sure, baby. Let's go."

By the time we make it down the stairs and onto the beach, the cloud-ridden sky is orange and pink from the evening sun.

Damn, it's gorgeous, and she said she fantasizes about having sex on a beach. I'll bet she's never had access to a private one before.

Maybe I can make her fantasy come true.

"Carter, would you be..."

My throat grows thick. I halt my step and turn towards her. I lift my hand and graze her cheek with the tips of my fingers. "I don't want you to be this nervous."

Her smile is tight. "I was going to ask if you would be really disappointed if we didn't have sex tonight?"

I would be. In fact, right now it feels like I might die if I don't fuck her, but she can't know that. I want her to trust me.

I smile. "A little, but it's way more important to me that you're comfortable."

She stares at me for a long moment, and I can almost see those thoughts of hers darting around in her head and clicking into place. I love that she's always thinking. I love that she's so methodical about everything. She's the most adorable person I've ever met.

Her smile reaches her eyes this time. "The best part of how brutally honest you are is that I believe you when it counts."

"Why would I lie to you?" The question rolls off my tongue without hesitation, and it makes my stomach hollow.

No more lies. Honesty is important to her, and she deserves the world. From now on, I'll be brutally honest even if it hurts her, just like I promised I would on the night we met.

She averts her gaze from mine. "Guys will usually say anything when they want..."

"How much experience have you had, if you don't mind my asking?"

She purses her lips as she seems to think about my question. "Not much. There was one guy who I did more with than all the others."

Graham.

Fuck. I don't even want to think about him. I hate the idea of her beneath him, giving him that furrowed-brow look she gives me as he pushed into her for the first time.

What's wrong with me? I didn't think I gave a fuck about virginity. It's all so stupid.

But the idea of someone else being her first and always being significant to her...

Always being remembered as "the guy who took my virginity," while I'm just the guy she's using to get TikTok views...

Fuck. I need to stop thinking about it.

"But that was a bad experience for me. He was..." She shakes her head. "He was not for me."

It's a balm to hear her say that. Graham said essentially the same thing. *"She was boring." "She just laid there."* Even back then —before I knew her—I made fun of him for not being able to make her come.

I was only teasing. What did I care back then?

Now, I'm dying to fuck his memory out of her mind. I want to slam my cock inside her and tell her she'd better enjoy it, because it's the only one she'll get for the rest of her life.

You're mine now, Vanessa Gallo.

Oh fuck. This is new. Am I really fantasizing about a monogamous relationship with her?

I glance down at my hand, and sure enough, it's shaking again.

Vanessa

Those icy-blue eyes are fixed on the sand. Gone is the relaxed, charming Carter I normally see. He's been much more reserved and almost tender tonight, as if he's trying to put me at ease.

Now is my moment. I just need to do it.

When I take a step toward him, his head shoots up, and his gaze falls to my mouth.

"I want to kiss you," I say.

He stares at me for a long moment. What is that expression? I've never seen it before. "Okay," he eventually says.

I press up to my toes and set my lips against his. Even in the chilly air, they're deliciously warm. At first, he only pouts his lip while I nibble at them, but when I slip my tongue into his mouth, he grabs me by the waist and yanks me against him. His strong grip cuts into my skin, but his kiss is soft.

When he finally pulls away, we're both breathless. We stare at each other. "I've never wanted anyone this much," he says.

I can trust that he means it, and the thought sends a tingling thrill up my spine. This is the advantage of choosing someone so brutally—sometimes painfully—honest. Those words would be a line coming from anyone else.

I'm going to do this. What a magical way to lose my virginity, on the sand of a private beach. If I pass this moment up, I'll always regret it. I can do this.

I can have meaningless sex and enjoy it.

Even if I can't enjoy it. Even if the shame comes back, this will be a good first step.

My gaze runs over his tall, hulking form. This is so different than I imagined my first time would be like all those years ago. I thought it would be with my husband. I thought it would be in the bed, and he would be the initiator.

Look how far I've come.

When I reach for the waistband of his jeans, his eyebrows shoot up his forehead. "Whoa there, baby," he says breathlessly.

My stomach sinks. God, how awkward. I look away and tuck a strand of hair behind my ears.

"Hey." His voice is gentle. "It's okay. I liked it."

His hand settles on my cheek and drifts down to my nape, calming my jittering nerves. I return my hands to his jeans, keeping my gaze fixed on his hips. I fumble with the button, so he lowers his hand and helps me. After I unzip them, I set my hands at my side. I'm not quite ready to pull his pants down.

"Are you sure you want to start this party out here?" he asks. "It's probably not going to live up to your fantasy. You're going to find sand in unspeakable places for the next month. No joke."

I chuckle, though my voice is a little tight. He must sense my jitters, because his smile fades. After setting both hands on my cheeks, he presses a kiss on my mouth. "You don't have to be nervous with me. Everything you do makes me happy."

It's such a sweet thing to say, I could almost cry.

Fuck.

I need to get my emotions in check. The last thing I want to do is cry during my first time. That would be even more pathetic than a panic attack, and yet...

Somehow, I don't think Carter would mind. He's nothing like Graham. I can't even imagine seeing disdainful bafflement in those kind eyes.

I take a deep breath, trying to let all of my nerves go on my exhale.

It seems to work. I grab his face and meet his eyes. When those blue eyes grow hooded, I take that as my cue. I press my lips against his and immediately slip my tongue into his mouth. He releases a groan that I feel in my belly. I move my tongue frantically, and he seems to like it. He matches my pace, grabs my hips, and yanks them against his. When he grinds them into my belly, I release a low moan.

"Oh God, Vanessa," he whispers against my mouth. "You're heaven."

Only belatedly do I recognize his hand is already inside my panties. When his fingers find my clit and start rubbing up and down, a tingling pressure begins to build in my core.

"Lean into it. You can take it."

"Yes," I pant, wiggling my hips against his touch. A jolt of electricity sizzles through my body, making me cry out.

"That's it." His touch grows more rapid. "Oh, my beautiful girl. Give me more of those sweet sounds."

Beautiful girl. I love it when he talks to me like this.

"Carter, I want you now."

"Soon, baby. Come on my hand first. Let me feel you."

"No," I whimper. "I want your... You know."

His fingers halt. "Cock. Say it."

I swallow. "I want your...cock."

He releases a loud groan that vibrates through my body, making me almost dizzy. I don't think I've ever been so aroused in my life.

The next thing I know, I'm being lifted into the air. After plopping me roughly onto the sand, he starts peeling off my leggings along with my underwear.

It's happening. I'm going to lose my virginity soon. And the cold, sick shame is nowhere to be found. My body is all heat and anticipation.

Thank you, Jesus. Thank you for answering my prayer.

The ripping of plastic tells me he's putting on the condom, and my stomach does a little turn. His face appears in my view, and it's only after he sets his body on top of mine that I realize he's completely naked. Nervousness flutters in my stomach, but it's a pleasant sensation this time. His body is so big and warm. His thick, hard cock presses into my thigh, and instead of fearing it, I'm ready. I'm ready for the pain of losing my virginity.

It will be cleansing.

Carter's fingers return to my clit, and he starts rubbing faster and lighter than he did a moment ago, making my body grow as taut as a drum. I thrust my hips upward to get more of it.

"No. You said you wanted my cock. You'll wait like a good girl."

"No," I whimper. "Now. Please now."

"How could I say no to my girl?"

"Don't say no." The words feel like a sob pulled from my chest.

His fingers drift lower and swirl around in my slippery wetness. "Oh fuck, you're soaking for me. This pussy is aching to take my big cock."

"Yes! Now!"

The sensation comes so quickly, I scream before I even know what it is. Fullness and sharp pain. Stretching and filling me everywhere. Water coats my eyes, and I jerk upward to escape the pain.

"Oh fuck." Carter's voice is brittle.

I take a deep breath and blow it out through my pursed lips. "Virgin. Did you forget?"

He's quiet for a long moment. When I glance at his face, his jaw is tight, and his gaze is fixed on my shoulder.

"It's okay," I say. "I'm glad you were so turned on you forgot. It means I wasn't acting like an awkward virgin."

He continues to stare at my skin, his breathing rapid. My God, does he really feel so bad he can't speak?

Chapter Ten

C arter

Oh fuck, what have I done?

Of course Graham was lying. He's always trying to compete with me. Why did I assume his story was true? Why did I think earnest, sincere Vanessa would deceive her followers? Something happened with Graham—just like she said—but it wasn't sex.

Not everyone lies. Not everyone manipulates.

Least of all this sweet, beautiful, perfect girl. When I'm finally able to lift my gaze to her face, I see concern in those big brown eyes, and it's like a knife in my heart.

She's worried about me, because she thinks I got caught up in the moment and forgot she was a virgin. She doesn't know that I assumed she was lying without even giving it much thought.

I have to make it up to her.

I have to make her first time incredible.

"Baby girl, I'm so sorry." When I lean in to kiss her, she grimaces. Probably because my cock moved farther inside her and hurt her again. When I start to pull back, she wraps her arms around me.

Oh God, her touch is heaven. She's holding me, and I don't deserve it.

"No." Her voice is gentle. "Stay where you are. Please."

My throat grows tight. "Baby, I'm hurting you."

"It's supposed to hurt."

I grit my teeth. "No. Not this much. I shouldn't have slammed into you. I should have been much, much gentler."

"I like that it was hard. It was symbolic. It was a 'fuck you' to my virginity and to purity culture."

She has that adorable furrow between her brows—the earnest frown that I've come to adore—and a strange lightness settles over me. I've just hurt her, and she doesn't care. Because she trusts me.

This is what love feels like.

I'm inside her, and the sun is setting over us, drifting behind the ocean. Pretty soon it will be only her. With no lights on the beach, it will be the crashing ocean waves and our bodies.

Her heaven might be some place in the sky that really only exists in her head, but my heaven is here. Inside her.

Holy fuck. I love her, and it's not going to fade away.

I've been deluding myself.

But it's okay. Everything is okay when I'm with her.

She's paradise.

I lift my fingers and brush them over the soft skin on her cheeks. "Thank you for trusting me."

She averts her gaze. "You feel really good."

I laugh as I press a kiss against her cheek. "Don't lie, baby girl. I probably feel like I'm splitting you open."

"Yeah, but it's kind of hot, especially when you say it like that."

When I laugh louder, she wiggles her hips. "Oh, that was nice," she says. "You feel like a vibrator."

I'm probably smiling like an idiot as I look down at her, and I don't care. I don't care if she can see how much I love her.

I'm keeping her.

This was meant to be.

Here I thought a part of me was broken—that I wasn't able to love—but it turns out that part of me was only buried somewhere deep and opaque. This girl found her way in. She didn't even have to try. She just walked earnestly forward, and she found me.

Now, I'll never let her go.

It's only her from now on.

I press both hands on her cheeks and kiss her hard. "You'll tell me if it hurts too much, right?"

She nods frantically. "I was so close before. I want you to make me come."

"Of course you do, dirty girl."

She presses her hips against me and moans. "I love it when you give me names."

I'll call her every precious name that comes to mind. My beautiful girl. My love. From now on, nicknames will only be for her. No one else.

I pull my cock out of her and press it back in, trying to help her adjust to my size. "I'm going to fuck you all night."

"Yes."

I pull out a little farther this time. "You're going to scream my name."

"Yes, Carter."

She wraps her arms around my shoulders, and I let my body sink into hers. She's so tight and hot. I'm not even moving, and it's still paradise.

I move inside her as slowly as I can. When her eyes widen, a wave of warmth washes over me. "You okay?"

"Yeah, the discomfort is starting to go away."

I kiss her nose. "Good."

"Your penis is really big."

I laugh. "Anything would feel big to you right now. Alright, I want to try something different, but you have to let me know if I hurt you."

"Does it involve pulling out of me?"

"For a minute."

She grips my shoulders, her dark-brown eyes boring into mine. "Can you hold me and kiss me for a minute first?"

My chest seizes so tightly the breath leaves my lungs. I didn't think it was possible to love someone this much. "Sure." My voice is just above a whisper.

I lower my mouth to hers and drink her in. There's nothing but her, the wind brushing over my back, and the lull of the crashing waves. I could live this way forever. I could have no one else but her and be perfectly content.

This is what love is. It's big and small at the same time. Big because my heart is so full it could explode. Small because it pulls me into this quiet place where nothing else exists but her.

Fuck, she's turned me into a sap, and I don't even care.

Her slippery tongue presses against mine before she pulls away. She stares into my eyes. "I still don't feel any shame. Why do you think that is?"

Because we're soulmates.

I swallow and look away for a moment while mist starts to gather in my eyes. Fuck, am I really going to cry during sex?

I don't even care. She's transformed me into a new person, and I don't even miss the old Carter.

"I think our bodies were made for each other," I say, my voice tight.

"Yes. That animal chemistry."

"Animal." The chuckle pulled from my chest makes my cock move into her tightness. I clench my teeth to fight the urge to ram it harder. Instead, I lift my hand and graze my fingers over her cheek. "My practical, unromantic girl."

"You're even sweeter than me during sex. It's funny. You're such a dick, and yet—"

I grab her chin and press her head into the sand. "Don't call me names. Unless you want to get punished after this."

Her eyes widen. "Ooh, I think I'd like that. Can we...try things like that?"

I groan as I press a kiss against her mouth. "We're going to try everything."

And I mean it. My whole life will just be this girl right here. My beautiful, earnest, precious Vanessa. I'm going to do everything in my power to give her everything she's always wanted. She can work for pennies by running a non-profit, and I'll make sure she can still travel the world. I'll make millions by growing OvuTrac, and she can have whatever she wants.

A gust of wind sends a chunk of hair over her face, covering her eyes. When I brush it away, her gaze locks on mine. As I stare at that adorable pointy chin and those sparkling brown eyes, a heaviness settles over my body. This is the most important moment of my life. This and the day I marry her.

Holy fuck.

I gasp out an almost hysterical laugh, and her brows draw together. "What?" she asks.

I lean in and press a soft kiss against her mouth, slipping my hand between our bodies and feeling down until I find her clit. "I'll tell you later. First, we're going to try something. Flip around."

Her eyes widen. "You want to...do me from behind?"

She's so prim when she says "do me" that I can't help but smile. "Yeah, but I'm going to go real slow. If it hurts, we'll stop." I brush a strand of hair behind her ear. "Can we try it?"

She nods. "I trust you."

My throat grows too tight to speak. Trust. Oh God, I don't deserve it. Not after all the lies I've told her. Not after slamming inside her because I believed that dipshit Graham over her.

I groan as my aching cock pulls out of her, and she flips over onto her belly. God, she's so graceful when she moves. I grip her hips and lift them so that I can position myself, and the sight of that tight ass and glistening pussy is enough to make me come right now.

After guiding my cock forward until I hit her wetness, I press inside her gently, giving her time to get used to me from this angle. It takes me about a minute to work my way inside. When I'm in to the hilt, I wrap my arms around her shoulders and pull her body tightly against mine, slipping my hands up until I find her small, perfect tits. She moans as I rub my thumbs over her nipples.

This is heaven.

I don't believe in God, but I believe in her.

I pull out slightly and thrust back in, and she moans. "That's it, beautiful girl. You can take it."

"Yes," she pants.

When I thrust into her this time, an almost unbearable electricity shoots into my gut. I settle my fingers on her clit and start rubbing in the rhythm I've learned she likes.

"Oh, I love that!"

I yank her back into my chest. "You're such a good girl. I'm so proud of you taking a cock like this on your first time."

She whimpers. "That's so hot. I don't know why it's hot, but it is."

I laugh as I pull her tightly against my body and press my mouth to her ear. "It's because you're a dirty girl, aren't you?" After thrusting my hips to the hilt, I grit my teeth to withstand the wave of electricity coursing through my insides. "You wanted cock all those years you were trying to be good, didn't you?"

"Yes!" she pants.

I rub her clit in a circular motion, and she clenches around me, sending stars into my vision. Good God, she's a dream fuck. It's never been this good before.

After squeezing her, I lick the inside of her ear. "I could fuck you forever, beautiful girl. I want to do nothing but fuck this sweet pussy."

"Carter! I think... I'm..." Her body trembles, and she thrusts her hips into my fingers.

"You can do it." I brush my lips over her cheeks. "You don't have to work for it. Let it happen."

She thrusts harder. "No, it's going away..."

I lift my hand to her throat and squeeze. "Stop." My voice is hard. "I told you to let it happen."

"Oh! I like that."

"What, baby girl?"

"I like it when you choke me."

My gut clenches as laughter bubbles out of me. "Filthy girl." I kiss her cheek. "Listen to Daddy, and I'll do it more. Let yourself come. Don't chase it."

She relaxes into my arms. Oh God, I could hold her forever.

I lick the sweat from her neck as I increase the pace of my fingers. Her body grows taut, and I put my mouth to her ear. "Come on my cock, beautiful girl. Do it for me."

She screams and whimpers as her pussy pulses over my cock. Her sweet little sounds send a flood of electricity through my whole body. I let out a roar as I thrust my hips into her tightness.

I've never felt pleasure like this.

I squeeze her tightly as the last pulse of come shoots out of me. "Fuck!"

"Carter," she whimpers.

At my final spasm, I pull her into my chest and collapse next to her on the sand.

We lie silently for several minutes before she releases a sleepy sigh. Is this heaven for her, too?

It can't just be me. This love is too big for it to be one-sided.

She must love me, too.

Vanessa

Jesus, I had no idea it could be that good.

My body is warm and limber, just like it was a few days ago

when he fingered me in the storage room. I'm free of the sick cold-ness that usually follows an orgasm. How is this possible?

A chill settles over my body as I relax in his hard arms. Please say he's not my antidote. Not Carter Blake, UC Santa Barbara's campus player.

Just imagine if he of all people is the only person in the world who has the animal chemistry I need to make my body feel good. He's already done with me. He's probably right now thinking about when he can leave.

How humiliating.

No. Thoughts like that are silly. I'm only twenty, and I have a whole life of sex ahead of me. Carter isn't special. I'm just inexpe-rienced.

He was the perfect first step, because he made me desire sex instead of fear it.

When he pulls me tightly against him and kisses my cheek, a bit of the coldness returns. This feels so good. I've already had an orgasm, and yet I don't want him to stop holding me. Does this mean it's beyond animal chemistry? Does this mean I have real feelings for him?

It's probably just my upbringing. I feel this affection for him because I was taught that love and sex go together. These feelings aren't real. Sex can be an expression of love, but it can't create love out of thin air. My body still believes what it was taught, even if I now reject it. It will probably take multiple sexual partners before my body catches up.

"I have sand everywhere," I say in an effort at lightness.

He snorts. "I told you. You'll still have sand in your ass crack weeks from now. Mark my words."

My throat grows tight, and I swallow to ease it. "You've had a lot of beach sex?"

His lips brush against my neck. "Just once before."

"On this beach?"

He's quiet for a long moment. "Yes, but this feels like it was the first. It's never been like this before." He nuzzles my neck. "It's never been this good."

My stomach flips over. "You mean...sex in general has never been this good?"

"Yes," he answers without hesitation.

I twist around to look at his face. His eyelids are heavy, and sweat beads glaze his forehead. His expression is unreadable.

"Do you really mean that?" I ask.

"I do."

A deep, delicious warmth settles over me, like a soft blanket. I gave the campus player good sex. That should give me confidence when I have sex next time, even if whoever it is doesn't make me feel as good or as comfortable as Carter.

"Can I ask you a question?"

"What, baby?"

"How many sexual partners have you had?"

"I get tested pretty regularly, love."

"I'm not worried about that. I'm just curious. You're really good with the clitoris."

His deep chuckle rumbles against my shoulder. "Is that a hint? Do you want me to give it a little more love?"

"No, I'm really just curious. I want to dissect your past."

"My inquisitive girl." His eyes grow heavy-lidded, and his throat works. He reaches out and strokes the hair around my temple. "I don't know how many people I've had sex with. I didn't count."

"Do you..." I lick my lips. "Do you remember all of them?"

His smile holds, but he narrows his eyes on my face. "Where are these questions going?"

"I'm not sure."

He leans in and kisses my nose. It's something he's been doing a lot lately, and I wish he wouldn't. I don't want to remember his affectionate gestures when I'm trying to enjoy sex with someone else.

"I don't think I remember all the women," he says. "Maybe I

could if I tried. I do remember the handful of guys I've had sex with because they were something new."

"You're bisexual?"

"I'm not really sure." He shrugs. "I prefer women, but I've been attracted to some guys."

"The way I was raised didn't allow for me to even consider it. To this day, I get scared even thinking about touching or kissing girls, even when I know it's normal."

He leans in and trails kisses from my jaw and down my neck. When he reaches my collarbone, he pats the sand away and starts using his tongue. By the time he reaches my nipple, he's sucking my skin.

He's so touchy, and it makes me feel so much.

Too much.

"That's really sad," he says. "I don't think it's the same for me, though I haven't thought about it too hard. All I know is that I've wanted more women than men. Do you think it's the same for you?"

I shift my gaze to the purple sky. Thoughts about girls always made me feel such a deep, sinking shame that I'd rationalize them away. I told myself thoughts like that came from the devil when I was young.

"I don't know," I say. "Our early experiences are so formative. Maybe being raised the way I was permanently fucked up my sexuality from what it would have developed into naturally."

"No. You need to stop thinking that way. You're perfect the way you are. You just need to unlock what's in here." He places his firm palm on my belly. "I'm going to help you do it."

I frown. "Are you saying you want to do this again?"

His lips close, and his eyes widen.

"I just figured this would be our only time," I say.

His expression grows bewildered. Did I say something wrong? God, I wish I knew the rules. I wish I hadn't been so sheltered when it comes to this stuff. I felt the same insecurity with

Graham. I didn't know what to say after my panic attack. I didn't know how to smooth everything over.

His gaze lowers to my shoulder. He stares at me for what feels like an eternity before finally looking up. When he does, his eyes are an icy blue. "We haven't gone live yet," he bites out.

Jesus, what is this? Why does he seem angry?

"We can do that tonight if you want."

His jaw clenches. "I don't want that. I think we should..." He inhales a shaky breath through his nose. "Try some more things first."

"You mean sexual things?"

"Yes."

Jesus, what is going on? I thought he only did one-night stands.

"I don't know if that's the right move for me. I probably need to start looking for another partner."

His eyes grow huge, and a chill skitters down my spine. What is that look? If I didn't know any better, I'd think it was horror.

"No, you don't." His voice is eerily quiet.

I frown. "Don't what?"

"You aren't going to be looking for another partner."

I blink once. "You mean...before we go live?"

He shuts his eyes for a moment, his jaw working. "Yes," he eventually says, though he doesn't sound quite as firm as he did a moment ago.

"Why not?"

"Because you're mine." His nostrils flare. "Until we go live."

Mine. The word shoots into my gut and clenches around it like a fist. If I didn't know any better, I'd think he was trying to tell me he wants a relationship.

But that's crazy. Carter Blake doesn't do relationships, and as flattered as I am that I gave the campus player good sex, I can't let it go that far to my head.

He's brutally honest. If he wanted a relationship, he would say so.

And anyway, a relationship is not the right move for me. I can't uphold my upbringing by committing to the man who takes my virginity just because I'm too weak to stop myself from getting attached to him.

"Okay... Well, when do you want to go live? I always assumed it would be right after—"

"In three weeks," he says. "And during that time, you'll fuck no one but me."

Heat washes over me, clenching my jaw. It can't be a coincidence that he's only mentioning my fidelity. What a typical fuckboy. He clearly has no plan on being faithful to me, and yet the idea of me having sex with someone else is unpalatable.

I glare at him. "Why three weeks?"

His eyes widen minutely. "I don't have... I was hoping I could time our Live with when Beach Burger goes public."

"I'm sorry, what?"

He shuts his eyes and pulls in an unsteady breath. "It's a long story. Do you think you can do this for me?"

I shake my head slowly. "This is the strangest conversation I've ever had, especially coming from the campus player. So you're saying you want to wait three weeks before we go live—for something that has to do with Beach Burger—and I have to be faithful to you during that time?"

He stares at me for a long moment. "Yes."

I lift both brows. "Are you not going to have sex with anyone else?"

His expression softens. "I don't plan on it."

"You don't plan on it," I bite out. "And yet you're practically demanding that I be faithful to you."

"I am demanding it. I won't go live with you at all if you aren't faithful to me."

My nostrils flare. "You don't have to. I'll go live on my own. Or better yet, I'll go live with the next guy."

His gaze narrows on my face, and then he smirks. "You think

so?" His words are light. "You were having such a good time finding candidates before you chose me."

I roll my eyes. "I hardly gave anyone a chance. I went on one date. I could find someone if I really looked."

"We'll see about that. Let's see how much fun you have trying to find another guy. Let's see if he can make you feel as good as I can."

Coldness runs through my veins, making my whole body grow still. How could he say something so cruel? How could he remind me of the way my body is broken just to prove a point?

I avert my gaze, clenching my teeth. "I don't think there's anything special about you. It's just sex. Maybe I should try fucking Ethan—"

I gasp when he grips my chin roughly. "You will fuck Ethan over my dead body."

I stare up at his wild eyes. He looks positively feral.

"I already told everyone in the frat to stay away from you," he says, "and that means not a single one of them will even glance your way."

My nostrils flare. "Then I won't go after a frat boy. Or I'll find one who isn't afraid of you. Armaan's a fifth-year senior. He'll do whatever he wants—"

I close my lips when Carter's nostrils flare. His whole body is vibrating with rage. I can feel it like the heat of the afternoon sun.

What is this intense reaction of his? He looks like he wants to grab me by the throat, and for some strange reason, that sends a simmering heat into my core.

My God, how quickly things went from hot to cold to hot again. How is it possible that we were snuggling a few minutes ago?

"You think Armaan will fuck you after this? You think you have that kind of sway with these guys?" Carter's fingers cut into my skin, though I'm not sure he's aware of it. "You don't. He's my brother."

I stick my finger in my throat. "You frat boys and your brotherhood. You all only rushed to get laid. I doubt your bonds run as deep as you think."

"Try it." His voice is quiet and void of expression. "See what happens."

A thrill runs through my veins. Did he really just threaten me? Why did it make my pussy tingle?

It's kinky, this fight we're having. We're lying here naked outside after we just had sex, and we're fighting about something stupid. Bickering, really. It's not like he really cares about me or my fidelity.

What would happen if I took it a step further? What if I did something crazy, like bite him?

Before I have a chance to second-guess anything, my mouth is on his hard forearm, and my teeth are clenching around his skin.

"Fuck!" he shouts, loosening his hold on me, and I use the opportunity to crawl from under him and dart away. I only make it a few feet before his hard body crushes me to the sand. My head slams down, and the breath is knocked out of me.

"You want to play, little girl?" His voice is lighter than before, but I know that anger still simmers below the surface. I bet he'd love to let it all out by fighting me.

"I don't want to play. I want to fight."

He wraps his arms around me and presses a kiss against my cheek. "You have to let me know if I'm too rough."

"I will."

He flips me onto my back. After grabbing my wrists, he pins them above my head. His hard body settles over mine, pressing me firmly into the sand. "I don't know how you're going to fight me when you can't even move."

I try to wiggle my hips, but they stay firmly in place. "I was an orange belt—"

He bursts into laughter, and it makes my skin heat. Fuck, he's so hot.

And so mean.

"An orange belt." His tone is almost affectionate as he kisses my nose. "God, you're so fucking cute. Alright, baby girl. Use those moves..." His voice chokes, and he shuts his eyes and laughs quietly, as if unable to speak. "Use those karate moves on me right now."

I make my body grow limp as I stare up at him with pouted lips. "I just want you to kiss me."

"Ah, my beautiful girl." He kisses my cheek. "I know this trick."

I lift my head to his neck and kiss it softly. His breath catches, and I smile. "It's still going to work."

"You're going to have to try a little harder than that."

I nuzzle my nose against his chest. What would he like? He's a talker during sex. Maybe he'd like it if I talked to him.

"Carter, all I want is your..." Oh fuck, this is going to be hard for me. But I can do it. I can be filthy. "Big cock again."

He groans. "Oh, I like where you're going with this." He squeezes my wrists so tight it almost hurts as he grinds his hips into mine. "Tell me more."

"It's the best cock I've ever had."

He gasps out a laugh. "Considering it's the only cock you've ever had... I don't love that one, but you're on the right track."

I widen my eyes to look innocent. "It's the only cock I've ever had, and the only cock I'll ever want."

Something sparks in his eyes.

Ooh, he likes that. But what kind of kink is it? Jesus, I hate how inexperienced I am. I don't know how to play on his level.

I'll just have to keep trying.

I wiggle my hips, and surprisingly, he lets me move. "It's the only cock I'll ever have."

"Yeah, that's right." His eyes are molten, and his jaw is hard. "You'll never take another cock but this one."

His words send heat through my body. God, he's so deliciously naughty. I love this kink, whatever it is. I love playing like we're really lovers.

Given the stupid argument we had a minute ago, you'd think we were.

"I don't want another one," I say. "I only want yours. I only want you to fuck me."

He grabs my neck and squeezes it tightly. His bright-blue eyes bore into mine. "Why is that, baby girl?"

Electricity fills my gut, and I whimper. God, I love being choked, but I have to keep my head. I've turned him on, and now I can get away.

"Because..." My lips close. Gosh, what do I say next? "Because I love it. I love you."

Heat washes over my face the moment the words are out. What a stupid thing to say. Carter's hold on my wrists loosens. Did I stun him? I avert my eyes from his, unable to bear his laughter.

I'm so bad at dirty talk.

What if he thinks I mean it? I did just lose my virginity. Hopefully, he knows I'm playing.

"Obviously, I don't mean that," I say. "I don't know how to talk dirty."

He doesn't say anything, and Jesus, I could die.

When I'm finally able to look his way, his expression makes my breath catch. His blue eyes are fixed on the sand over my shoulder, and they look almost...melancholy. But why?

Good Lord, this whole experience has been so strange. Here I was, afraid he'd be making excuses to leave me moments after we had sex. Instead, he went from rage to playfulness to...whatever he is now.

I just hope he isn't feeling sorry for me because he thinks I've caught feelings.

I swallow. "Did I really weird you out?"

"No." His voice is soft.

I stare at him, wishing I could absorb his thoughts. Why isn't he making fun of me?

He presses himself up from the sand and pats the sand from

his thighs, looking so comfortable in his nudity I envy him even in my turmoil.

"Well, this was definitely an unforgettable first time." I force out a laugh. "I never imagined biting would be involved. Or arguing about..." I frown. "Whatever that argument was about."

"I need to go."

The urgency in his tone sends a ripple of humiliation over my skin. Here it is. Now he wants to leave me. All because I'm bad at dirty talk.

He really does think I caught feelings.

Chapter Eleven

C arter

Her movements are jerky as she puts her clothes back on. She's obviously embarrassed for what she thinks was bad dirty talk after a playful fight.

It would have been bad dirty talk coming from anyone else. From her, it was so catastrophically worse. Will I ever get over the emotional rollercoaster of tonight? It feels like I've come back from war, my body and spirit forever marred.

All from a short fuck on the beach.

It was so much more for me, and I thought she was right there with me. Even if she didn't love me fully, I thought, at the very least, she wanted exclusivity after this.

God, I'm a cocky bastard. Why did I think I had her in the palm of my hand when all evidence pointed to the opposite? She's been telling me from the beginning that this is supposed to be a one-time thing to help her "fix" her body through meaningless sex.

I'm the one who put meaning into it. She has no idea what's really going on.

She doesn't know she crushed me.

And she can't know. Oh God, she can't know this power she holds over me now. I would be at her mercy, like a dog begging for her affection. Just the thought of it is like red ants crawling all over my skin.

I can't tell her how I feel until I know she's mine.

After pulling her shirt down her stomach, she shoots me a tight smile. "Well, I guess the moral of the story is that I need to work on my dirty talk."

I try to force a smile, but the muscles in my mouth are too tight. Fuck, will I ever be able to smile again?

"You should maybe work on the biting, too," I say as I button my jeans.

She frowns. "You didn't like that?"

"It was a little weird."

She looks away, looking so sweetly dismayed I want to take her into my arms. I shouldn't be such a dick to her. I would have liked her playful bite if my heart hadn't been breaking at the time.

"Um..." She uses both hands to tuck her hair behind her ears. "I'm really embarrassed."

I grunt. "Don't be."

"Really? You're so weirded out you want to leave."

God, I do want to leave. I need a moment to myself. I can't show her compassion when I'm nursing my own wound.

"I'm so confused by you," she says. "Five minutes ago, you wanted me to be faithful to you for three weeks before we go live —and I assume you wanted to have more sex during that time— and now you can't get away from me fast enough."

"I'll get over it. We can talk about everything tomorrow."

"Well, this has officially been the strangest night of my life. And the most embarrassing. I think..." She stares at me for a moment before taking a step back. "I think I want to go on a quick run. You can go ahead and head home. Have a good night!"

She doesn't waste a moment before taking off and jogging down the beach. At first, I can only stare at her loose-limbed form as she trots gracefully over the sand. When it registers that she's running away from the awkwardness, I roll my eyes. "What the fuck do you think you're doing?" I call out.

She halts for a moment before turning around. "I need to run my embarrassment out of my system."

"No." I shake my head. "Not when it's dark out."

"I don't care. I really need a run."

Irritation flares through my veins. "You're not running alone at night."

"What do you care? I'm doing it."

When she takes off again, I sigh heavily. It takes a moment for my listless body to snap into action, but it doesn't matter. Once I start running, I gain on her within a few seconds. She's quick but too small. When I catch up to her, I yank her against my chest.

Fuck, why does it have to feel so good to hold her?

Witch. She's cast a spell on me. That's the only way to explain how she made me fall in love with her when I was incapable of it before.

I lift her and set her over my shoulder, giving her ass a hard slap when I'm done. Fuck, I want to slap her ass for days. Turn it red and raw for what she put me through tonight.

"Looks like I'm going to have to take you back into the house myself."

"I'll just head back out here after you leave."

When I slap her ass even harder, she gasps.

"I'll lock you in the basement. I'm not even kidding. It's a lounge with a couch, bathroom, and walls of wine shelves. You'll be fine until morning. I'll even give you food."

She giggles. "That's kind of kinky."

I roll my eyes. "Everything's kinky to you. Even love." A wave of despair settles over me, but I don't think she can tell. I did a good job of making that sound like mockery.

"I'm sorry I'm not good at dirty talk. I don't really love you, so stop—"

I slap her ass so hard, she yelps.

"Just shut up and promise me you won't go out running tonight."

"Can we talk about the three-week thing?"

"We'll talk inside, but only if you promise."

She groans. "I promise I won't go running tonight."

Vanessa

"Why do you want to wait until Beach Burger goes public to go live?"

He takes a sip of the amber liquid, setting it on the counter when he's done. The second we got into the house, he rushed over to the living room bar and pulled out a bottle of his grandpa's scotch.

"My grandpa is planning to announce me as his new chief of staff in a few weeks. I've told him over and over again that I'm planning to take the job with OvuTrac, but he hasn't taken me seriously." He smiles, but it looks forced. "If I announce my relationship to him on our Live, he'll finally get it. You know how important traditional Christian values are to him. You might be a Christian, but you're definitely not traditional."

The words seem to settle into my skin first, making it prickle, before it registers what he's trying to say. A ball of ice forms in my stomach.

He's using me.

Fuck, why does it hurt? I knew he was using me to win the bet. Why does this feel so much worse?

"Ah." I try to swallow but find my throat is too dry. "You want to use my 'virginity show' as a fuck you."

"Exactly."

"This seems..." I lick my lips. "I get that you have a lot of resentment—a lot of justified resentment—but this seems..."

"It's none of your business."

A pang shoots into my chest. His tone is so remote. Gone is the warmth from earlier. Thank you, Jesus, for not allowing me to misread any affection into his request for three weeks of fidelity. It had nothing to do with me.

And everything to do with his ego.

I clench my jaw. "I don't understand why you want me to be faithful to you."

Life enters those remote eyes, and he looks much more like the Carter who kissed me everywhere and called me his beautiful girl. "Because..." He closes his mouth and breathes in through his nose. "I'd feel better that way. I think it's safer if we only have sex with each other for the next three weeks, and—" His eyes grow hooded as he smiles "—it will be my thank-you for letting me use your TikTok platform. There's so much more than what we did out there. I'll make pleasing you my mission these next three weeks, and we can make videos together for your TikTok if you want."

My stomach flips over. Now he's on to something. There's no reason to limit our sexual encounters to one time when he's so good at pleasing me, and three weeks isn't enough time for me to get attached to him.

Please, Jesus. Don't let me get attached to him.

Plus, my followers would love to have him in my videos. He's a celebrity on campus, and he'd be able to provide the perfect outsider perspective.

"Alright, let's do it."

His eyes widen. An emotion flashes over his face... It's gone so quickly that I can't read it.

"But I have my own demands," I say.

He smiles before lifting his hand and grazing a thumb across my cheek. "And what are those, baby girl?"

"I need us to...try things at least three times a week."

He chuckles. "Try things? What exactly do you mean by that?"

"Don't be a dick. You know what I mean. Sex stuff. I guess like...blowjobs and anal and stuff. Anything else most people who have sex do."

His brows shoot up. "Well, I wasn't expecting you to be so blunt after you talked around it."

I nod. "You know how much I value honesty."

His expression softens. "I do. Why is that exactly? I mean, I get why honesty is important, but why is it especially important to you?"

I wave my hand. "It has to do with the way I was raised. I won't bore you with it."

He takes a step in my direction, his brow furrowing. "It won't bore me. Nothing about you bores me."

The kindness in his voice tells me he really means it.

"My whole world was shaped by people with an agenda. They weren't lying. They believed what they taught me very deeply, but whether they meant to or not, a lot of it permanently fucked me up. It was lies. And even though they didn't mean to lie and manipulate me, the damage was real."

"Yeah," he whispers. "That makes sense."

"I felt gross and disgusting and uncomfortable in my skin. I hated my body. I knew I was pretty, but I felt ugly. I couldn't understand it. Why would following God make me feel that way, especially when I was created in his image?"

"Oh, Vanessa." His voice is just above a whisper. "That's fucking awful."

My eyes prickle, and I look away to gather myself for a moment. Why am I getting emotional when I've said these same words so many times to friends and in my TikTok videos?

"Yeah," I rasp. "But thankfully, I had wise people to help me see the truth. God is good, but he can't protect me from everything, not even from his own teaching—or the warped way that some people interpret it. He wants me to figure it out for myself because he wants me to be strong. And he's here to walk with me and comfort me through it." I smile tightly. "Look at how far I've come. I just lost my virginity on the beach."

He stares at me for a long moment. "You dazzle me."

Warmth drifts over my skin. I love it when he compliments me, especially with that reverence in his voice.

"Anyway," I say, not wanting to get any more emotional. "Do we have a deal?"

He doesn't answer right away, and I find myself searching those blue eyes of his to figure out what he's thinking.

I don't understand Carter nearly as well as I thought I did. Nothing about tonight was what I expected.

"Let's do this, Gallo."

Chapter Twelve

C arter

Three weeks. I have three weeks to make her love me.

I'll make myself invaluable to her. I'll devote myself to pleasuring her and meeting her emotional needs.

I can do it. I mishandled the situation because I didn't realize this tenderness in my chest is really love, so I withheld it from her. I should have shown her what a miracle she is from the beginning.

Going forward, I'll worship her.

And no more lies. She deserves nothing less after what she shared with me tonight. She deserves the world.

The strangest part of all of it is that I don't even care about that damn Live anymore. I don't care about humiliating Grandpa. When I suggested that we wait three weeks, I was mostly just grasping at any excuse to be with her longer. It doesn't really matter when I make the announcement. Whether it's tonight or three weeks from now, it'll cause just as much of a scandal given that the company is going public so soon.

I don't even care about any of it anymore. It all feels sort of petty now.

Goddamn, I think Vanessa has transformed me permanently.

When I pull up at the frat, the murmur of voices and booming music drifts from the house. Goddamn it. All I wanted was some quiet time—to fall down on my bed and forget about how I flew to heaven and then crashed back to the ground. Looks like I'll be the one taking a night stroll on the beach.

After hopping out of my car, I head for the trail down to the sand. I grab my phone from my pocket and pull up my mom's name on the call list.

She picks up immediately after I press her name. "Baby, is everything okay?"

I smile. She used to call me "baby" when I was a little boy. After I told her it embarrassed me, she stopped. She took it very seriously. Now, it slips out only when she's emotional.

"Sorry," I say. "Is it late?"

"It's eleven," she nearly shouts.

"That's not late for me."

"Why are you calling?"

My smile grows at her exasperated tone. "I met a girl."

"Oh... Someone special?"

My smile fades. "Yeah. Really special."

"Oh my God. I've never heard you say that before. I was worried you were a sociopath."

I gasp out a laugh as I walk out onto the sand. The ocean wind blows my hair into my eyes, and I swipe it away.

"I need you to help me," I say.

"How could I possibly help you?"

I glance out at the water. "She's a really good girl. A Christian."

"Uh-oh."

"Not like that. She's not a prick like Grandpa. Or a spineless twat like Grandma."

"Carter Harrison Blake. I don't appreciate you calling my

mother a twat. No matter what she's done to me or to you. That's a gross word, anyway."

"Well, it happens to be the best way to describe her. She absolutely wants to see you. It's so obvious whenever I see them. She's dying to hear how you're doing, but—"

"Really?"

The hope in my mom's voice makes my heart clench.

I swallow. "Yeah, but she's too much of a spineless twat to do anything about it. She lets Grandpa rule everything. Anyway, I don't want to talk about them. I need you to help me with Vanessa."

"Vanessa," she repeats. "I bet she's really pretty, huh? All the Vanessas I knew growing up were pretty."

"She's fucking gorgeous, but that's not even why I like her."

My mom snorts. "I'm sure it doesn't hurt."

"No, but Mom. Oh my God, this girl. She's so smart and such a genuinely good person. She's curious about everything." A smile rises to my lips. "Sometimes I'll say something so stupid, and she'll analyze it with this little frown on her face. I just love talking to her. I want to be with her all the time."

"Wow..." Her voice is breathless. "You sound like you're in love with her."

I scoff, and I don't know why. I'm usually open with my mom. Why don't I want to tell her the truth?

This itching vulnerability. I fucking hate it.

"Anyway," I say. "I need you to help me charm her. I majorly fucked up because I didn't realize how amazing she is at first. Maybe you could call me on Thursday when I'm with her and pretend you need something? Then I can start chatting with you. I won't be acting. We'll just talk like we normally do, which I know will charm the hell out of h—"

"No, I'm not doing that."

I roll my eyes. I knew she would make a show of resisting at first, though eventually she'll give in. "Why not?"

"It's a lie. Even if we're being sincere together. It's still a lie. I don't like it. Why would you even need to do this? I hate that you manipulate people when you don't need to. You're already so sweet and so handsome—"

"Mom, I need this." I lower my voice and try to keep the smile from twitching on my lips. She'll be able to hear my smile in my voice, even if it's small. "I really fucked up with her. Please do this for me."

She stays silent for a moment. "Now you're manipulating me."

I grin. "Is it working?"

"Yes, sadly." She groans. "Alright, if I do this, am I allowed to tell her about it someday? Make a big joke of it and say, 'You won't believe how much Carter was trying to impress you.'"

I grin. "If you meet her, that means I've won. You can tell her whatever you want when she's officially my girlfriend."

"You've won? Do you hear yourself? Are her feelings a competition? Are you on *The Bachelor*?"

"As if this isn't always how it is with dating. We always make ourselves look better than we are. And you don't have much room to talk when you lied to Dad and said you were eighteen, so—"

"Alright!" she growls. "Please don't go into that. I was very drunk and living with two asshole parents. I wouldn't have lied like this. For no reason, it seems. Why are you going to this much trouble?"

My throat grows tight.

I love her

"She's really special, Mom."

She sighs heavily. "Alright, as long as you don't lose all feelings for her tomorrow. You've always had such a short attention span. I don't want this girl getting hurt."

"She won't," I say with complete confidence. "I'm going to make her so happy. After I win her over."

I mean it. I'll never hurt this girl. How could I when my heart is bursting with love for her? I would sooner die.

.   .   .

Vanessa

After rinsing the dish way longer than necessary, I hand it over to Carter. He shoots me a questioning frown as he lifts the towel and takes it from me.

Shit, my cheeks must be pink. I'm nervous around him, and I hate it.

This is my first time seeing him since we parted ways on Tuesday. He texted me yesterday asking if we could start our "activities" after our shift at Gospel House. My stomach has been in knots ever since.

Before, I was worried about my own body—what I would feel when we had sex. I was worried the delicious warmth that always comes from being around him would go away and the cold, sick shame would return.

Now, I have a new fear.

What if I can't please him? The first time we had sex, I was a novelty. Maybe that's why he enjoyed it so much. He's notorious for losing interest in his sexual partners. What if my inexperience makes him lose interest in me?

His big, bulky arms flex as he wipes the towel over the plate. He washes dishes so deftly, with such grace.

"Why are you staring at my biceps, Gallo?"

I roll my eyes, though my cheeks grow even hotter. "You have very big arms."

He grins, and those adorable dimples make their appearance. "Do you want to touch them?"

Even in my embarrassment, I can't help but smile back. "Later."

He takes a step in my direction. "Only if you're a good girl."

Pressure grows in the pit of my stomach, fluttering to my groin. My God, I love the way he talks. Livvy has told me that Cole says these kinds of things to her, but it always sounded bizarre. He's like an older brother, and the idea of him spanking my sister and tying her up—like I know he does—always grossed me out a little.

Now I understand.

"Carter, could we..." I close my mouth. Damn it, I'm a good communicator. Why is this hard to bring up? He's already seen me at my most vulnerable. Somehow, asking this question is more difficult than lying naked in his arms, exhausted and sated after having sex.

I'm startled by the pressure of his hand on my arm. It's a little wet from the sink, but it's still deliciously warm and hard. "What, baby girl? Don't be embarrassed to ask."

God, his voice is so kind.

"Do you know what I'm going to ask?"

He smiles. "I have a feeling you're going to ask for something sexual."

I huff out a brittle laugh. "Yeah, I was wondering if we could try some kinky things, like role playing and costumes and stuff?"

His eyes widen. "You really want to?"

"Yeah..." I clear my throat. "I liked when you... When we fought on the beach."

He sets the plate on the counter and walks so close we're almost touching. After grabbing my face, he leans forward and stops just before our lips touch. His breath brushes over my mouth. "I'll give you whatever you want, beautiful girl. I just want to make you happy."

Heat shoots between my legs. "Does it make *you* happy? You said it was awkward on Tuesday."

He groans. "I wish I hadn't said that. It wasn't awkward. I'd love it if you bit me again." A smile rises to his mouth. "Especially in the middle of an argument."

I avert my gaze. "I guess I should have asked first."

"Hey." He touches my chin, guiding my head up to meet his gaze. "You're safe with me. You don't have to be embarrassed. I won't make you feel that way again, and we can try whatever kink you want."

"Have you done that kind of stuff a lot?"

"I have," he says without hesitation.

Icy jealousy twists in my stomach. Where is this coming from? I know he's a manwhore. Why on earth would I be jealous over this?

This is just meaningless sex, and only for three weeks.

A buzzing sound cuts through the silence, and Carter's blue eyes widen. He steps away and grabs his phone from the counter. "It's my mom. I have to grab this."

He swipes his thumb across the screen and lifts the phone to his ear. "Hey, Mom."

When the faint, muffled sound of her voice comes in, Carter's expression softens and his lips quirk. Good Lord, how cute. He's really happy to talk to his mom.

"I'm just at the shelter with Vanessa," he says, smiling at me.

Does she know who I am? He said my name like she should know it. Warmth rushes through my veins. If he talks about me with his mom, maybe he cares about me a tiny bit.

No. I can't start thinking that way.

"But I can talk for a second..." He looks at me. "Do you mind? I should only be five minutes."

Yikes, that's my cue. How embarrassing that I've been sitting here eavesdropping. Am I really smiling right now while I stare at him? I need to get out of here.

"Not at all," I say quickly before heading towards the door. "I'll give you some privacy."

"No!" His voice is sharp. "You're fine. I just didn't want to be rude and make you wait forever."

"No, it's fine." I slip outside into the back parking lot.

Just before the door shuts, his voice reaches my ears. "Vanessa! It's okay—"

The heavy metal door slams, and his voice is cut off. I exhale a long breath as I walk to the palm tree at the edge of the lot.

The tangy scent of ocean hits my nose, calming my insides. This is all okay. Carter can really help me. Even if he puts me on edge in moments like this, I feel completely at ease when he touches me.

A player might be scary outside of the bedroom, but that's just because I don't know the rules. I don't know how I'm supposed to behave, but I can learn.

The door opens and slams shut, and Carter's big footsteps sound behind me. "I told you that you didn't have to leave."

Why does he sound so irritated? I was just being polite.

"I don't like eavesdropping," I say.

When he comes into my view, those blue eyes are rolling. "It wasn't a private conversation."

"Why are you so annoyed with me?"

His gaze snaps to my face, and he stares at me for a moment. "I'm not." His voice is much gentler than it was a moment ago.

"You certainly were Tuesday." I swallow. "After I told you I loved you, I mean. I'm still recovering."

I avert my gaze, unable to look at his expression. If I catch even the faintest bit of pity in his eyes, I might not be able to have sex with him again.

I'm startled when he wraps his arms around me and pulls me into his chest. He nuzzles his nose into my hair, and I relax into him. God, I love how affectionate he is.

"I'm sorry," he says. "It was just a bad day for me."

"Well, isn't that lovely. It was my first time having sex, and it was a bad day for you. I guess that was a line when you said it was the best sex you've ever had."

"It wasn't a line." His tone is firm. "It was...something else that bothered me."

When I look up at him, that big notch at his throat is rising and falling unsteadily. "Is something going on with your mom?"

His eyes narrow in confusion for a moment before he grunts. "No. I told you that wasn't an important conversation. She was calling because she... She and I are really close. I'm probably her best friend, actually." He laughs. "It makes me feel kind of bad for her."

I grimace. "Me too."

His lips part. He stares at me for a moment before lifting a hand high in the air and slapping my ass. The crack of a sound echoes through the parking lot before I feel the sting on my skin.

My forced giggle is light to disguise the heat pooling in my belly. I'd love to rub myself against him, but I'm still too shy. Maybe later.

"That didn't even hurt," I say, pressing my head against his chest. "And I was just teasing. I bet you're a great best friend. You're so much sweeter than I thought you would be."

He rubs my back with the tips of his fingers. "You are too. I had all kinds of preconceived notions about you based on your TikTok."

"Me too," I say. "About you, I mean. Because of your reputation."

His fingers make their way over my shoulder, up my neck, and to my earlobe. He caresses it with his thumb and forefinger. "We're going to get very close over the next three weeks. That's what sex does."

"For everyone but you, you mean."

His body grows still.

"Don't worry," I say. "I'm not going to get clingy."

I'm startled when he grabs my face and meets my gaze. His pale-blue eyes bore into mine. "Let yourself feel whatever you feel while we do this. Being in your head is never a good thing when it comes to sex. Don't fight your feelings. Can you do that for me?"

I swallow. "You say that now, but you know if I show any signs of having feelings for you, you wouldn't be able to get away from me fast enough. Like the first time we had sex."

"No." His grip on my face grows tighter. "When I told you that you're safe with me, I meant it."

My throat grows tight. I know exactly what I mean when he says I'll be safe. If I start to fall for him, he'll be kind. He won't make me feel foolish. He'll probably even want to be friends after our three weeks are up.

"Can you do this for me?" he repeats.

"Yes," I say in the end, because I find I can't deny him.

Jesus, please protect my heart over these next three weeks.

Chapter Thirteen

C arter

Armaan doesn't answer when I knock on his door, so I let myself in. When I walk into his room, he's lying on the couch by the window and staring up at the ceiling.

"Are you high?" I ask almost rhetorically. Armaan is always high. Even on a Friday morning before class.

"I took LSD," he says.

I grimace. "Are you insane? I thought you said you have a midterm."

"Term paper," he corrects. "In creative writing. It's due at midnight. It's a ten-thousand-word short story."

I sit down on the chair across from him. "I hope you've written most of it already."

"I haven't written a word." His voice has a dreamy quality. "That's why I took LSD. I'm writing it right now. In my head."

"I don't think it works that way. Your story's probably going to be pretty shitty."

"Probably. You want to write it for me?"

"Nope. But I'll give you a plot idea if you help me out. It will only take five minutes, and you won't have to get up from the couch."

"Deal." He flips onto his side. "What do you need?"

"Holy shit." I grimace at the sight of his face. "Your eyes are black."

"My pupils are dilated."

"You look like a demon. Go look in the mirror, and you'll have your story idea. Something about a family being haunted."

He nods sluggishly. "I like that. It'll be from the demon's perspective."

"Good call. Now help me with Vanessa."

He frowns, and his eyes dart side to side. He seems to be processing my sentence, but at a much slower rate than normal.

Great. Of course he had to take a powerful hallucinogen just when I need his help.

"I thought she picked you," he says. "Did you fuck it up already?"

"No, she chose me, and we had mind-blowing sex, but I want more than that. I know you're not going to believe me, but I want to be in a relationship with her. She makes me feel things...I've never felt before."

"You sound like you're in love." He frowns. "You sound like Logan."

I chuckle. I do sound like our love-slut friend who graduated last year—Armaan's closest friend. Logan fell in "love" about twenty times just in the three years I knew him.

This isn't the same at all. My love for her is permanent, but Armaan doesn't need to know how deep my feelings run. Not until I have her locked in.

"Holy shit," Armaan says. "You look like Logan right now. Your eyes turned green and everything...fuck." He smiles slightly. "Hey, Logan. I miss you, brother."

"Goddamn it. You're tripping out. You're not going to be able to help me like this."

"Naw, man. I'll help you. You still have Logan's face, and I love Logan more than I love you, so I'll do a better—"

"Okay, then help me quickly, before I turn into someone you hate. I'm going to spend the next month blowing Vanessa's mind. I'm going to become a guy in a rom-com. I'm going to, like, take her to a fancy clothing store after it closes and let her pick out whatever she wants, or—"

Armaan shakes his head sharply. "That's the guy she doesn't pick. She never picks the rich guy."

"Yes, she does," I say. "That's a scene from *Pretty Woman*. I've seen that movie a hundred times with my mom. She picks the rich guy."

"That's the exception. Usually, she picks the poor guy."

"Well, I'm not the poor guy. So just keep your mind on movies where she picks the rich guy."

"Statistically speaking, she picks the poor guy way more. Vanessa's going to see you doing rich-guy things, and deep down she'll be like, he's not the one."

I groan. "This is the dumbest fucking argument I've ever gotten into. You're not helping me."

"You got to do church shit with her. Watch every single one of her purity-culture videos, and do stuff related to that. That shit means a lot to her. You need to be extra sensitive about it."

I open my mouth to insist that I have been when it strikes me that he's right. Maybe I've been more sensitive than the other guys pursuing her, but that isn't saying much. I could do much more.

"Damn, you're brilliant," I mutter.

"Yep. Now give me my story plot."

"Simple," I say, standing up from the chair, itching to get home so I can watch every single one of Vanessa's videos. "Pick your favorite movie and swap out all the characters and scenes with something similar. Instead of a shark, it's a demon. Instead of a romance, it's two people who hate each other becoming buddies. All stories are exactly the same. I learned that in a creative writing class my freshman year, and I basically wrote my own version of the first Iron Man for our final project."

He stares at me for a long moment, his dark brows slowly pulling together. "That's not helpful. Thanks for nothing."

I chuckle as I walk toward the door. "You're welcome."

* * *

She adjusts the head of the tripod before plopping on the couch next to me. "Okay, this is my plan. We'll talk about how we're going to spend the next several weeks trying a bunch of different things to help me."

"It's so clinical." I grimace.

She glares at me. "Yes, it's clinical. I'm treating my body shame the way a clinician would. I'm even using techniques I learned about in my abnormal psychology class."

My chest twinges, and I grab her hand. "Maybe you don't have to approach it that way. I've already shown you how good it can be. You don't feel shame with me."

The thought alone already made me feel like a king, but even more so after binging nearly half of her videos this morning.

It's strange how different I felt watching them this time around. A few familiar videos popped up, and I saw a completely different girl than I did even just a few weeks ago. It was only her nervous primness that made her seem insincere—the way she enunciated her voice and widened her big Disney princess eyes. She wasn't trying to entice creepy college guys—that was going to happen no matter what, beautiful as she is. She's just not relaxed on camera, not fully. She puts on her presentation face, probably the same one she used in speech class freshman year.

How could I have hate-watched this adorable girl when all I want to do now is smother her with kisses?

Fuck, I'm getting sappy.

Love is strange.

She shoots me a hard look. "I'm not going to risk losing progress. We're going to try everything there is to try. All sex acts and kinks. I want you to teach me how to deep throat and swallow come—"

She shrieks when I grab her by the waist and set her on my lap. "If you keep talking like that, this is going to be a very different kind of video."

When she smiles shyly, I kiss her on the nose.

"I'd never do that," she says. "At least not with the campus player. Maybe with my future hus—"

When I flip her onto her belly, she shrieks. "We'll start working on kink right now. I'm your dom, and you're not allowed to talk that way. There's no one but me. Don't talk about fucking other people. Even your future husband."

Who will be me, goddammit. Even though she doesn't know it yet.

When I pull up her dress and reveal that adorably tight ass, she wiggles her hips, making my dick twitch and stir. I lift my leg and clamp her thighs between my own. I grip her cotton panties and yank them down.

"Why is your ass so tan?" I ask. "What kind of bikinis do you wear?"

"Oh em gee! You're killing me! Just spank me already."

I laugh. "Oh em gee? I don't think I've heard anyone say the letters like that."

"I have a hard time saying, oh my God. It wasn't allowed when I was little."

"Don't change the subject. Why is your ass so tan?"

"I'll tell you after my spanking."

I bring my palm down on her skin with a resounding crack. "You don't make the rules. You'll tell me now or get spanked again."

She releases something between a moan and a gasp. "I'm Italian," she says. "I have olive skin."

SLAP!

She groans this time.

Dirty girl. She likes being spanked.

"Don't lie to me." I rub her warm skin, now darkening from my palm. "You're not tan in between your cheeks. She squeals when I pull her ass cheeks apart with my thumb and forefinger. "You've been tanning."

"Okay, fine! Livvy and I lay out naked on her roof."

I grit my teeth. "Can anyone see you?"

"It's none of your business."

SLAP!

She gasps. "Maybe her neighbors can. I doubt they look."

"How do you know?"

"I don't, but it's unlikely."

"Honey, have you seen yourself? Don't do it again. No one is allowed to look at you naked but me."

She wiggles. "For the next three weeks."

Since she's not able to see me, I take this opportunity to roll my eyes. "Yes, for three weeks you belong to me and only me."

And then for the rest of your life.

"I never thought you'd be so possessive."

SLAP!

"You don't get to talk back to me..." I pinch my fingers between her pussy lips and spread them open. "You obviously like it. Fuck, you're soaking wet. We'd better do this video soon. Daddy's getting impatient."

She moans. "Daddy. I really like that."

"Do you?" I dip two fingers inside her pussy, plunging in and out quickly.

"Yeah." She groans. "I don't know why. It makes me want to sit on your lap while you're...inside me."

I groan, but it sounds almost like a growl. "Alright. Get up now. I'm getting too turned on. If you keep talking like that, I'm going to maul you in this video."

I grab her by the waist and set her next to me. When her long, mermaid hair falls in front of her face, I lift both hands and brush the thick strands away, unable to keep from smiling. "People are going to think I just fucked you."

"That's okay. We can't have any embarrassment when we do this. It's real and raw. That's why it resonates with people."

"I don't think that's why it resonates with guys in my fraternity."

"Well, I know I've helped a lot of young evangelicals, along with helping myself." She gets up and walks to the tripod. "You can let me do most of the talking. Stop me if I say anything that makes you uncomfortable. You can even be with me when I edit so you can—"

When she sits back down, I press a quick kiss on her cheek. "That won't be necessary. Say what you need to say. If it really helps you, who cares if you embarrass me?"

Her eyes brighten. "Do you really mean that?"

Damn, this is working like a charm. Thank God I thought to go to Armaan. He does sometimes have brilliant insights. Vanessa cares deeply about her purity-culture TikTok, and all I have to do is sit here and talk about fucking her, which is what I already want to do. I want the rest of the world to know that she's mine.

"Of course," I say. "I already have a bad reputation. Talk about whatever you need to."

The warmth in her eyes makes me want to kiss her again, but I force myself to turn to the front-facing camera on her phone. She slides close to me on the couch and reaches a hand out to the screen.

"Alright, it's recording." She turns to me and narrows her eyes as she stares at my face. That tiny hand of hers reaches out and fluffs up the hair at the crown of my head, and I could die from the pleasure.

I love having her like this—touching me like she owns me.

"I'm guessing you're going to edit this out," I say.

"Maybe." A plastic smile spreads across her face as she looks at herself on her phone screen, but it doesn't look devious to me anymore, only practiced and prim. "You're well known on campus, so I might leave it in. It'll intrigue people to see us so familiar with each other."

"But they're already going to know I'm fucking you."

"I know." She arches her brows as she stares at her reflection. "But fixing your hair isn't sexual. It's more intimate."

Yes, it is. Heartbreakingly intimate.

I think I might die if I don't win her.

"Leave it in," I say.

"Okay, I'm going to start." She faces the camera head-on, straightening her spine and lowering her chin. "Purity culture made it impossible for me to enjoy my body," she says, enunciating her words slowly.

"Ness," I say. "Just talk normal."

She frowns. "What do you mean?"

"I mean, people can understand you just fine. You don't have to talk like you're teaching English as a second language."

Her eyes widen. "Am I talking that way?"

"You're not meaning to?"

"No..." Her expression grows bewildered.

"You're still adorable," I say. "You're just not yourself."

"No, no. This is good. I didn't notice it. And for the record, you don't want to enunciate slowly when you're teaching English as a second language either. You want people to catch the natural patterns of speech when teaching any language."

I grin. God, she's so fucking cute. "Thank you. That'll be helpful since, you know, I teach ESL for a living."

"What you said is really important for me to know, and no one has ever said it before." She frowns. "I think it's probably because you're such a dick."

My skin heats. It used to amuse me when she called me a dick, but not anymore.

"I didn't mean to sound like a dick," I say in a softened voice. "I really think you're adorable in your videos. Obviously, I'm not the only one who does, since you have almost every guy on campus—"

"No, stop." She lifts a hand. "I don't want any more flattery. I already know you think I'm cute. I need more constructive criticism."

I gasp out a laugh. "Alright, beautiful girl."

"I want you to stop me whenever I do something unnatural and give me an idea of how to fix it."

"You can't fix perfect, love."

She grimaces. "Shut up. Do you want something from me? Some kind of... I don't know...sex act that you're afraid to ask for?"

"No." I set my hand on her thigh and squeeze. "I'm not afraid to ask for anything."

"Then why are you being so nice to me?"

She genuinely means it. Damn. Did I really fuck up this hard? How did I not show her how special she is from the beginning?

When I don't answer right away, she turns back to the camera. "I'm going to have to edit the hell out of this, but I might leave some of these parts in." She smiles. "I'd love for people to see the campus player kissing my ass."

"I'm going to be licking it later tonight. Should we take a video of that, too?"

"Alright, shut up." She lowers her chin. "Two nights ago, I lost my virginity." She turns to me. "How do I sound?"

I tilt my head. "More like yourself."

She nods once. "I'm going to be talking about my journey through my recovery from sexual shame with the man who's helping me with it all. You probably notice him from the Greek scene. He has quite a reputation for having a lot of sex."

"Wow." My skin prickles. "This is way more uncomfortable than I thought it would be. I don't know how you do this."

She smiles. "You'll get used to it."

"I can say filthy things without thinking twice, but hearing you talk about me while I'm sitting right here is...strange."

She narrows her eyes. "Let's try something different then. I'm going to let you talk. Why don't you tell the camera about our first time?"

"Holy shit, are you serious?"

"Yeah." Her brow furrows, though the ghost of a smile touches her lips. "This is what I do on here. I can do all the talking if you're uncomfortable."

"No, no. I can do this." I huff out a laugh before turning toward the camera and taking a deep breath. "When it comes to sex, I really like novelty. I don't know why, but the idea of..." I swallow. "The idea of having a new partner is really exhilarating for me. For the first time—"

I glance Vanessa's way, and her gaze is riveted on my face. Fuck, this is important. I need to somehow show her how important she is without giving her the power to destroy me.

Fuck, it's such a delicate balance. How much is too much to show?

"For the first time," I say, "I'm exhilarated by the idea of having sex with one person. Everything is new for her, and that makes it feel new for me, too. I'm excited to...help her work through her religious trauma."

When I turn to her, she has a glowing smile, and it makes me want to throw her over my shoulder and beat my chest. That was good. Really good. And the strangest part of it is that it is the truth. For the first time in my life, I don't have to manipulate in order to get what I want. I don't have to calculate my next move. This must be what love does. I can use my heart instead of my head.

And my body. For the next three weeks, I'm going to make this woman feel things she never thought were possible. She won't even be able to imagine moving on to another sexual partner, not when the one she has is an expert at making her come.

Vanessa

. . .

"My beautiful girl." He blows on my nipple. "You taste like candy."

I smile as he kisses a trail from my chest to my navel. "There's no way I taste like candy."

"You're like candy to me. Especially here." He hums as he buries his face between my legs, and my spine goes rigid. Before I get a chance to think, I grab his head and lift it.

"No," I say. "Not yet. I'm...not sure if I'm ready to go down on you. Afterward, I mean."

He frowns up at me. "You don't have to. This is about you."

"I know, but..." I swallow. "For some reason, it makes me feel self-conscious when I'm the only one...feeling good."

When he snorts, a chill skitters over my skin. "Why is that funny?"

"It's funny you think I wouldn't love licking your pussy."

The skin on my chest and face grows warm and tingly. Does he really mean it? Carter isn't one for empty flattery.

"Baby girl." He grips my thighs and spreads them apart, his eyes glittering as he stares between my legs. "I'm hard as a rock just being close to it."

My belly catches fire. "Really?"

"Oh yeah." That faraway voice and those almost hypnotized eyes turn my legs into melted butter. My thighs fall open as I relax into the bed. "You were made for me. I feel it every time we're close. Your scent." He lowers his head and inhales deeply. "I want to put you on a plate and eat you for dinner."

I slam my palm over my mouth as laughter bubbles out of me.

"I mean it." I hear a smile in his voice. "If it'll help you feel less self-conscious, you can let me come on you afterward. I'll probably be seconds from exploding after I've had my mouth on you."

I jerk my head up. "You want to come *on* me? Where?"

"I don't know..." His heavy-lidded gaze drifts over my body. "Your ass. Your tits. Your stomach." He sets one hand on the center of my belly. "Your skin is so pretty, coming anywhere would turn me on."

My God. I knew people did things like this in porn, but I never imagined that real people would enjoy it.

It's fascinating.

"What is it about putting your...come on me that turns you on?"

His brow furrows. "I don't know. It'll feel good."

I shake my head sharply. "No, I need you to give me a real answer. I find this really interesting. I think I want to watch you while you do it, so my stomach would be the best choice. It'll give me the best view."

"My inquisitive girl." His smile is almost piteous, and yet somehow, I'm not embarrassed. There's affection in his eyes, even if he finds my request strange. Has that affection always been there?

It makes my heart flutter.

"You're so fucking cute," he says. "Alright. Let me think about this. I guess I like...marking you. It's a dominating thing, I guess. I'm a primitive guy." He shrugs. "Sorry."

I wave a hand. "Sex is primitive. That's been my whole problem. The body doesn't listen to reason."

"Why do you think I'm able to make you feel good?" His blue eyes bore into mine. "What do you think that means?"

Our gazes hold for a long moment. I have no idea why he's been able to pull me out of my head and make me forget my shame, and for the first time, it doesn't scare me.

I trust him.

"I'm not sure," I say. "But I'm not going to think too hard about it. Alright, can you go down on me now?"

He grins. "My pleasure."

He buries his head between my legs, and just the heat of his breath sends a wave of pressure into my gut. He inhales deeply and groans. The first brush of his hot tongue makes the pressure balloon, and I lift my hips to his mouth to get more of it.

"Good girl," he rasps. "Give me more of this delicious pussy."

"Carter!" I whimper.

"That's right, baby. Say my name."

He's so delightfully naughty. The up-and-down motion of his tongue grows more rapid, and electricity shoots throughout my limbs. Distantly, I recognize that his movements are skilled, probably from doing this so many times before, but it doesn't bother me.

I don't feel self-conscious anymore.

"Carter, I think I'm close."

"Come on my tongue. Let me feel you."

The pressure in my belly ignites, scattering my thoughts. I scream and thrash and say words that are too far away for me to hear. The heat of his tongue laps up and down my pussy as wave after ripple of ecstasy shoots through my limbs.

My body is like an empty vessel when it's over, but I'm somehow able to hear his voice. "Good girl. Time to mark you."

When I open my eyes, he's hovering over me with his cock in his hand. He grimaces as he stares at my belly, looking so unlike the Carter I know. This one is hungry and wild, like he would grab me by the throat if I tried to get away, and it ironically makes me feel like a queen.

I'm doing this to him.

I turned him into this primitive being.

"Oh fuck!" He hisses as liquid spurts from his cock onto my belly, warming my skin. "Yeah." He fists his cock up and down. "Take all my come. You're mine now."

"Yes." On instinct, I dip my index finger into the slippery mess and lift it to my mouth. When I hum in delight, his eyes grow huge.

"Fuck!" He collapses next to me and grabs my face. "You're perfect," he says as he presses a hard kiss on my forehead.

"So are you," I say.

I really mean it. These last few days have been spectacular, and I'm so grateful I found him.

I refuse to question it anymore. Jesus brought him into my

life for a reason. He makes me feel completely at ease in my skin, and I'll always be grateful to him.

Carter

I'm making progress with her. I can feel it.

She's a practical, unromantic girl. That analytical brain of hers needs to survey the situation and determine that it's safe before she loses her heart. Her pragmatism is one of the things I love most about her.

As we lay in my grandparents' biggest guest bedroom, I reach out and stroke her face with the tips of my fingers. Fuck, it hurts to love someone this much. I would die for her, and yet she's still unsure about me.

I wish I could chain her to me. Keep her around even if it's against her will. If she ever got away, I'd have to chase her and charm her right back into my arms.

"What are you thinking about?" she asks in a sleepy voice.

I smile as I lift my hand and run my fingers through the soft strands of hair around her cheek. "I was thinking how I'm kind of in the mood for In-N-Out."

Her sleepy eyes crinkle at the edges. "And here I thought you were thinking about how beautiful I am."

I lean forward and press a kiss against her lips. "That too."

"You're not even a good liar."

I chuckle. Oh, baby girl, if you only knew.

"I can't imagine eating In-N-Out in your grandparents' big fancy house," she says. "It feels like only aged, grass-fed beef would be allowed."

I shake my head. "This house has seen so much takeout. My grandma doesn't know how to cook, and I was a picky eater growing up, but very low brow in my pickiness. If it wasn't Kraft mac and cheese, I wouldn't eat it.

Her expression grows stern. "Naturally. What kid eats the gruyere and black forest ham mac and cheese?"

I pull her tighter against my chest. "Exactly."

"So you spent time with your grandparents when you were a kid? For some reason, I had the idea that you didn't see them at all until you were a teenager."

"They reconnected with my mom when I was ten, but I didn't start spending summers with them until I was a teenager. Going to visit my dad in Idaho didn't seem as fun as the beach after about fifteen."

Her eyes narrow. "What's the deal with your dad? You're obviously not very close to him."

I shrug. "There's nothing wrong with him, but he and my mom were both teenagers when she got pregnant. I get the idea that he was kind of a..." I laugh. "Kind of a dipshit when I was really young. They broke up when she was still pregnant with me, and I don't think he helped my mom very much until I was about five or so. He and my other grandparents moved to the Midwest when I was in junior high, and after that, I started spending summers with them."

"Did your dad help your mom financially?"

"He paid her a little child support, but he's never made very much. My mom and I struggled a lot growing up. She still lives in a shithole in Ventura. One of the first things I'm going to do when I start making good money is buy her a nice house."

She smiles at me with such a tender look in her eyes that my heart squeezes.

Please love me, Vanessa. I want to be able to say the words. I want this itching vulnerability to go away.

"You're such a caring son," she says. "I never would have expected it."

I lift a finger and touch the tip of her nose. God, I love her nose. I love everything about her. "It doesn't feel like being a caring son, because it's second nature. I've been doing it since I was ten."

She frowns. "What do you mean?"

"That was when I started spending time with my grandparents, who are obviously loaded." I gesture around the room. "They wouldn't give her any money, but they'd give it to me." I smile. "Rich people don't know how much regular things cost. I'd tell them my football equipment cost two grand, or that summer camp costs five. They'd give it to me no questions asked."

When her eyes grow huge, I laugh humorlessly. "It sounds shady, but I wouldn't have done it if we weren't desperate."

Yes, I would have. I'd have done it just for the pleasure of swindling money from them.

"And what did you tell your mom?"

"What do mean?"

"When they gave you money, I mean. Where did you tell her it came from?"

"Um... Well, she knew. She knew I got it from them."

Her eyes widen. "She was in on it?"

My skin heats. "You say it like it was a conspiracy. Like she was sending me out to con them. It wasn't like that. My mom and I have always been a team. She was only sixteen when she had me. She was a kid herself."

"Wow," she whispers. "That's a big responsibility."

"It was. I don't know how she did it."

"No, I mean for you. You essentially had to be a full member of the household when you were just a kid. You had to help her make sure the bills were paid. That's a lot for a kid."

"It really wasn't... I mean, I didn't think about it that much."

"No, it was just a part of your life. You didn't know anything else."

I stare at her for a moment, trying to gauge her tone. She sounds almost...irritated, like she's judging my mom for my upbringing.

Maybe she's getting protective of me. My body grows light and airy. I ought to be defensive on my mom's behalf, but not at this sign that Vanessa is starting to care about me. She doesn't know my mom. If she did, she'd see how much she loves me. How none of our financial struggles were her fault.

"I had a great childhood," I say. "My mom did the best she could with money, but it was hard having almost full custody of a kid *and* having to work full time with no education."

"I'm not saying it wasn't hard for her. I just think you should acknowledge the fact that you had a lot of responsibility as a kid. The kind most kids don't have."

The back of my neck prickles. I never thought about it this way. Our financial precariousness didn't make me unhappy, even if it should have. I always knew everything would be okay, one way or another. That we'd figure it out together.

My biggest struggle was her emotional state. She needed me. I was her best friend, and the change in her life circumstances— being cast out of her community—left her a little fragile. I was always afraid I couldn't compensate for what she'd lost.

I had to lie to her sometimes. She'd ask me if Grandpa and Grandma ever talked about her, and I'd make up these silly little stories. *"For some reason, Grandpa wanted me to tell him all about your new job. He asked me a million questions, and it was weird."* She'd probe me for more details—always with heightened color and a slight smile—which told me it was the right move.

"It's good for kids to have responsibility," I say. "It prepares them for adulthood."

Her brown eyes grow huge. "You think kids should have that kind of responsibility? I was responsible for cleaning my gecko's cage growing up. Not putting food on the table."

I stroke her cheek with my fingers. "You had a gecko?"

She leans into my touch. "I did. Laurence."

"Laurence?" I burst into laughter. "What a name. Did you call him Larry for short? Larry the Gecko."

"Considering his full name was Theodore Laurence—from *Little Women*—he should have been either Laurie or Teddy, but my family all called him Laurence."

"Oh, Vanessa. That's so cute. I bet you were such a serious

little kid."

Her brow furrows. "Why do you say that?"

"Because you would have been a little version of you now, and you're always analyzing everything. You find the whole world interesting. I fucking love that about you."

Her smile fades as she stares at me. Fuck, did I really use the word "love"? I have to be more cautious. She has to be under my spell before I can tell her how I really feel.

"Tell me about your family," I say to change the subject. "How do your parents feel about your virginity show?"

That bewildered look fades into a smile, and my racing pulse slows. "My 'virginity show.' I ought to add that to my TikTok bio."

"Not without paying me, Gallo. I'm going to patent it."

Her smile holds. "My parents have a don't ask, don't tell policy. They know I bash purity culture on TikTok, but they don't want to know about it. Neither of them watch my videos. Livvy was very open with them about the deconstruction of her faith, and it was a big struggle for them. I think they're trying to stay blissfully ignorant with me, and I'm fine with it. It's really none of their business."

"That's true." I kiss her cheek. "Do they know about me?"

She rustles around on the bed, turning onto her back so that I can't see the expression in her eyes. "They do," she says, her voice faint. "My mom wanted me to invite you to Livvy's engagement party, but I told her I wasn't sure. It'll be after our Live."

My hand trembles. I want to tell her there's no end date to our relationship. I want to tell her I love her.

Instead, I turn to my back. "Tell her to count me in," I say. "And would she mind if I steal you for your birthday weekend? I'd like to take you out of town."

"You do?" Her voice is full of curiosity.

I smile. "Yep, I have a whole trip planned."

And if everything goes right, you'll be in love with me by the end of it.

Chapter Fourteen

Vanessa

"I can't believe there's a line for a Wednesday night beer pong tournament." Saanvi frowns as we stand outside the Alpha Lambda Xi. "They play beer pong every damn night."

I wrap my arms around my shoulders to fight the cold. It's odd that Carter hasn't come out yet to bring us inside. I texted him right after Saanvi and I parked, which was about fifteen minutes ago.

It's silly to fear that he's with another girl. He demanded my fidelity and promised his own in return.

Still, he didn't get the reputation of campus player for nothing.

After two weeks into our three-week commitment, it's time to finally admit to myself that I've caught feelings. It was inevitable. He acts like we're a real couple. When we attended his weekly dinner with his grandparents, he showed me almost as much affection as when we lie in bed together after sex. He kept his fingers on my thigh or my shoulder or even entwined in my hair all night, and he kissed the tip of my nose whenever I said something that amused him.

Plus, we're leaving tomorrow morning for my birthday trip, and he gets this huge grin on his face whenever I ask him about it, like he's just as excited as I am.

It's only natural that I'm falling for him. This is what happens to a person who was trained to associate love and sex. It doesn't mean I won't be able to have good sex after these three weeks are over.

I only hope that it won't hurt too much to leave Carter behind.

"Carter's going to lose his mind when he sees your dress," Saanvi says, her gaze drifting down to my hips.

I smile. The bare skin on my chest would normally make my stomach a little queasy, but imagining Carter's eyes on my body makes me tingly everywhere instead. The way he looks at me naked makes me feel like a goddess.

I never thought this feeling was possible before I met him.

The girl in front of us turns around, rolling her eyes. "Apparently, the tournament is full, and I don't think they're going to let anyone else in."

"Full?" Saanvi scowls. "It's not even a real tournament. They'll be so drunk at the end of the night that the brackets will get messed up. No one ever knows the real winner."

"Only girlfriends are allowed in now, I guess," the girl says.

"Well, I'm a fraternity sister," Saanvi says, "and Vanessa's a girlfriend."

The girl furrows her brow. "Which one of them is your boyfriend?"

Just as I open my mouth to tell her I don't have a boyfriend, Saanvi speaks over me. "Carter Blake. She knows how to keep the player in check."

"Saanvi!"

A satisfied smile touches Saanvi's lips. "It's the truth."

"Carter Blake," the girl says. "I can't believe that. I never thought he'd get a girlfriend."

"She has him wrapped around her finger," Saanvi says, and the girl's eyes grow huge.

I don't know why it should make my stomach flutter. He's not my boyfriend, and enjoying this kind of attention is just vanity. I didn't think I was this silly.

"There's my girl."

It's Carter's smooth voice. He hovers over me as his gaze drops down my skimpy dress. "Goddamn. Do you want me to drag you to my bedroom right now?"

My stomach flips over as I kiss him on the cheek. "Later. I'm excited to play beer pong. I've never done it before, so Saanvi and I practiced earlier."

His brows raise. "With beer?"

"Oh, no. We filled red cups up with a little water." I grin. "I have really good aim."

He sucks in a smile. "Practicing beer pong with water. Could you be any cuter?"

"Don't be condescending." When I punch his shoulder, he yanks me against his chest.

His warm breath tickles my ear. "I don't know how I feel about this." He tugs at my short skirt. "I'd like it in private, but the other guys are going to have their eyes on your ass all night, especially during the tournament."

"That's the point. I'll make them miss their shots. Plus, I'm trying to get used to being in public with my skin showing. I'm starting to feel more comfortable doing it."

He presses a hard kiss on my mouth. "In that case, show off that ass all day. Thankfully, I'm the only one who knows it in the biblical sense of the word."

A moment later, he whisks me into the main room of the frat. There are two ping pong tables and a large whiteboard with tournament brackets.

"Alright," he shouts. "I don't care who's won so far. My girl's here, and she's ready to play."

"She can be my partner."

A chill runs down my spine at the sound of Graham's voice. Oh my God. What is he doing here?

Don't let him see how much he affects you. Be cool. You can do this.

I take a deep breath through my nose before turning in the direction of the voice. Graham has a slight smirk on his face. "Hey, Vanessa. It's been a while."

I force a smile. "It has. How's geochemistry going?"

His smile falters. "That was two quarters ago."

Of course it was. It's been months. Why does seeing him again make it feel so close? Why do I feel like he's staring at my bare tits as they bounce up and down like he did when I paced the floor during my panic attack?

"Your videos have been popping up lately on my For You Page," he says. "I saw you picked Carter to help you with your... religious trauma."

Is there malice in his tone, or am I imagining it? He isn't an asshole. He's just a dumb boy who lacks the skills to handle the complicated emotions wrapped up in a woman's sexuality. I couldn't expect him to understand.

Then again, I couldn't imagine Carter looking at me with that same disdain if I had a panic attack before sex.

"Yeah," I say with forced a smile. "I know it seems strange to pick the campus player, but he turned out to be the best person to help me."

"Yeah, I'll bet Carter's seen everything. He doesn't get weirded out easily." Graham's smile doesn't quite reach his eyes. "I'm glad you found someone who works for you. I was worried you'd have a hard time."

My skin heats. That wasn't my imagination, was it? He's being smug. He's trying to embarrass me. Why would he bring that up in public with Carter right behind me?

"She found someone who actually knows where the clitoris is located." Carter sets his hand on my waist and tugs me against him. "That was her number one requirement after you."

My stomach flips, and I turn to Carter with huge eyes. He has that adorable little smirk on his face. "Don't worry, baby girl. He knows I'm just teasing him." He pats Graham hard on the back. "She had a pretty low bar when she was looking for guys. I guess I should thank you for that, huh?"

Graham laughs, but it sounds forced. "Dude, you're embarrassing her."

"Am I embarrassing you?" Carter leans in and kisses the tip of my nose, and warmth seeps through my veins.

How did he know exactly what to do? I only told him a handful of details about the Graham incident, and yet he handled the situation exactly how I would have wanted. The tension has been diffused, and now I'm pretty sure Graham is at least as embarrassed as I am, if not more so.

"No," I say, "but let's change the subject."

"Perfect timing." Carter gestures at the ping pong table to our right. "They just finished up our game. Alright, Vanessa and I are taking over. I don't care who was on the list."

The next hour passes in a blur. Carter and I play three rounds of beer pong, and he barely takes his hands off me. Any time I make a shot, he kisses me. In between turns, he wraps his arms around me.

I feel the intense gazes of people around us, and it makes my belly flutter. His behavior must be unique to me if everyone is so transfixed by it.

My assumption is confirmed when Lacey pulls me aside later that night. "Girl," she says. "What did you do to him? I've never seen him like this before."

After all the beer from the tournament, I can't stop myself from beaming at her. "He seems to have a thing for virgins raised in purity culture."

She looks over my shoulder at Carter. "You're disgusting!"

Her speech is a little thick, probably from the shots she took with Carter earlier. "You have a virgin kink! She just told me."

"Stop talking to her!" Carter exclaims. "I don't trust you with my girl. You're going to tell her things I've done."

Lacey grins wide. "That's a great idea, actually. Come to the bathroom with me."

As Lacey pulls me in the direction of the hallway, I turn to Carter and giggle.

"Don't listen to her about anything," he says.

Lacey holds my hand as she guides me to the bathroom. "He's only saying that because he used to talk so much shit about you."

My eyes widen. "What are you talking about?"

"Oh, just about your purity-culture show, and how it was cringe. He's totally eating his words now." She tugs me inside the bathroom and shuts the door. "You should have heard him a few nights ago. He got drunk at my sorority and couldn't stop talking about you."

My heart squeezes. I wish I didn't like hearing that so much. It's going to make it that much harder to move on when these three weeks are up.

"Plus, he's not even looking at any other girl." Lacey stumbles a little as she stands from the toilet. "And that's so weird for him. He won't even let girls sit on his lap anymore."

I can't stop myself from grinning. Jesus, I must be drunk.

"When I first watched your show where you said you picked him, I was like, no fucking way! Vanessa Gallo would not choose Carter to take her virginity. I've been watching your TikTok for months now, by the way. I think you're a queen. Our culture is so fucking gross when it comes to women's sexuality. I love how you're just like, 'Fuck patriarchy. I'm getting some dick!'" She giggles. "Still, I did not expect you to pick someone like Carter. I thought for sure he must have lied to you."

The back of my neck prickles. "What do you mean?"

She waves a hand. "Oh, you know Carter."

"Um..." I lick my lips. "You probably know him better than I do. It's only been a few weeks."

"Oh, it's not that big of a deal, really. He's just a good liar." She turns to the mirror and runs her fingers through her long blond hair. "Like, a scary good liar. He could seriously be an actor, he's so good at lying."

When I don't respond, Lacey turns to me. "Oh my God! I'm scaring you. It's seriously not a big deal. It's not like he lies about important things. Just stupid stuff, like..."

She keeps talking, but I'm too in my head to listen. Lacey's known Carter for a long time. Why would she say something like this if there's no truth to it?

Of all things someone could say about Carter, this is the very last I'd expected to hear. He's always been so brutally honest with me.

I can't think about this now. Not while I'm buzzing from all that beer. I'm bound to say something stupid to Carter. Even if he were a good liar, what's it to me? He's not my boyfriend.

Besides, this is one person's opinion. For all I know, Lacey might not be a very insightful person. Maybe she assumed Carter was lying about something when he wasn't.

By the time I make it back to Carter, I'm able to smile and kiss him on the cheek.

He pats my ass. "Did she talk any shit about me?"

"Lots." I grab the red cup from his hand and take a small sip. "Apparently, you talk about me all the time. About how beautiful and amazing I am."

"Naturally." His smile is big and sweet, so why does it unsettle me?

I didn't hear relief in his voice. I'm only imagining it after what Lacey told me.

Chapter Fifteen

C arter

She smiles as she sets the plate of pancakes in front of me. As she walks to the other side of our small patio table, my gaze drifts to her bare legs. She's wearing one of my giant T-shirts, just like she did on the night we met, which seems like a lifetime ago.

I love that she wanted to make me breakfast in this messy kitchen just after a party. All we had were just-add-water pancakes in the pantry, because our chef brings his own supplies Monday through Friday. I told her I wanted to take her out for breakfast, especially with the weekend I have planned, but she wanted to stay here and cook for me.

She's treating me like I'm her boyfriend.

My body is so light I could float away, especially after the fear that gripped me last night. I almost broke out into a cold sweat when she disappeared with Lacey, who could've told her how I lied to Ethan about how she was interested in a relationship with him.

What would Vanessa think? She'd assumed I was match-making that day on the beach. For someone who values honesty as much as she does, she'd probably think I'm a sociopath if she realizes how I tricked him into thinking Lacey cared about him just to get Vanessa to myself.

The worst part is that there are so many lies. Lies that wouldn't have meant a thing to me if I hadn't somehow deceived Vanessa into thinking I'm brutally honest by nature.

Fuck, what would she do if she found out from someone else that I thought she wasn't a virgin? She might never speak to me again.

I have to tell her. It would be so much worse if she found out from someone else, and she could easily hear stories from my brothers, especially when one of them is drunk.

It's not the right time to confess, though. She has to be in love with me first.

Beach Burger goes public in six days. She'll be in love with me by then if I have to sell my soul to the goddamn devil.

"So..." I start, and she glances up from her pancakes. "For your birthday festivities, I have a big plan to help you with your body shame, but I'm a little hesitant about it. I know it's a whole complicated thing, and I don't want to make it seem like I know better than you do about how to get over it."

Her brow knits. "Okay...let's hear it."

"Well..." I bite my bottom lip and scrape it with my teeth. "I have something planned for tomorrow, but it's kind of up in the air. I think you should be pretty happy about it, but I'm worried it's not... That I overstepped. At the same time, I want it to be my birthday present, so I don't want to tell you what it is."

She straightens her posture, her eyes growing adorably wide. "Oh..." The inflection in the small word tells me she's pleasantly surprised, and the tension leaves my shoulders.

"Would you rather me just tell you what it is so you can be prepared? Or do you want it to be a surprise?"

"I want it to be a surprise," she says immediately.

"But what if you hate it? What if I really did overstep?"

She stares at me for a long moment, her lips lifting at the corners. "I trust you."

My throat grows tight. I force a smile as I avert my gaze from hers.

I don't deserve that trust, but I'm taking it anyway. I need it if I'm going to make her fall in love with me over the next six days.

After I have her love, I'll confess.

Vanessa

Warm fingers press into my thigh in a gentle squeeze. "Wake up, beautiful."

I jerk up to see that we're parked on the side of a street. "Are we in Malibu already?"

He smiles, and it's a relief. He was oddly quiet for the hour-and-a-half drive from Santa Barbara. The silly, infatuated girl in me feared that he's finally getting tired of me. Two weeks of fidelity is probably a lifetime to the campus player.

I told myself over and over again that it doesn't matter. We have a deadline no matter what, and he's already helped me so much.

Still, the idea of the warmth behind those eyes cooling... Of again seeing the dismissive, blasé version of Carter who brutally admitted he only wanted me to win a bet...

Jesus, please help me not to get too attached.

"I have a surprise for you before we check in at the hotel," he says.

My stomach flips over. "Another one?"

"This one isn't as big as the one I have planned for you tomorrow, but I think it should be fun." His smile grows mischievous. "For both of us."

"What is it?"

His hand trails up my thigh. "I was able to get this sex shop booked after hours, and we have an appointment with them in..." He glances at the clock on the center console. "Five minutes from now."

My mouth drops open. "You booked an appointment with a sex shop? Why?"

He chuckles. "Why do you think, baby girl?"

Heat pools in my belly. "Are we going to buy toys or outfits?"

After kissing my jaw, I feel his smile against my skin. "All of the above. I want you to pick out whatever you want. Take time exploring the shop. Try things on. No one will be around but me. I'll fulfill whatever fantasy you have. You can let your imagination run wild."

An almost hysterical giggle bubbles out of me. "I don't know why, but I feel...embarrassed?"

He runs the tips of his fingers up my spine and settles them on my nape. "I figured you would be. That's why I booked it after hours. The person I talked to said the employees can even stay in the back room while you shop, if you want extra privacy."

I nod jerkily, my breaths coming in fast. "I can do this, right?"

"Of course you can. You've already shown me you're a freaky girl. You can pick out whips and paddles. You can dress as a schoolgirl or a French maid or whatever you want. You seem to like it when I tell you what to do, so I can dress like a cop or your headmaster or whatever. Or...if you'd like, I can dress up like a French maid or a schoolgirl, and you can spank me." He threads his fingers into my hair. "I really mean it when I say this is for you. I'll do whatever you want."

"And you won't..." Nervousness tingles over my skin. I can't believe I'm about to ask this, but I have to. I need his reassurance before I can let loose. "You won't make fun of me?"

He grabs me by the shoulders, his eyes boring into mine. "Are you being serious right now?"

"Well...I know you wouldn't really make fun of me. You

wouldn't ridicule me, but sometimes you can be a little...snarky, I guess."

His jaw clenches. "I would never make fun of you about something like this. How fucked up would that be? The whole point is to help you get over your sexual shame. And even if it wasn't, you can't be comfortable with sex unless you can trust your partner to accept you for who you are."

Jesus, sometimes it feels like he was picked out just for me. Who else could say something more perfect? Before I know it, warm water is dripping down my cheeks. Oh my God, am I crying?

Carter's eyes become saucers. "Baby girl, are you okay?" There's so much kindness in his tone, I almost can't stand it. My chest heaves, and another stream of tears falls down my face.

"Yes." I wipe under my eyes with the pads of my fingers, trying to prevent mascara from dripping down my cheeks. How embarrassing to show up at the sex shop with trails of grayish black under my eyes.

"What's wrong?"

"I don't know." I take a shaky breath. "I'm just overwhelmed."

But I do know.

Trust is the key to my body. Trust is the antidote to shame, and I've never trusted anyone more than I trust Carter.

I have to stop lying to myself. I'm not ready to say goodbye to him in a week.

My heart is breaking at just the thought of it.

Chapter Sixteen

C arter

A little notch forms between her brows as she tugs at the skirt of the French maid costume. She's had her signature thoughtful expression the whole time we've been here, and I've been fighting the urge to take her into my arms. I've forced myself to play it cool, not wanting to spook her.

I'm *this* close to winning her heart. I can feel it.

Those tears had to mean something. A practical girl like her wouldn't cry over a trip to a sex shop if it hadn't touched her deeply.

"This is the tiniest duster I've ever seen." Her nose wrinkles as she brushes the white feathers across her palm. "And it's too soft to pick up any dust."

I smile. "It's not actually for dusting."

"I know, but you'd think for as expensive as it is, they'd at least make it functional."

"It is functional. It has a different function."

Her eyes grow wide. "What?"

My smile fades. Sometimes I forget how innocent she is. All of this is new to her, and I'd be a dick to tease her.

I place a little kiss on the tip of her nose. In a way, it's new to me, too. I've never done these types of things with someone I loved before.

And I'm never going back to my old life.

"What would your best guess be?" I reach out and stroke a feather with the tip of my index finger. "They made it nice and soft for a reason."

"Oh!" Her eyes grow huge. "I don't know why I didn't think of that. It's for tickling, isn't it?"

I smile lazily. "It's for torturing."

"Torturing me or you?"

Heat shoots into my groin at the thought of her brushing that thing over my bare skin. "Either one. Remember, this is all about you. Do you want this outfit? I'll go set it down on the counter with the vibrators."

That serious frown returns to her face. "I'm not ready to pick one yet. I want to explore a little more."

"We can get more than one. Fuck, we can buy the whole store if you want. Anything for my beautiful girl."

She grins. "Maybe we'll get it then, but it's not going to be the main event. I haven't found that one yet."

I pat her ass. "Get to it then. I'm already half hard picturing you as a French maid."

I spend the next twenty minutes pretending to look at my phone but secretly watching her while she explores. I don't want her to feel like she's under my scrutiny, but she's too damn cute for me to look away.

I never thought it was possible to be so enthralled with someone as she completes the most basic of tasks. I thought my friends were so stupid when they fell in love. It didn't make sense how one person could hold their interest when there are so many people out there. Now I understand.

I don't want anyone else but her.

A little while later, she walks over to me holding a plaid skirt and a tiny white button-up shirt.

"Catholic schoolgirl," I say. "Perfect for a good Christian girl."

"That's what I'm thinking." She lowers her voice to just above a whisper. "I was thinking how much I need to be praised. I'm a teacher's pet. I like getting positive feedback from everyone, and I love it when you...say sweet things to me in bed."

I nod. "You have a praise kink. I've noticed that."

She wrinkles her adorable little nose. "Is that what it's called?"

"Yep."

She nods slowly as she stares down at the outfit, clearly deep in thought. Abruptly, she looks up at me, a determined expression on her face. "I don't want to be spanked or punished tonight. I want you to tell me how good I am. I'm so used to feeling terrible about myself for being sexual. That's my default. I want to behave whorishly and have you tell me I'm wonderful."

I grin. "That'll be easy."

Vanessa

I throw open the bathroom door for effect, lifting my arms in the air to give him the best view of my skimpy Catholic schoolgirl costume. The cold air on my skin feels as natural as Carter's warm hands.

Maybe my body really has changed.

For the first time, I'm ready to take charge in the bedroom. I don't have to let Carter guide what we do. I have power when we're naked together, and it's time to use it.

I'm going to show him how grateful I am.

There's no way in hell I'd be wearing a Catholic schoolgirl outfit right now if it weren't for him. I've made more progress in two weeks than I expected to cover in a year of meaningless sex with multiple partners. To show my gratitude, I'm going to push him to his limits tonight.

I only hope that I can. I've learned a lot in the few sessions we've had, but Carter is extremely experienced. Will I be too vanilla to really surprise him?

His gaze roams my body, down and up and back again. Those blue eyes are molten. He walks in my direction, hovering over me when he gets close. "My prim little girl." His hand trails up my thigh before settling on my bare ass cheek. "I can't spank you? Only praise?"

I smile. "You sound so disappointed."

"No, I'm happy doing whatever you want, but can I earn the right to spank you? Maybe by praising you extra good?" He presses two fingers against my clit. "What if I make you *feel* extra good? What if I give you the best orgasm of your life? Can I spank you then?"

"Ooh, I like that idea." I lean into his rapidly moving fingers. "That feels really nice."

He removes his hand and grabs me by the waist. After lifting me into his arms, he carries me over to the couch and sets me on his lap. His fingers immediately return to my clit. "You're my good little girl, and Daddy wants to make you feel good. Daddy loves this sweet pussy."

Heat curls through my veins. God, I love how he talks. I never knew I needed praise so badly.

As his pace grows rapid, I thrust my hips forward, and a moan slips out of my mouth.

"Is this good enough, baby girl, or do you need my mouth?"

I hum. "Your mouth."

In an instant, I'm set on my back, my skirt is pushed up, and I'm doused out of my haze. I set my hand on his. "No, Carter. Wait."

He frowns. "You don't want me to lick you?"

"I do, but maybe later." I sit up straight and smooth down my skirt. "I want to be your whore tonight."

He grins and leans forward. After rubbing his mouth against mine, he takes a little nip of my bottom lip. "You already do it so well, beautiful girl." He grabs me by the waist and pulls me to his lap. "Your little pussy makes Daddy happy. It's so tight and hot and sweet."

I relax my head against his shoulder. "You always make me feel so beautiful."

He squeezes me tight. "You're my girl."

I lift my head and look into his eyes. "You're my headmaster, and I'm your student. Teach me what you like. Tell me exactly what you want. Praise me when I do a good job." I smile. "I will do a good job because I'm a teacher's pet. I'll give you the best orgasm of your life. I'll make you see God."

His smile grows indulgent, like he thinks my audacity is naïve, but I don't care. I'll show him I'm right. "Is that right?" he asks.

I pout my lips and flutter my lashes. "You don't believe me?"

He smirks, looking much more like the cocky Carter I met—whom I've rarely seen since the night we first had sex. His hands grip my hips, and he sets my feet on the floor in front of him. "Let's see what you got, Gallo."

I take a step back and spread my arms wide. "Would you like me to strip first?"

He leans back into the back of the couch and rests his elbow on the arm. "That's a great idea."

I smile as I start to unbutton my tiny shirt.

"Stop. Panties first. Hand them over when you're done."

The heat in his voice makes my stomach turn over. I reach underneath my skirt and pull my string panties down my thigh. Once I step out of them, I toss them onto Carter's lap.

He grabs them and immediately brings them to his nose. His eyes fall shut as he inhales deeply, humming afterwards. "Good girl. Now bend over the bed and spread your cheeks apart."

Heat suffuses my skin. Even in my wildest masturbation fantasies, I never imagined exposing myself in that way.

"You can do it," he coaxes. "Every part of you is beautiful. I want to see it."

I nod quickly and turn around before I lose my nerve. I extend my stomach over the bed and shiver when cool air hits the dampness between my legs. When I grab my ass cheeks and pull them apart, he releases a deep groan that shoots right into my clit.

I guess this isn't so difficult after all.

His big footsteps sound over the carpet before a finger presses inside my pussy. I take in a sharp breath.

"Nice and wet. Good fucking girl." The sternness has returned to his voice. The thumps on the ground tell me he's dropped to his knees, and my gut clenches in anticipation.

"Can I lick you?"

"My ass, you mean?"

"Does that scare you?"

"No..." I frown. "It sounds interesting, actually."

A deep rumble of laughter echoes through the room. "My inquisitive girl."

Wet heat hits my skin suddenly. His slippery tongue moves up and down, shooting bolts of lightning through my whole body. Before I know it, I'm whimpering.

"You like feeling my tongue in your ass, huh?" He pats my butt. "It's perfect, just like the rest of you. Now I'm ready for that sweet pussy. You're going to ride me."

His weight pulls at the bed as he sits down. He lays back and sets his head on his hands. "I don't feel like doing any work. Unzip my pants and pull out my cock."

I smile at the sight of him, resting on the bed, waiting for me to ride him like he was born for it. His ease with his body is one of my favorite things about him. It's made me feel more comfortable in mine.

After tugging down his jeans, I free his rock-hard cock from his boxers. It bounces a little before resting on his stomach.

"Unbutton your shirt so I can see those gorgeous tits," he commands.

I do as he says.

"Good. Keep everything else on."

"Even my boots?"

"Yep." He smiles lazily. "I want to remember that you're my student. My eager little pet."

I glance down at his cock, which now has a bead of moisture at the end of it. Damn. He must be much more turned on than his lazy demeanor suggests.

This is good. This means I can blow him away if I do this right.

I scoot over his body and stand up on my knees. "Okay, tell me exactly how to do this, and I mean *exactly*. I even want you to grab me by the hips and show me your favorite rhythm."

The sound pulled from his chest is something between a laugh and a growl. "My favorite student. Just the prim way you talk makes me want to explode. Okay, grab my cock and guide me in. Nice and slow. It's important that you get comfortable before you start moving."

I nod once as I do as I'm told. His cock slips in easily, wet as I am, and with a few adjustments, I'm able to get it all the way in. He's big and full between my legs, but my body is accustomed now after the handful of times we've had sex.

"Do I feel good?" I ask.

"Perfect."

The tightness in his voice makes me look up, and the sight of him makes my stomach flip over. His eyes are glazed, and he's clenching his teeth.

I'm doing this to him. I have this power.

When I straighten my spine and cup my tits with my palms, he gasps. I smile slowly. "Do you like this?"

"Yes," he rasps. "Rub them."

As I move my hands in circles, my nipples tingle under his intense gaze. I rock forward, and his long, low groan tells me he liked it. His cock slides in and out, inch by inch, filling me with its delicious length.

"Oh, fuck." He grimaces, looking almost in pain as I rock back and forth.

Jesus, I feel like a queen having him at my mercy like this.

I never imagined having power during sex, even as I started to break away from purity culture. On the contrary, I thought I'd be putting my body under the power of a man. It terrified me.

I pull up from his cock and spear it back into me.

"Jesus Christ!"

My smile is a little smug. "Am I doing a good job?"

"Yes," he pants, his lips quirking. "You're going to fucking kill me."

Suddenly, I stop. "Did you forget to praise me?"

He moves into a sitting position and pulls me against his chest. His mouth moves to my ear. "You're a fucking miracle, Vanessa Gallo."

The words wrap around my heart like a blanket. I move away to look at his face, and his eyes are full of...yearning. I think he really meant it.

Our gazes stay locked as I continue to move, and even in his ecstasy, that expression doesn't waver. The next few moments extend like a lifetime between us. I see us panting and sweating and holding each other years from now, when our bodies have become so familiar to each other that they're almost indistinguishable.

It's only when he finds his release that our mystical connection breaks. He releases a roar, and a flood of euphoria fills my body as we come together.

Minutes later, as I lie in his arms, I'm still thinking about it.

Oh God, I think I love him.

But how can I trust it? How can I know that my primitive brain isn't playing tricks on me after years of being trained that sex, love, and monogamy are inseparable?

Chapter Seventeen

anessa

After taking a bite of my breakfast burrito, I shut my eyes and hum.

"Good?" Carter asks, and I hear a smile in his voice. Just before I got into the shower this morning, I told him I was in the mood for breakfast burritos. By the time I was dressed, he'd researched all the breakfast places within a ten-mile radius of our hotel, and this one had the best reviews on their breakfast burritos.

I can't believe how much effort he's put into making my birthday trip as perfect as it can be. Is he trying to tell me something?

When we made our agreement, he told me he wanted to use these three weeks to thank me for letting him use my TikTok to call out his grandpa. Could this be part of that thank-you, or does it mean more?

He's hardly even mentioned going live since then. In fact, the one time I tried to talk about Beach Burger going public and the logistics of our Live, he brushed it off and told me we'd figure it all out later.

I think he might be falling for me. I think that's what this trip is about.

And I'm going to ask him, even if I'm scared of the answer. He's brutally honest, so I won't have to worry about him making up an excuse to soothe my feelings.

I need to know. I won't be able to sort out my own feelings until I have a grasp on his.

"Delicious," I say. "The chorizo is cooked perfectly. It has little crispy bits in it."

His smile grows. "The best part."

"How's your omelet?"

He cuts off a big chunk of egg and scoops it up with his fork. "Not nearly big enough. I'm ravenous after last night with you."

I giggle. This is my first out-of-town trip with a guy, and it's just as fun as I'd hoped it would be.

He winks, and my belly flutters. I love how flirtatious he is all the time. I bet he'd be the type of boyfriend who would still be affectionate and playful even years into the relationship.

Jesus, am I really doing this? Am I really imagining a relationship with the UC Santa Barbara player? Just because I think I might love him doesn't mean he feels the same.

Even if he is falling for me, would he be willing to change that much? Monogamy would be a big step for someone like him.

"So..." His lips purse to the side. "The surprise I told you about is going to arrive soon."

I set my fork on my plate. "Arrive? What does that mean?"

"So..." He expels a breath through closed lips. "Rachel Moore agreed to meet with us this morning. She's stopping by when we're done with breakfast. She was able to block out about half an hour with you, and she's happy to make a video for your TikTok—"

"Are you fucking kidding me?" I shout.

His eyes grow huge.

"Sorry." I laugh, setting my hands on my hot cheeks. "You just really surprised me."

"I hope it's a good surprise."

I shake my head, my vision a little blurry. "Incredible."

His smile is so warm I can almost feel it from across the table. "So you're saying I delivered?"

"Yes, you delivered! How did you even make this happen? I've been emailing her for months."

"She said she hasn't checked that email in a year. Apparently, her inbox was full, and it was stressing her out. She actually seems like kind of a mess, which I liked. She was very relatable when I talked to her on the phone, but I originally got a hold of her by DMing her on Instagram."

"Instagram..." I mutter.

Damn, why didn't I think of that? Why was I so professional in my approach? Her videos are so relatable. I should have reached out to her in the same style as her videos, like Carter did.

"Oh, damn," Carter says. "She's here."

He lifts his hand high in the air and waves. When I turn around, Rachel is walking purposefully in our direction. She smiles at me as she approaches our table, and my stomach flips over.

"Are you *Ness*?"

I smile at her strange emphasis on my nickname. "Is that what he called me when he talked to you?"

"Oh yeah." She scoots into our booth next to Carter, smiling mischievously at him. "He said it so many times it almost felt like he was name-dropping. Like if I called LeBron James, Bron Bron to show that we're besties."

Carter lifts a brow. "Lebron James is your bestie? I would have asked you to invite him if I knew. That way I could've had something to do while you two talk about your woo-woo Christian shit."

Rachel smiles at me, shaking her head. "Our woo-woo Christian shit. Ness, you should pretend to cast a demon out of me just to scare him. My friends and I used to love doing shit like that in front of my atheist husband when we were newly dating."

I tuck a strand of hair behind my ear. "I went to a charismatic church growing up, so if I ever really want to scare Carter, I'm going to start speaking in tongues. Then he'll think *I'm* possessed by a demon."

Carter frowns. "Are we talking about Christianity right now or horror movies? I seriously can't tell the difference."

"Oh, Carter." Rachel sets her hand on his shoulder. "We haven't even scratched the surface of our woo-woo Christian shit. It can get a lot weirder." She turns to me. "Has he been to church with you?"

"Only once, but the church I go to now isn't nearly as weird as the one I grew up in."

She nods. "Most of us get a little less woo-woo with age. So, only once, huh? How long have you been together?"

"Oh, um…" My gaze falls to my plate. "We aren't exactly—"

"Two weeks," Carter says. "Our anniversary is today, actually."

Rachel grins. "Your two-week anniversary. How sweet. I remember those days…"

Rachel keeps talking—something about her and her husband—but I find myself unable to listen.

Carter is looking at me with such determination, like he's daring me to contradict him.

What does that mean? Did he only tell Rachel that to spare her a complicated explanation, or is he trying to tell me something?

I'll know soon. I'm going to ask him as soon as Rachel leaves.

"Oh my Lord, I'm blabbing on and on," Rachel says, pulling me out of my head. "I'm sorry, I always ramble."

"Don't apologize." My cheeks heat. God, I have this one opportunity with her, and I'm daydreaming about Carter. "That's why people find your Instagram so relatable. I could learn from you. Mine are always so polished, and I come across like a girl scout."

"It's cute though," Carter says, lifting his hand and poking the tip of my nose.

"Eww," I say. "Don't patronize me when I'm trying to improve. You've already implied that my videos are cringe, and I only have this short time with Rachel."

Rachel smiles. "He's just so in love he has stars in his eyes."

Carter smiles sheepishly, but surprisingly, he doesn't correct her, and hope flutters in my heart.

It makes me bold.

"Rachel, before we make our video, I want to ask you something. It's something I've always wanted to ask you, but it's pretty personal."

She smiles. "Go for it. You should know from my Instagram that nothing's too personal for me."

I nod. "That's what I thought, but I wanted to make sure. Anyway, I remember you saying in one of your videos that you never really enjoyed sex with your first husband because of the way you were both raised. Because it felt shameful for both of you."

She snorts. "That's correct, girl. We had years and years of bad sex before he finally cheated on me, and—" She raises a hand in the air "—Praise Jesus that he did, or else I might still be having bad sex."

Carter laughs, but I find that I'm too nervous to join him. The question I'm about to ask... He's going to know. He's going to know what I'm hinting at.

"What if you had really good sex? Is it possible that sex can make you feel like you love someone even when you don't?"

"What do you mean?"

"Like, say you had a fling when you were just starting to deconstruct your faith and break away from purity culture. You and I were taught that sex and love go together. Do you think your upbringing could have made you vulnerable to feel love when it wasn't there?"

She purses her lips to the side, narrowing her eyes. "I never really thought about it. I was a huge ho for about a year after I divorced my ex-husband, but I never felt like I loved any of them."

"What if you had?"

Her gaze drifts to Carter and back to me. Her expression doesn't change, but she knows. She knows why I'm asking this question.

My gut churns, but I force myself to hold her gaze.

"I don't think I would have thought too hard about it," she says. "Purity culture has done enough damage that we shouldn't have to be constantly second-guessing our feelings."

Her answer is so simple, and yet my eyes prickle. She's right. Why am I overthinking everything? Why am I letting my upbringing drift into every sweet moment of my life?

The last few weeks with Carter have been magical. I want him. I want to be with him, and it's time to start finally trusting myself.

I only hope that he feels the same.

Carter

"Wow," Vanessa says. "I can't believe that just happened."

I smile. "Did it help you?"

"I think so..." She glances down at her lap. "I'm glad I got to ask her some of the questions that have been on my mind for a while."

I am too. My God, I am too. I've barely been able to contain myself since she asked Rachel that last question. My thumb is pounding against the table, and I've been constantly shifting in my seat.

I think she loves me.

"You were really yourself with her," I say. "You went deep

right away, even if it felt uncomfortable. Since we only had a half hour, that was the right move."

She smiles abashedly. "I learned it from you. I used to be so much more guarded with people I didn't know, but you're so honest, even about your flaws. It inspires me."

A cold hand closes around my heart. I hate it when she does that. I hate when she tells me I'm honest.

What if she finds out? What if this all goes away?

"Carter, I want to talk to you about something."

My pulse starts to race. This is it. If she wants more than our three-week commitment, I'm going to find out now. Fuck, I'm ready to burst out of my skin.

"I realized something last night that..." Her gaze drops to her plate, and she purses her lips. I want to tell her to get on with it—to stop torturing me—but somehow, I'm able to maintain my placid expression.

Or at least, I think I am.

Maybe my anxiety is all over my face.

"I hope it doesn't freak you out," she says. "I can't think about that. I just need to say it."

I swallow. "Okay..."

"Being with you has taught me that trust is the key to making my body feel good. I've had good sex these past few weeks because I trust you so much. It's beyond trust, I think..." Her dark-brown eyes lock on my face, and my pulse pounds like a hammer against my throat. "I think I want to be with you long term. I don't want this to end in a week."

The world around me starts to buzz, and my head grows so heavy I nearly fall forward.

I did it.

She's mine now.

"Really?" My voice is strangled.

She frowns. "Does that weird you out? I know relationships aren't really your thing. I would definitely want us to be... I'd want monogamy. Not just a casual—"

"Fuck yeah, we'd do monogamy. Are you crazy? Do you think I'd be okay with you fucking anyone besides me?"

"Oh." Her big brown eyes are huge. "So then, you feel the same?"

I stand up and walk over to her side of the table. Her eyes are saucers now as I scoot into her booth. Without wasting a moment, I grab her face and kiss her with all the hunger and love and agony that's tormented my heart since the moment I met her. By the time I pull away, both of our chests are heaving.

"Does that tell you how I feel?" I ask.

"Yes," she says breathlessly, but she doesn't really know, because I'm not ready to tell her.

I'll tell her I love her soon. This itching anxiety—the fear that she'll vanish if I make the wrong move—will go away with time.

I've never been in love before. It's understandable that I'm gun-shy.

Chapter Eighteen

V anessa

A gust of wind brings the scent of cinnamon, making my stomach rumble. I look up from my textbook in the direction of the smell. Oh, that's right. The campus market makes fresh pastries on Friday mornings. I'm just about to get up and go get one when my phone chimes.

> Carter: I'll be there in 5 mins, baby girl. Don't order without me or I'll spank you in public.

A tickling sensation fills my belly, and I can't stop myself from grinning, even though I know I must look silly. I love it when he threatens to punish me.

The last week has been a delightful blur, and distinctly

different from the arrangement we had before our trip to Malibu. Within twenty-four hours of coming back to Santa Barbara, Carter was already planning a trip to Ventura so I can meet his mom. Even his body language has become more possessive. He almost always has a hand on some part of my body, and he looks at me like he wants to eat me for dinner.

I'm silly for loving it so much.

But also nervous.

He told me this morning that he wants to talk to me about something tonight. My initial reaction was hope. I thought maybe he was going to tell me he loves me, but then I remembered that tomorrow marks the end of our original three-week arrangement.

If he still wants to embarrass his grandpa, I shouldn't discourage him. Even if I think his plan is childish, it's really none of my business.

"Vanessa?"

I jerk up to see a dark-haired man smiling at me. It takes me a moment to recognize his face.

Derek.

I smile back, surprised at how genuine it feels. Who cares about the past? Sure, he used our shared religious background to win the fraternity bet, but he wasn't the only guy who tried to manipulate me. Several of his brothers volunteered at Gospel House to make me think they really had an interest in charity, and Ethan used me to make a girl jealous. If I wasn't angry with them, I shouldn't be angry with Derek.

Besides, his deception made me value what I have with Carter that much more.

"How are you?" I ask. "I haven't seen you around the frat much."

He grins as he sits down next to me. "I've been pretty slammed with classes lately. I've actually been a good student since I moved out of the house and into my own apartment, so I haven't wanted to break my streak."

I snort. "Carter never seems to get much work done, and I see why. There's always a beer pong tournament going on, even on a random Wednesday night."

He stares at me for a moment, his expression thoughtful. "I heard you two are a thing now, and I'm happy for him. I saw him at our fraternity meeting yesterday, and he seemed so different than he was even a few weeks ago."

My stomach flutters. "Really? He still seems like the same old Carter to me."

Jesus, am I really fishing for reassurance? I know Carter is different now that we're together. I see it every day. I don't need Derek to confirm it.

Still, I love hearing stories from his friends about how much he's transformed.

"Hell, no. Don't tell him I told you this." He glances around the area, as if looking for Carter. "But yesterday, he called you his future wife, and just a month ago, he was telling all the guys you weren't really a virgin."

My body grows cold. "What?"

His smile fades. "Oh, shit. I figured... I thought Carter would have told you by now since it wasn't a secret. He said it multiple times. I figured you... When you finally, you know... Fuck." He scratches the back of his head.

I shouldn't believe Derek. He's already manipulated me once, but something about his words and body language ring true. He doesn't seem like he's lying, and what would he have to gain by telling me this now? Carter has already won the bet. Besides, I've already been told once that Carter is a liar.

And I chose to ignore it then.

"He said it multiple times?" I ask.

"Yeah, but it wasn't like what you're probably thinking. It was sort of offhand. He would just say things like, 'You know she's probably not even a virgin, right?' but that was before he really knew you."

"Yes." My voice is brittle. "But he never told me. We're now officially in a relationship, and he never once mentioned that he thought I was lying—to hundreds of thousands of people, by the way—about being a virgin." I grimace at the thought. "What a creepy thing to lie about. My whole TikTok is about how I think the virginity construct is harmful."

He shuts his eyes, obviously upset that he's going to get in trouble with Carter, but I couldn't care less.

How could Carter have withheld this from me when he's been so brutally honest about everything else? The very night we met, he admitted—

A prickle of foreboding electrifies the back of my neck. Oh, Jesus.

Carter told me a lot of things on the night we met.

"Derek..."

"What?"

I swallow to ease the tightness in my throat. "Did you ever announce to the guys in your frat that you were going to take my virginity and win the bet?"

His incredulous expression tells me everything I need to know.

"Oh my God, he really is a liar."

"Vanessa..." Derek shuts his eyes for a moment. "I'm not sure what Carter told you, but... Just try to go easy on him. I've always felt that there's a lot going on in his life that he doesn't talk about. I don't think it's a coincidence that he had so much sex and no relationships until you. I think he has a hard time letting people in—"

"It's not an excuse to fucking manipulate people." When Derek blinks rapidly, I realize I nearly shouted in his face, and I don't care. "I have a hard time letting people in, too, because I've been manipulated by people my whole life. You have religious trauma, too. You of all people should understand."

Derek's expression grows pained, and my head grows fuzzy.

How could Carter have done this to me? How could he look at me with that tender, heavy-lidded gaze when he lied to me like this? Not just lied. He was so convincing, and I've told him again and again how much I value his honesty.

Fucking fuck. What is wrong with Carter?

"Oh, God..." I mutter. "Is he... Is he just using me for something? Do you have something going on in the frat? Some other bet?"

"No." Derek's tone is urgent, no doubt because Carter is his *brother*.

Their stupid brotherhood.

"Carter isn't that bad. He's a little...manipulative sometimes, but he's usually pretty open about it. If you call him out on it, he'll own up. Trust me, he really likes you."

"Hey."

It's Carter's deep voice. When I glance up, his brows are drawn. His blue eyes urgent and probing.

He knows.

He fucking knows.

That's how devious he's been. It's all a big secret that everyone knows but me, and Carter can see just by looking at Derek and me together that the secret is out. Holy fuck, what kind of things does he say about me at his frat meetings?

Jesus, I thought I loved him.

I thought I loved him, and now I'm learning that I don't really know who he is.

What if there is another bet going on? What if he told all of the guys that he got me to fall for him, and they all laughed at me?

"Hey, man," Derek says. "She's a little upset, because of something I said."

"I can see that." Carter's tone is accusatory, as if he's angry with Derek, and it makes my skin crawl. Do I mean so little to him that he can't even confide in me? He can't be honest about his past lies?

He doesn't love me. Not even close. Our relationship was all a game to him. Am I just like his grandparents in his eyes? Was he just trying to humiliate me the way he plans to humiliate them?

Holy fuck, what if he took videos of me naked or something?

No. Now I'm spiraling. I'll have a full-blown panic attack if I let my thoughts go this far. I take a deep, shaky breath in an attempt to slow my racing pulse. I need to talk to him.

Not now.

After I've calmed down.

I stand up from the bench and fix him with an accusing look. His face is pale and drawn, and I don't give a fuck. I would probably even enjoy it if my heart wasn't breaking. Without speaking, I brush past him and walk away.

"Vanessa!" Carter's tone is frantic. The pressure of his hand halts me, but I yank myself away from him.

"I'm going on a walk," I say.

"I'm coming with you." His tone is hard, but his speech is rapid. He's panicking.

Good. He deserves it.

"No," I say. "I need space from you."

"Absolutely not." He grabs both of my arms and pulls me around to face him. "We're talking about this."

When I pull away, he lets go of me immediately. "We will talk," I say, "but if you press me anymore, it will be our last conversation. Ever."

The terror that fills his eyes should be satisfying. Why don't I find it satisfying?

His chest rises and falls rapidly. "When can we talk?"

"I don't know. I'll call you."

With that, I turn around and dart away. I can feel his gaze boring into my back, so I speed up my pace.

Chapter Nineteen

C arter

My hand is shaking when I reach out and grab my phone. Fuck, my whole body is trembling. This isn't a good sign.

If I'm going to save myself from this nightmare, I have to keep a clear head. I have to come up with a way to convince her that I'll never lie to her again. All of the lies came from the old Carter. I've become a new person since I fell in love with her.

Goddamn it, why didn't I tell her I love her? The moment we made it official in the restaurant would have been the perfect opportunity. If I tell her now, she's going to think I'm lying.

Why isn't she here already? It's 7:03, and she's never late, not even by three minutes.

This isn't good. This isn't good at all.

"Is he in his room?" A sweet, distant voice asks, and the wave of dizzy relief that descends over me causes me to sway forward. I have to set out my foot to stop myself from falling over.

Keep it together, Carter!

She can't see this turmoil, or she'll think my lies were way worse than they were. She can't find out that I've been dreading this moment from the moment I realized I loved her.

She taps on my door, and I want to rush over to her, but I stay in place for a moment before walking at a normal pace. When I open the door, I have to keep myself from reaching out and grabbing her. She looks so beautiful with her dark waves hanging over her shoulder. If everything goes well, I'll have her beneath me, and my fingers will be entwined in that soft hair.

Eyes on the prize, Carter. Keep your head.

I gesture for her to come into my room, and it's only when she's standing in the golden light from my window that I realize her eyes are brighter than usual.

Because she's been crying.

Oh, fuck. Why did I do this? Why did I lie to this perfect girl? I had a gut feeling on the night we met that she was special. Why did I have to scheme?

"Are you going to start talking?" There's an edge to her voice. "Or are you going to force me to ask you the question?"

My pulse pounds like a hammer against my throat. "I'm... I want to make sure I know what you're upset about."

She huffs. "Are there so many lies that you don't know where to start?"

"No..." When I reach out to touch her arm, she takes a step back. The sight of it is like a knife in my chest.

"Ness, just please hear me out before you start thinking the worst."

She stares at me for a moment before nodding.

I exhale a shaky breath. "I'm sure Derek told you that he didn't really tell everyone he was going to take your virginity."

She rolls her eyes. "No, he didn't have to tell me. I guessed after he told me you told the whole frat I wasn't really a virgin."

Oh fuck. A rope coils around my lungs, making it hard to take a breath. "Yeah... Before I knew—"

"Why didn't you say anything?" she shouts, and I jerk back.

I've never seen her in this much distress. Her eyes are huge and bright, and her lips are quivering.

I just want to take her in my arms. I need to find a way out of this so I can hold her soon.

Before I lose my mind.

"I didn't... It didn't seem like it needed to be said. I realized you were a virgin the night—"

"Oh, you mean when you slammed into me?" She crosses her arms over her chest. "And here I thought you were just excited."

"Graham told me you guys had sex, okay? I'm a fucking idiot for believing him over you. I should have known he was lying after getting to know you, but I just didn't think that hard about it."

"Yeah, probably because you think everyone's a liar like you." She grimaces, her mouth trembling as if she's on the edge of her composure, about to break down into tears.

Why can't this nightmare be over?

"How could you think I would lie to my followers like that? You knew me before we had sex..." She shakes her head, her eyes growing unfocused. "I told you how I felt about being manipulated by the church growing up. And the whole time, you were manipulating me—"

"I wasn't!" I shout. "I love you! I love you so much it's fucking painful. I'm not good at being open about my emotions. That's why I lie sometimes."

Her gaze snaps to my face, and fire grows behind her eyes. "No. Your lies were deliberate. You lied to manipulate me, and you were very good at it. I didn't even think to question your lie about Derek, because you seemed so sincere. You're an actor. I can't trust anything you say."

Her words are like needles pricking all over my skin. I loved having her trust.

And I've lost it.

"I'm not an actor. I'm just... I'm able to lie well when I really want something. I realize in retrospect that it was a sign of how much I was drawn to you. I must have wanted you really badly to have fought that dirty. I wouldn't normally... I don't lie like that all the time."

"No." Her tone is hard, her nostrils flaring. "Only when you really want something, and apparently, I'm one of those things. Am I supposed to be flattered?" She takes a step in my direction. "What exactly do you want me for? Obviously not a relationship. You can't have a relationship when you lie to someone like this."

"I don't lie like this!" I can't keep myself from shouting. "I'm trying to tell you that!"

"You do lie like this!" she shouts back. "You did lie like this, and I am so done with being lied to. A year ago, I chose to be honest with myself and the people who were raised the way I was, because it was the only way to heal from the damage of my childhood. I need honesty. I need trust." She inhales a shaky breath. "And here I thought I loved you, but I didn't even know you."

Loved.

Oh God, she loved me, and I destroyed it.

I want to die.

"Please..." It's all I can say before my voice quivers. Warmth streams down my face. I try to wipe the tears away, but my hand is shaking too hard.

"I need to go," she says, and it's like being sent to the executioner. Once she goes, it's over. I have to figure out a way to make her stay. To make her believe that I love her too much to lie to her again.

In the end, my thoughts are too fragmented to find any words at all. She walks out of my bedroom and closes the door.

Chapter Twenty

C arter

"I hope it's not cold," my grandma says as she pours tea into a tiny cup. "It's been sitting out here for a bit."

"I'm sorry I'm late." When I reach out to grab the cup, my hand is shaking.

I haven't stopped shaking in three days. I notice it every time I grab my phone to see if she's texted me back.

She hasn't.

Every moment that passes fills my stomach with sick dread. If I can't think of a way to make her forgive me, I'll live in this constant state of agitation forever. I can't have peace without her.

She was my heaven. Now that she's gone, I'm in hell.

"It's okay."

Grandma's voice is gentle as she stares at me. Is that inquisitiveness in her eyes? I hope not. I don't want to talk about anything.

"What's Vanessa doing?" she asks.

A sharp pain slices into my chest, but with a concentrated effort, I'm able to keep from grimacing. I hate when people ask about Vanessa as if she still belongs to me. As if she should be here right now.

"Probably at Gospel House."

Grandma is quiet for a moment, and her curiosity vibrates between us. God, please help her not to ask.

I don't think I can bear it.

"Probably?" she asks, and I can't stop myself from flinching.

"Yeah, we...broke up."

There's a long pause, and I take a sip of my tea. It's tasteless. No wonder I haven't been able to eat in days.

"What happened?"

Her voice is relaxed and neutral. Unlike my mom, who I know would be emotional. I couldn't tell her anything about what happened. It's my grandma's calmness that draws me out of my gloomy cave.

"I fucked everything up," I say. "I don't think I can fix it."

"How did you...*fuck* it up?"

Hearing my proper grandmother say fuck would probably make me laugh under different circumstances. Now, it's painful. I used to love it when Vanessa said fuck, too, always with such emphasis, like she was making up for all those years of not being allowed to say it.

"I lied to her," I say, "and she found out."

"Lied about what?"

I wave a hand. "Stupid shit. I was just trying to win her over in the beginning. I manipulated her, and she found out."

My grandma sighs heavily. "I thought it might be something like that."

My head jerks up. "Why do you say that?"

She gives me a pitiful look, like I'm asking a question with a stupidly obvious answer, and my bafflement expands like a balloon.

"Honey, do you think I don't know who you are?"

My incredulity must be all over my face, because she smiles. "Oh, you think I'm your naive granny? You think I don't know that you've been using our money to finance you and your mom's life for the past decade?"

When my cheeks heat and I avert my gaze, she laughs.

I figured she picked up on it a few times—I didn't always put enough effort into my lies—but it never occurred to me that she knew the extent of it.

I thought she would have put a stop to it if she knew.

"We're such a fucked-up family," I mumble.

"Everyone is fucked up in some way. It's not just our family."

"Our family is especially fucked up. I shouldn't have had to lie to you guys. You shouldn't have cut off my mom."

"You're right."

Heat tingles over my skin. "You agree with me?"

She blinks hard. "Honey, our relationship with your mom is very complicated. I regret the stance we took when she was a teenager. We told her she had to either repent or live on her own. We truly believed that letting her sin under our roof was putting her salvation in jeopardy. We thought we were doing the right thing, but—"

"Bullshit!" My jaw clamps shut, and I take a deep breath through my nose. "You kicked a teenager out on the street."

She sets her teacup on the little plate in her hand. "It wasn't quite like that. She chose to live with her friends—"

"Yes, and then she eventually had nowhere to go. And you guys didn't help her."

"We made a lot of mistakes."

"Yes, you did."

"I don't want to make excuses for us, but your mom didn't always make it easy to have a relationship with her."

"You didn't even try."

Grandma purses her lips and turns to look out at the ocean. "We did, but your mom wouldn't accept half measures. She wanted us to embrace her back in our life and in our church community. Your grandpa wasn't willing to do that."

I frown. "Are you saying you tried to reconcile with her?"

"A few times. How do you think we were finally able to see you?"

My head grows fuzzy. "What do you mean 'finally'? Do you mean... Did you try to see me when I was little?"

"Are you kidding me?" She raises her brows. "You're our grandson. We begged to see you, but she was extremely protective of you for a long time. She didn't trust us with you, especially since we weren't willing to invite her back into our life."

"I don't blame her."

She sighs. "I don't either. We even tried to reach out to your dad once when you were a little older. We were going to try and visit you during one of your summers in Idaho—which was a big mistake. She warned us away from you after that."

I lean back in my seat. "Good for her."

My grandma's smile is a little sad. "Do you hear yourself?"

I shrug. "I'm on her side. Sorry if you don't like it."

"It's much more than that. The two of you are a unit. You take care of each other."

"That's how it should be."

Her brows shoot up her forehead. "That's how it *should* be? You're her child. You shouldn't be taking care of her."

Rage flares through my veins. Just as I open my mouth to defend my mom, Grandma lifts both hands. "I'm not saying she isn't a good mother. In many ways, she did a far better job with you than we did with her. We were never as close to her as she is to you. There were stark boundaries between parent and child. It's how your grandpa and I were raised, and it was a little too rigid. Unhealthy, even. But I don't think the way you were raised was ideal either. You were the man of the house when you were only a kid. You weren't able to go out and get a job and really take care of the family, so you had to maneuver your way through it. No wonder you manipulated Vanessa. It's what you're used to doing to get your basic needs met."

I'm just about to protest when a memory drifts into my mind. *"You had a lot of responsibility as a kid. The kind most kids don't."* It's Vanessa's sweet voice whispering in the dark, when her warm, naked body rested against mine. It was a sign of protectiveness, and it made my heart clench.

Back then, I dismissed it. I figured she didn't have all the information. She didn't know how hard it was for my mom to raise a child when she was a kid herself.

"I was sort of like a caregiver growing up," I mumble.

"Yes, you were."

"But it wasn't Mom's fault. Being a teen mom was overwhelming for her. And you know my dad didn't do shit for her until I was older."

"Your mom is a grown woman. She's not a teen mom anymore. You're still taking care of her."

"I know, but..." My lips close. I hate that I can't come up with an excuse for her. "She did her best," I eventually say.

"I know she did. She loves you fiercely. She's a tiger mom. But just because we do our best, doesn't mean we don't fall short sometimes."

I nod once, and even that small movement feels like a betrayal. "So you think... You think I lie and manipulate because I can't help myself?"

"No." Her tone is hard. "You're a smart kid. You could figure something else out. You lie and manipulate because it's the easiest way for you."

Her words are like a dagger in my chest, and I can't stop myself from flinching. Fuck, I'm selfish. Vanessa deserved the world, and because I prioritized my own comfort, I withheld from her the one thing she values most.

Honesty. Vulnerability.

What could I possibly do to fix it?

"Maybe, I could..." I scratch my head. "Maybe I could make

myself really vulnerable. Maybe I could tell Vanessa every single lie I ever told her, even the ones she doesn't know about."

"I think that might be going a bit far." Grandma frowns. "Why would you want to hurt her even more?"

"Because it's the only way she can trust me moving forward. If I reveal things—things I have no reason to tell her—maybe..." I shut my eyes. "Maybe it's the step in the right direction. Maybe she'll feel like there's at least the potential for trust."

"You'd be willing to do that for just the *potential* of trust?"

I swallow, my eyes misting. "I'd be willing to do anything."

Chapter Twenty-One

anessa

My sister's car isn't in the driveway when I pull up, but thankfully, I have a key. I used to come here pretty often to study on their balcony while she and Cole were at work. I haven't done it much lately, and I'm sure she's noticed.

When I get to the front porch, I reach into my purse and search around for my key. Just as I start to unlock the door, it opens on its own. Cole stands in the doorway. "She's still not home." He sounds a touch exasperated. "She said she would only be gone an hour, but it's been three."

I can't help but smile. The biggest problem Livvy and Cole have in their blissful relationship is how much Cole worries about her. Carter's lies would be incomprehensible to either of them.

"Your life is going to be a nightmare when you have kids," I say as I walk inside. "What are you going to do when they stay out past curfew?"

"They aren't going to stay out past curfew." He keeps his

eyes on me as I follow him into the kitchen. "I'm going to be strict as hell. I'll have to be to make up for your sister. All they'll have to do is cry, and she'll give them anything they want."

"True. I always used tears to get her to forgive me when she was mad."

He grabs a glass from the cupboard, and I sit down at the table and take in the view of the ocean. Just at the base of those cliffs in the distance is where I lost my virginity.

It was magical, when I'd expected it to be scary. I trusted him so much.

How ironic that the man who taught me that trust is the key to getting over sexual shame turned out to be one of the least trustworthy people I've ever known.

Cole sets a small tumbler of amber liquid in front of me. My head jerks back. "What is this?"

"Tequila." He smiles. "Good tequila, too, so don't shoot it. Sip it."

I grimace. "I want to die at just the thought of sipping tequila."

"Just try one sip."

I lift the glass to my nose. The chemical smell alone tugs at my gag reflect. After taking a deep breath, I lift it to my lips and take a tiny sip. It's spicy and woody, heating my throat as it trails down. "That really isn't too bad."

He takes a sip of his own. "Told you."

"I'm guessing you served me alcohol because Livvy told you about Carter."

He leans back in his chair, swirling the liquid in his glass. "She did. But I also noticed you haven't been around much since we got engaged. I thought maybe some tequila might loosen you up to tell me why."

I wince. "Is Livvy really upset about it?"

"What do you think?"

I groan. "I think if I told her I was jealous that her sexual shame vanished overnight when mine has been such a struggle, she'd think I don't love her as much as she loves me."

He takes a sip before setting his tequila on the table. "Have you ever met your sister? If you told her that, she'd wish she could bring her sexual shame back just to make you feel better."

I shut my eyes. "She's a much better person than I am."

"She's a better person than most people, but that shouldn't stop you from confiding in her. She's strong. She can take it. Besides, she could probably help you. She didn't get over her sexual shame overnight. I don't know where you got that idea."

My head jerks up. "She didn't?"

He frowns. "Of course not. It's been one of the biggest struggles of her life, just like it is for you. We were working through it for probably the first few years we were together."

I stare at him, dumbfounded. How could this be? She certainly never said anything to me.

"But she made it sound like sex was always so magical between you guys..."

He smiles lazily. "It was magical, but that's only because we trusted each other so much. She was able to talk about her struggles with me, and she knew I was willing to work through it with her."

Tears prickle behind my eyes. Oh, fuck. I don't want to cry, but how can I not when that's exactly how it was with Carter? I wasn't afraid of him seeing my struggles. I wasn't worried about having a panic attack, because I was sure he would be kind and understanding.

Who knows if I was right? Maybe he would have mocked me behind my back.

Yet even with everything I know now, I can't imagine him doing that. At times, he was so in tune with my emotions and attentive to my needs. He couldn't have faked all that, could he?

"I can see you're thinking about Carter," Cole says.

I sigh heavily. "Yes."

"What did he do?"

I lift my glass and throw the rest of the burning liquid down my throat, slamming the glass down afterward. "He's a liar. I don't even think he really liked me now that I look back on everything. He had this whole...stupid scheme to humiliate his grandparents using my TikTok. I think that was the only reason he dated me."

Cole snorts. "That's ridiculous."

"You have no idea how utterly manipulative he is. How good he is at lying. It's scary."

Cole shakes his head. "I'm not defending him. I'm sure he really fucked up. But I know he really liked you because I could see it. I barely talked to him that day he came to church, and I could still see it. He actually reminds me a lot of myself when I was his age."

I shake my head sharply. "He's nothing like you. If he seemed like it, it's because he's such a good liar."

"Yeah, he's a liar because he's so insecure. Do you remember how I used to be with Livvy? How possessive I used to be?"

"You never lied to her."

"No, she was so sweet I didn't have to. Instead, I hovered over her. Made sure everyone around me knew that we were best friends. That she was basically mine. I was doing anything I could to keep her to myself."

I nod slowly. "I do remember that."

"I did it because I was insecure. I knew she cared for me, but I felt like I could never be enough for her because I wasn't a Christian. That's probably why Carter lies. He feels like he isn't enough for you."

"There's no reason for him to feel that way. He gets any woman he wants. He's a fuckboy."

Cole shrugs. "I was a fuckboy, too. Mostly because I was trying to distract myself from the woman I thought I couldn't have. Trust me, fuckboys are all secretly insecure."

I wish it were true, but Carter's as comfortable in his own skin as anyone I've ever met.

Then again, he did say he isn't capable of loving anyone besides his mom, that he thinks he's broken. Could it be that he's afraid of love, and that's why he lied?

No. I can't think this way. I'm trying to make excuses for him because I want them to be true.

The front door opens, and my sister's musical voice floats into the kitchen. "Is my Nessa here?"

Cole's face melts into a boyish smile. God, I love how much he still worships my sister.

My chest aches. Carter gave me looks like that, too.

Livvy walks into the kitchen with a reusable grocery bag on her shoulder. "I bought so many snacks. Flaming Hot Cheetos and Dr. Pepper, and when we're ready for sweets, I got Sour Patch Straws and two bags of those Italian chocolate chips Nonna used to buy. The ones that are shaped like flying saucers."

My mouth drops open. "Where did you find them?"

"World Market." Livvy grins. "They only have them every once in a while."

"Alright, gorgeous girls." Cole walks over to Livvy and gives her a smacking kiss. "I'm going upstairs to watch some baseball. No teams I give a shit about are playing, but I can make the sacrifice if it means giving you a real girls' night."

I wrinkle my nose as I look at my sister. "Would you be annoyed if Cole joins us? I feel like he might have some insight on Carter."

She shoots Cole a cheeky smile. "Some fuckboy insight. Yes, he would have that."

Cole glares playfully at her before turning to me. "I'll join you guys later, but I think you should have some alone time first. Don't you?"

I give him a knowing look before inviting my sister outside onto the deck. As we watch the sun set behind the ocean, I tell her why I've been so distant these past few weeks. After we both shed a few tears, we finally start our long overdue wedding planning.

Chapter Twenty-Two

C arter

"That looks new," I say to Armaan. "What happened to Bong Solo?"

Armaan's gaze grows hooded as he presses a ball of weed into the tiny glass bowl. He's always so deft and precise when he packs his bongs. "He broke. This is Logan Henderson."

I frown. "You just straight named it after Logan. Not even attempting a bad pun? What about Logan Bongerson?"

"No." Armaan presses his index finger into the bowl over and over again, packing down the weed. "Logan got me this for my birthday, and I miss him."

"Now you get to kiss him every day."

Armaan nods once as he lifts the glass tube to his mouth. "Several times a day."

After inhaling deeply, Armaan hands me the bong along with a stick lighter. I light the bowl while I inhale the thick smoke. My head grows fuzzy for a moment, and I see Vanessa's gorgeous, sparkling eyes and sweet smile.

Fuck, I miss her.

It's been four days, but it feels like an utter fucking eternity.

When I groan, Armaan looks up at me with sleepy eyes. "Please tell me you didn't just say you want to get high when you really want to whine about Vanessa."

"Did Saanvi tell you?"

He grimaces. "I'm not telling you a goddamn thing. I'm on Vanessa's side."

"You talked to Vanessa?"

Armaan's hooded eyes fall nearly shut. "Let me repeat myself. I'm not telling you a *goddamn* thing."

I groan again, and this time, it sounds like a growl. "Your loyalty should be with me."

"It should be, huh? But it's not."

I lean forward, setting my elbows on the table. "Okay, now you have to tell me. What did she say? She obviously told you a lot. I need to know. Tell me."

He stares at me for a long moment. "No."

I roll my eyes, shaking my head. "Fuck you. Don't forget that when you cheated on your ex-girlfriend, I was the one that drove you to her apartment so you could beg her to forgive you. I didn't judge you once."

"Yeah, you did."

I expel a shaky breath through my nostrils. "Yeah, I did a little. At least I didn't cheat on Vanessa."

He shuts his eyes and leans back in his chair. He sits like that for a while, and if I didn't know him any better, I'd think he'd fallen asleep. But this is what Armaan does when he's thinking deeply. "Maybe you didn't cheat on Vanessa, but you did the same thing I did with Brenna."

I huff. "Which is?"

"You blamed her for your own shit, and you took it out on her."

"What exactly is my own shit?"

He stares at me for a long moment. "I don't know exactly, but I don't think you would lie like you do if you weren't seriously fucked in the head."

"Thanks, bro."

"You're welcome."

"I didn't come here to talk about my issues. I need your help with something."

"I'm not doing anything that concerns Vanessa."

"I don't need you to do anything big. I just need you to make sure she watches something."

He scowls. "What are you talking about?"

"I'm going to post a TikTok telling the honest truth about everything, and I want to make sure she watches it."

At first, he just stares at me with a sleepy expression. As if coming to some kind of conclusion, he breaks out into a low chuckle. "Oh my God, Carter. No. I'm not doing that. And that's for your sake. You don't want to do that."

I grit my teeth. "Why not?"

"Because it's embarrassing."

"That's the point."

"It's a bad idea."

"I disagree."

He lifts a hand. "You fucked it up with her. She's not going to forgive you. You can't charm your way out of this. Religious girls aren't charmed by fuckboys, anyway. You had your shot, and you ruined it."

My throat grows tight, and mist rises to my eyes. Oh God, no. Please say I'm not going to cry in front of Armaan. Fuck, what is in this weed? I look away, blinking away the moisture in my eyes.

"Oh my God." His voice is almost panicked. "Please tell me you aren't crying."

"I am crying. You should feel terrible."

"Fuck. Are you really crying?"

"Yep. And the only way you can make it up to me is by getting Vanessa to watch my video."

"Oh my God! I fucking hate you. I thought you were really crying."

I look at him earnestly, hoping he'll see my desperation on my face. "Will you do it? I don't care that you're on her side. To be honest, I kind of admire you for it. I love her, and I want her to have everything. Even your loyalty, when technically, I should have it, but this would mean the world to me."

His eyes narrow on my face. "I feel like you're playing me right now."

"I am, sort of. It's all I know. You should feel sorry for me. I'm so fucked in the head that I don't even know how to not play people."

He rolls his eyes. "Alright, I'll do it, but not because of your sob story. Only because you would do it for me, and I'm not sure which of us is the bigger asshole."

I pat his shoulder. "Good man."

Vanessa

When Saanvi pauses *House of the Dragon*, I turn to her. She's wincing as she stares at her phone.

"What's up?" I ask.

She sucks in her lips and then lets them out slowly. "Armaan is outside. He has some food from our grandma."

I frown. Why does she look upset about this? "That's great. I'd rather have something your grandma made than order Doordash."

She winces. "He also said... He wants to show you something."

My stomach flips over.

Carter.

Whatever he wants to show me has something to do with Carter, and my heart is fluttering like a moth in my chest. I knew Carter would try to apologize somehow.

I can't lie to myself. I've been waiting for his apology and going crazy after a week of not hearing from him.

I miss him.

"I'm sure it has something to do with Carter," she says. "Do you want me to tell him you don't want to see it?"

I open my mouth and close it. I should say no. Carter is so good at manipulation. Whatever Armaan has to show me is bound to tempt me to reach out to him.

Somehow, I don't care.

"I want to see what it is."

Saanvi's eyes crinkle at the corners. "I'm really glad you said that, because I'm dying of curiosity."

A few minutes later, Saanvi lets Armaan inside. He carries a large box into our kitchen.

"What did she send?" Saanvi asks.

"A bunch of stuff," he says, "but I took all of my favorites."

"You always do."

Armaan sets the box down and starts putting the containers inside the fridge. "They give you all the money, so I get the best food."

"So, Armaan," I call out. "Does whatever you have to show me have something to do with Carter?"

He doesn't look away from the fridge. "Of course it does. He's a pathetic mess. He even started crying yesterday when he was talking about you."

My mouth drops open. "Did he really?"

"Yep."

Saanvi squeals. "You did that, Nessa! You made Carter Blake cry."

My stomach churns. I don't want him to be that sad. I also don't want to feel sympathy for him when he broke my heart with his lies.

"What does he want you to show me?"

"It's really embarrassing," Armaan says. "For him, I mean."

Curiosity makes the hairs on my arms stand up. "What is it?"

Armaan sighs heavily as he shuts the fridge door and pulls his phone out of his pocket. "He made a video. He hasn't posted it on TikTok yet. He wanted to show you first. He wants you to let him know if it's too embarrassing." Armaan pins me with a hard stare. "The answer to that question is yes. You don't even need to watch it for me to tell you that, but I made him a promise."

My pulse pounds as Armaan walks over to the couch. What does he mean by embarrassing?

Armaan sits down next to me. When he holds up his phone, a video is already pulled up on the screen. The sight of Carter's face makes my chest tug. Why does longing have to be so visceral? I want to tug him out of that phone and plant kisses all over his face.

"Are you ready for this?" Armaan asks.

Nervousness is churning my gut, but I manage a nod.

"Alright, get ready for this rollercoaster."

After he taps the screen, Carter stays silent with a questioning frown on his face, probably because he's checking to make sure his phone is recording. Clearly, this video is unedited.

"This is my first time posting on my own," he eventually says, and the sound of that mellifluous voice curls through my insides. "Normally, I have my girl with me, but she's not here because..."

He runs both hands through his hair. My chest aches at the sound of him calling me his girl.

"Vanessa, if you're watching, I have to tell you something. I told you a bunch of lies. More than the ones you know about. To be honest, I'm so used to lying, I don't even notice I'm doing it sometimes. I probably told you lies I don't even remember, but I promise to tell you everything I know."

He sighs heavily. "I also withheld something important from you. Something I was terrified to say out loud. I think that's even worse than the lies I told. So I'm making this video to come clean.

The first lie you already know, but I told you another one that same night. I told you that I was only after you to take your virginity, like every other guy. But that wasn't true. The truth is that I knew from the beginning that I wanted to..."

He shuts his eyes tightly, and I wish I could reach out and touch him. I know what he's going to say.

"I wanted to do the thing I told you about. It has to do with my career and family, but I'm not going to say what it is because you already know. I won't name any names because it doesn't matter to me anymore. You were right that my plan was childish."

Armaan laughs, and it makes it hard to hear what Carter says next. "Riveting stuff, Carter. Maybe tell us all some of your inside jokes with Vanessa, too."

"Hush!" Saanvi's voice comes from behind the couch. "Go back a few seconds, Ness. Armaan, shut up. We need to hear all of it."

"This so cringe," Armaan says. "I'd really prefer not to hear any of it."

Saanvi hits his shoulder. "Then go away!"

"No, he made me promise to sit here and make sure Vanessa watches the whole thing."

My heart clenches as I lift my finger and press play.

"I don't give a shit about any of that anymore," Carter says. "It's honestly so hard for me to remember why it ever mattered. I think it was because...I didn't really know what I needed, and I was trying to fulfill what I thought I needed in all the wrong ways. You helped me see what I need. I need love."

When he shuts his eyes and laughs to himself, I want to reach out and hold him. This is hard for him to say. Someone who schemes as much as Carter has probably never been this vulnerable with anyone, let alone on a public forum like TikTok.

"It sounds really pathetic," he says, "but it's the truth. I need *your* love. And that's what brings me to the thing I withheld. Nessa, baby girl—"

"Oh fuck, Carter." Armaan cringes. "Not baby girl. Please."

Just as I press pause, Saanvi punches Armaan again. "Shut the fuck up or get out of here!"

"Yes," I say breathlessly. "I really need to hear this."

"Sorry," he says, and I press play.

"I've known I love you for weeks," Carter says. "I knew during our first... Our first time. I didn't tell you because I was terrified. Because I always have to have the upper hand with people. I always have to have power over them. I'm a coward. That's why I lie, Ness." He swallows. "I don't deserve you."

The video freezes, signaling the end.

"That's it?" Saanvi shouts. "What the fuck, Carter? I was expecting a marriage proposal."

"Oh, thank God he didn't take it that far," Armaan says, "But I wouldn't have been surprised."

I fight the tears threatening to spill out of my eyes. I don't know if I need Carter's love, but I want it more than I've ever wanted anything in my life.

Chapter Twenty-Three

C arter

Her name appears on the screen of my phone, and my heart jumps into my throat. I grab it so quickly from my desk that it falls out of my hands at first. I could die at the agony of waiting even another second to read it.

Before I know it, I've swiped the screen, and my gaze is scanning the words.

> Vanessa: Any chance you want to meet up?

I make myself take one deep breath before my thumbs start frantically typing on the screen. I press send without even checking to see if my words make sense.

> Me: There's nothing I want more.

It's not really true. I want this meeting to be over and done with. I want to be in bed with her, but I'm still pretty damn close to heaven just from getting this damn text.

It'll be hell waiting to hear what she has to say.

What if she wants to tell me to leave her alone? To stop making videos like the one I made a few days ago.

I can't think about that now.

Three dots appear to show me she's typing.

> Vanessa: When are you free?

> Carter: Right now.

> Vanessa: What about tomorrow morning before my religious studies class?

> Carter: I'll come to your apartment. How about we do 6, and I'll bring coffee?

The three dots appear and then disappear again. I'm almost dizzy as I wait for her response. Why am I so nervous? She's not going to back out now.

> Vanessa: 6am?? Are you crazy. My class isn't until 10.

> Me: I won't be sleeping tonight, so the earlier the better.

Vanessa: Are you implying you're nervous?

Me: No need to imply. I'm so nervous I'm about to shit my pants.

Vanessa: I can't tell if you're trying to manipulate me…

My pulse races, and I take a deep breath to calm it.

Me: I don't usually tell girls I'm going to shit my pants when I want to manipulate them. I'm more charming than that.

Vanessa: You're so good at manipulating that you probably know that being vulnerable is what I want.

I run a shaky hand through the hair at the crown of my head.

Me: I don't know what to say. If you don't believe me when I'm vulnerable, there's really not much I can do.

Waiting for her answer is agony. Finally, her response pops up.

Vanessa: I believe you. Let's meet at 8:30.
Don't come to my house. Let's meet on the
beach and take a walk.

I exhale a long, shaky breath. I have a meeting with her, and that gives me the opportunity to start proving to her that I'm safe.

Now, I just have to get through the next twelve hours.

* * *

After I finally drift off at four in the morning, I sleep fitfully, but exhaustion proves to be just what I need. It dulls the anxiety and gives me a hazy exhilaration, as if I've been drugged.

I'm going to win her back. I can do this.

The cool wind brushes against my cheeks, filling me with determination. She and I will be going on beach walks every damn morning. This will become part of my everyday life, goddammit.

When she appears several feet away, I could fall over at the sight of her. She looks like an angel in her bright-yellow sundress. Her long dark hair blows every which way. I want to touch it. I want to touch her.

I take a deep breath as I walk in her direction.

Be genuine. Be sincere. Wear your heart on your sleeve.

You can do this, Carter.

Her smile is cautious, and it makes my chest ache. Just last week, she would have wrapped her arms around me instead. I would have pulled her into a tight hug and called her my baby girl.

Fuck, I had everything, and I lost it.

"You brought the coffee?" she asks, and it's only then that I notice the puffiness under her eyes. She's not sleeping either?

I'm a bastard for feeling hope at the sight of it. I should be miserable that she's miserable.

But damn. It's comforting to know she might feel even a fraction of my agony.

I lift her coffee cup as she approaches me. "I went to this little place on the wharf. They didn't have your Mexican Mocha, but I asked them to put nutmeg in this one."

She smiles. "I just need the caffeine. I'll take anything."

I glance away, not wanting her to see my eagerness. "Did you not sleep well?"

She purses her lips and looks down at the sand. "No. I haven't been sleeping well since our...breakup, I guess."

I shut my eyes as a wave of euphoria washes over me. It has to mean something. Maybe she still loves me.

Maybe there's hope.

"I've been sleeping like shit, too." I keep my eyes fixed on a distant cliff as we walk along the water. "Every single night. I got used to sleeping next to you."

"Me too." She takes a sip of her coffee. "Plus, I've just been so torn about everything. I've been running every moment we had together over in my head, trying to figure out if what you said was true or not."

An unbearable heat claws through my insides. I hate that I've been my most vulnerable with her, and she doesn't believe me because of my stupidity.

Why was I so afraid? Why didn't I see that she's one of the kindest, most loving people I've ever known? My heart was always safe with her.

"I understand why you would do that." I choose my words carefully. "My lies have made it impossible for you to see what's real and what's not, but I promise you there will be no more lies. And I'll be honest about any lie I've told in the past."

She's quiet for a moment, frowning as she stares at her feet while we walk. I can see the intricate machine working in her head. My thoughtful, practical girl. As she looks up at me, her eyes narrow on my face. "That shirt you let me borrow...when my dress got all wet."

I wince. "Fuck, I forgot."

"I knew it! Parker bumped into me on purpose, didn't he?"

A wave of despair threatens to choke my throat, but it fades as soon as I open my eyes and catch the look on her face. She doesn't look upset. She almost looks...

Intrigued.

"So you really forgot?" she asks.

"Yes," I say right away. "Completely. It was so fucking stupid. Parker wasn't even in on it. He was too drunk. I had another guy push him into you." My hand is shaking so hard I slip it into the pocket of my hoody. "I'm a piece of shit, huh?"

I'm startled by the warmth of her hand on my arm. I desperately want to set my own on top of it, but I stop myself.

I can't be too eager.

"You seem...different. Less cool and collected." Her lips quirk. "I like it."

My throat grows tight. "I don't like it, but I like that you like it."

Her smile grows. "I feel like you would tell me anything right now."

"I would."

I mean it, too. I really would tell her absolutely anything. It's strange and exhilarating.

Freeing.

"I still feel..." A notch forms between her brows. "I don't know. Uncertain. I don't know if you're really changing or just trying to win me back. True vulnerability isn't just one revealing TikTok video. It's an everyday thing. Would you mind if we were friends for a little while before I... Before I decide if I can trust you?"

I grab her hand and pull her to face me, trying to show her in my eyes the love I feel in my heart. "You can have whatever you want. I'd take any part of you over nothing."

"And you won't... You won't try to get me to change my mind when I'm not ready?"

I gasp out a laugh. "You mean I won't try to manipulate you into doing something you don't want to do? No, baby girl. I'll never do that."

She nods, but she still looks a little wary. She glances down at our joined hands. "And what if I... What if I date someone else, would you still want to be friends?"

A coldness settles in my gut, but with effort I keep my expression blank. "Yes," I say with as much decisiveness as I can muster. "I wouldn't... I'd be cool."

Not on the inside. I'd want to die.

After I killed him, of course.

Oh God, I hope she never brings anyone around me. I don't know what I'd do. It would take everything within me to be nice.

Still, she seems reassured. She gives me the warmest smile I've seen all morning. "I'd like to hang out. I've missed you."

My chest pulls so tight I'm not sure if I can speak. It takes every effort not to reach out and touch her. "I've missed you like crazy."

The affection in her eyes makes the tight coil around my lungs snap and fall away, and I inhale what feels like my first breath in days.

Hope. There's hope.

Chapter Twenty-Four

C arter

My heart pounds as I walk up the stairs to her apartment. I have a question to ask her today, but I have to charm her first. Thankfully, I have plenty of time to do it.

We're spending the whole day together. It's been a week since our conversation, and she's been cautious but kind. We've met on campus a few times for coffee, never for more than an hour. Every time, I've tried to make our dates last longer, but she always has an excuse.

She's still wary of me.

But with each day, I'm making progress. She must be starting to see that she's not just a girl I want to win. She's a person who's inspired me to become something new, and if I can't have her, I can never go back to who I was before her.

Some people are that way. Like a chemical reaction, they become something else when they're combined, and there's nothing you can do to reverse it.

After knocking several times, Saanvi finally opens the door. "She needs help with her surfboard," she says. "It's huge."

I roll my eyes. "Ness," I call out. "Leave the longboard. I brought you a shortboard."

"No," she calls back. "I'm comfortable with my longboard because I learned on it."

I shoot Saanvi a knowing smile. "Well, you're going to relearn on a shortboard today. I don't even think I can fit your longboard in my car."

"We'll make it fit," Vanessa shouts.

I glance down at my iWatch. The best waves are coming in soon. "No, we won't."

Saanvi winces. "She's had it since junior high. It's her baby."

"It's a piece of shit."

"That makes her love it even more."

"Alright," I shout. "You can bring the longboard, but you're practicing on my shortboard at least once."

"Deal!" She emerges from her room with a giant yellow surfboard dragging on the floor beside her.

I shake my head. "You can barely even carry it."

"I can carry it just fine." She lifts the board from the ground and holds it at her side, but her steps grow slow and measured.

"You do realize we're going to have to walk. I can't fit that thing in my car."

She shrugs. "It's only a twenty-minute walk."

I roll my eyes. "And who's carrying that board during those twenty minutes, Ness?"

She grins. "It's only fair that the person with the most physical strength and endurance carry it."

"And who among us has the most physical strength and endurance?"

Her smile grows. "You."

"Exactly." I shake my head, smiling as I look at Saanvi. "I think she's bringing that board just to punish—"

I close my mouth at the look on Saanvi's face. It's thoughtful and almost...piteous. God, I must look so lovesick, but maybe it's a good thing.

It's vulnerability.

A few hours later, Vanessa and I are floating in the ocean, resting on our boards while the afternoon sun evaporates the salty water from our backs.

"Your longboard is better for floating," I say. "I'll give it that."

She grabs a piece of kelp from the water and rubs her thumb over the grainy leaf. "Floating is my favorite part of surfing."

I chuckle. "Yeah, I noticed. You take all the baby waves, and you rarely stand up. Why don't you just bring a boogie board? They're much easier to carry."

She lays her head down on her board and sighs. "I like having the option of being able to stand up."

The wistfulness in her voice warms me everywhere. I lift my hand and reach it out, ready to stroke the wet strands of hair around her face, but I stop myself just in time. When I pull my hand back, she looks up at me. "It's okay. You can touch me."

I can't help but release a groan. "How much can I touch you?"

She smiles. "Maybe just a little rub for now."

"Where?"

She laughs. "Wherever you were going to touch me."

"It just so happens, I was going to touch your pussy."

She punches me on the shoulder, and I'm so overwhelmed with this easiness between us that I reach out and stroke her hair like I wanted to before. I pet it, like she's a dog, but she doesn't seem to mind. Oh God, I've missed being able to touch her. During my darkest moments, I feared that I'd never get to do this again.

"Fuck, I love you so much." The words feel pulled from me, as if there's nowhere for them to go but out of my mouth.

She turns her head to the side and stares at me. She looks like she wants to say more but is holding herself back.

I understand. She's not ready to trust me yet.

But I still have to ask her my question.

"Do you think... I was hoping you could come with me to my grandparents' house tomorrow."

She frowns. "What's going on?"

"I need to tell my grandpa that I can't work for Beach Burger. The company went public last week, and we still haven't had a talk. I've been ignoring him. I even missed our usual weekly dinner."

"I can't imagine he's taken that well."

I snort. "No. He's calling me daily and leaving very un-Christian messages. I finally told him we can meet tomorrow, and my mom is driving up from Ventura."

Her eyes grow huge. "Your mom is coming?"

"Yep. She agreed we needed to all finally have it out, though I'm not sure if she's going to like everything I have to say. I'm going to tell them all how hard it was for me being stuck in the middle of their feud."

She reaches out and sets her hand on my shoulder, and I lean into her touch. "That's not going to be an easy conversation," she says.

"No." I blow out a breath between my closed lips. "That's why I'd like you to come with me if you can."

She's silent for a moment, and my ears are drawn to the whispered hum of the waves in the distance. "Why?" she asks.

"I just... I love you, and I know you have my best interest at heart. I know you're neutral. Everyone is probably going to get a little emotional, especially my mom. If you're there, I'll feel...safe, I guess."

She stares at me for a long moment. Did she get salt in her eyes, or is that glassy brightness for me?

"I'll be there," she says.

Chapter Twenty-Five

anessa

The next day, we're sitting in his grandparents' big dining room. It's evening, and the low sun casts an orange-pink glow over the table. The five of us sit with glasses of wine in front of us.

The polite and stilted conversation has now faded into silence. Carter looks up from his glass and gives me such a sad, pathetic look that I shoot him my warmest smile back to encourage him. I told him in the car that I'm willing to offer my opinion if he wants it, or sit silently and give him support. He chose the latter, which I'm grateful for. It would be hard to talk to his family about issues that don't involve me, but I'd do it. I'd do anything for him.

I love him.

I love him with all of my heart.

He looks around the table, and then his expression grows stern. "You're probably wondering why I asked you all to meet up. Recently, I did something..." He glances at me, his expression growing somber. "I hurt Vanessa really badly, and I realized something about myself. I'm a really manipulative person."

"Carter," his mom says, her voice gentle. "You say that like it's part of who you are. A personality trait that you can't change. The truth is that you made some poor choices where Vanessa is concerned, but—"

He lifts a hand. "Mom, please don't defend me. Please don't interrupt either. I have a lot to say, and this is..." He shuts his eyes briefly. "This is hard."

His mom's eyes grow huge. She's probably just as surprised as I am to see Carter like this.

"I'm sorry, baby," she says.

"It's okay." He smiles sadly at her before turning to his grandpa. "Your decision to disown my mom was reprehensible. I'm pretty sure you mostly cared about the company and the embarrassment of her pregnancy. If you try to tell me it was about your religion, I'm going to fucking throw up."

"Watch your language," Dan says.

"Oh, stop it," Nancy says. "It's not like we all haven't heard you say much worse, and with far less justification."

I widen my eyes at Carter, and he smiles slightly. I've never heard Nancy stand up to Dan, and based on the look on Carter's face, I doubt he has either.

"But the worst part about it for me was being caught in the middle of it. It was..." He narrows his eyes, as if searching for the right word. "Really fucking hard. Mom was really hurt, Grandpa. She used to cry on our drives back to Ventura after picking me up, and I'm pretty sure it was because she wanted to spend time with you guys, too."

His mom's cheeks turn pink. "I didn't... I don't remember that."

Carter's expression grows tender as he looks at her. "I know you were trying not to cry, and I'm sorry if I'm revealing your secrets. But I have to get this out, because I refuse to be in the middle of your feud anymore. Mom, I know you didn't mean for me to be. Probably none of you did, but..." He shuts his eyes and inhales a shaky breath. "It still fucking sucked. I was a kid, and you were all adults. It changed me permanently. It made me—"

"You're a Blake," Dan says, smirking. "One of the brightest kids I know. You didn't even have our wealth growing up and look at how you turned out. You're resilient."

"Dan," I say, because I can't help myself. "Carter has already asked for no interruptions because this is a difficult conversation for him. Please don't do it again."

Dan's mouth snaps shut, and his eyes grow wide. This is how he looked at me the last time I called him out for his insensitivity. My guess is that he's not confronted very often.

"I won't," he says. "I'm sorry, Carter."

Shit. I inserted myself when Carter wanted my silent support. I'm about to apologize when the words freeze on my tongue. He's staring at me with a small, tender smile. "My kindergarten teacher," he says, and there's so much love in his voice I feel like I could reach out and touch it.

I'm not going to make him wait a second longer. As soon as this conversation is over, I'm going to tell him I love him and want to be with him.

Carter turns to his grandpa. "I just have one last thing to say, and then I'm leaving. I'd like it if you could all continue this conversation after I leave. I think you all have a lot to say to each other, and this has already been exhausting for me."

"That's understandable, honey," Nancy says.

Carter nods. "I don't want to work for Beach Burger. I'm done with all of this shit. I already have a job lined up at OvuTrac, and it's something I'm passionate about. If you want the Blake legacy to continue, it should be through your daughter. She should be your successor, even if you have to spend the next ten years preparing her for it."

"Carter, you don't have to say that." His mom's voice is small.

Carter smiles sadly at his mom. "I mean it. Legacy is important to Grandpa, and you're his closest relative. You may not have experience, but you're smart as hell. You can learn."

He pins his grandpa with a hard stare. "But if you don't, it'll just have to end with you. I'm not doing any of this anymore. I'm not going to be in the middle of your petty drama."

Carter

I exhale a long breath after stepping out of the house. Fuck, that was awful, but it needed to be said. Hopefully, I'll feel better when I reflect back on the whole thing.

Thank God I had my girl with me. I couldn't have gotten through it without her. She was so sweet—so prim and stern when she stood up to my grandpa. I knew I could count on her.

Vanessa walks beside me, and I deliberately wait several steps before turning to her.

"Sorry that was so—"

She leaps onto me, wrapping her arms around me. "I love you!"

"What?" I frown, my heart beating like a cannon. "You do?"

"Yes," she shouts. "You were so brave in there. So brave and so vulnerable."

My throat grows tight.

"I'm so proud of you." Her voice trembles. "You didn't have to do that. It would have been easier not to."

Mist rises to my eyes, and I squeeze her. "I never would have if not for you. I would have acted like just as big of a child as my grandpa instead of saying what's in my heart."

"Don't give me credit for how brave you were in there. That was all you, baby boy."

I laugh softly, though my throat trembles.

She loves me. Finally hearing those words on her lips is like the first gulp of air after a near drowning.

"Baby boy," I repeat, "I'm not sure if I love that pet name."

She plants a hard kiss on my cheek. "What should I call you, then?"

I swallow. "Does this mean... Do you trust me again?"

"I do." She sniffles, and I squeeze her so tightly I'm not sure if she can take a breath.

"Don't cry, baby girl. I'm going to make you so happy."

"You never answered my question."

I frown, pulling away for a moment to get a look at her face. Her eyes are red, and her nose is a little runny, but she has a slight smile on her face.

"What question?" I ask.

"Your pet name. What kind of pet name do you want your girlfriend to call you?"

I shut my eyes at her use of the word girlfriend.

This is really happening. The misery is finally over.

When I open my eyes, I lower my chin to stare down at her. I lift my finger and tap the tip of her nose. "Call me Daddy."

She giggles and leaps into my arms, wrapping her legs around me this time.

Epilogue

V anessa

The wind brushes a strand of hair over my face. I wipe it away before I press the record button.

"My name is Vanessa Gallo," I say, "and I'm a non-virgin raised in purity culture."

Carter grabs me by the waist, and I squeal as he lifts me onto his lap. "Because I devirginated her."

I grimace and try to wiggle out of his arms, but he holds me still. I lift my phone high into the air so that I can capture us both in the camera. "That's the most disgusting word I've ever heard in my life. Never say it again."

He presses a kiss against my cheek before looking at the camera. "She's only saying that because we're recording. You wouldn't believe the kinky shit she's into behind closed doors."

I shush him and gesture with my head to the small group of people to our right. "We're at my sister's engagement party," I say. "And we're making this quick video so—"

"We're going to be making a video at our own engagement party a year from now. I'm going to put a giant ring on her finger."

My stomach flutters at his words, but I try my best to keep my lips from twitching while I roll my eyes. "I will not be getting engaged at twenty-two, so you're setting yourself up for a failed proposal."

He squeezes me. "I guess I'll just have to come prepared to get a yes out of you." His warm breath heats my ear. "I'll have to use my mouth."

I press the stop record button and twist around to look at his face. "You need to stop being so filthy in our videos. I'm going to get a violation."

"Ness!" my sister calls out as she walks up to our table. "We're going to take a bridesmaids picture. Do you know where Mari went?"

I frown as I glance around the beach. "No. I haven't seen her for a while."

"Pastor Brandon is missing, too," Carter says, and my sister's eyes grow huge.

I scan the beach one more time. "Oh my God, you're right!" I shoot wide eyes at my sister, and she smiles slyly back.

"I'll go look for Mari," she says.

"Hopefully, you don't see anything that traumatizes you," Carter says as she walks away.

I punch his thigh. "Don't! Mari has, like, fifteen family members here tonight. I don't want them to think—"

"That Pastor Brandon is probably groping her tits right now?"

"Hush!"

He pulls me close and kisses my neck. "I just want to be groping your tits right now. When can we leave?"

"Not for hours, but we can make a little trip to the bathroom." I purse my lips. "Are you okay with some kissing, or do you need a blowjob?"

He pinches my waist. "My prim little girl. I love the way you present my options. I can't believe you're offering a blowjob at your sister's engagement party with your pastor in attendance."

Warm contentment flows through my veins. I can't believe it, either. Just two months ago, I thought I would die an old lady without ever enjoying sex.

I press my lips against his. "I'm so glad I found you. Who knows where I would be if I hadn't picked you."

His blue eyes grow hooded. "For me, it was only ever going to be you, my shameless girl."

Next book in the Purity series...

LUST: A Forbidden Age Gap Romance

Mariana and Pastor Brandon's forbidden love story

Tropes: Age gap, dom/brat dynamic, jealous/possessive hero, forbidden love, TONS of angst

PRE-ORDER LUST NOW

Afterword

Thank you for your support and reading Carter and Vanessa's story. If you enjoyed *Shame*, I'd greatly appreciate it if you went to Amazon or Goodreads and told the world what you think.

If you want more Purity Series content, go to skylerma son.com and sign up for my newsletter.

Join my Facebook reader group:
Mason's Minxes

And follow me on social media here:
instagram.com/authorskymason
facebook.com/authorskymason
twitter.com/authorskymason

Also by Skyler Mason

Acknowledgments

Gabrielle Sands, you are my star, my perfect silence. You went from critique partner to one of my closest friends in the span of a year. Thank you for making me a better writer every day. Carter wouldn't be nearly as swoony without you.

My editor Heidi Shoham, I don't know what I would do without you. Every critique you've given me has made me a better writer. Thank you for helping me make this book shine.

My sensitivity reader Amrutha, thank you for your thorough feedback on Armaan and Saanvi's characters. I look forward to working with you in the future (*hint hint, readers* Armaan might be getting his own book!).

My proofreader Hazel, thank you for your thorough polishing of this book.

To my lovely readers, you have no idea how much I appreciate you. Your love of the Purity series has been overwhelming. I can't wait to give you the next book!

Printed in the USA
CPSIA information can be obtained
at www.ICGtesting.com
LVHW042107240124
769628LV00005B/966

9 781088 087596